What can be more frightening than a mist dragon jealously guarding its home? Surely not a four-inch faerie dragon.

Even a painting of a dragon can be dangerous if you look it in the eye.

Hunting dragons is no game. Being hunted by dragons is even less so.

Can a captured pseudodragon can give a wandering barbarian a new lease on life?

When a young gnome finds he can see through the eyes of a dragon, he becomes the most unlikely defender a great wyrm has ever had.

The only thing more stupid than telling your friends you've fed a dragon is bringing them to see it.

Red Wizards kill and steal for a book. But who can blame them when they hear the secrets this tome keeps?

Freedom can come at a high price, but no matter how much you're willing to pay, never try to buy it from a dragon.

A fang dragon stalks the streets, hunting prey more terrifying than the assassins sent to hunt it.

Dragons grow old and die just like people, and it's a very bad idea to disturb their graves.

When the most trusted among the dragons feel the Rage simmering inside them, even ancient alliances can crumble.

THE YEAR OF ROGUE DRAGONS

Richard Lee Byers

Book I
The Rage

Book II
The Rite

Book III
The Ruin
May 2006

Realms of the Dragons
Edited by Philip Athans

Realms of the Dragons II
Edited by Philip Athans

FORGOTTEN REALMS

THE YEAR OF ROGUE DRAGONS

Anthology

Edited by
Philip Athans

REALMS OF THE DRAGONS II
The Year of Rogue Dragons Anthology

©2005 Wizards of the Coast, Inc.

Cover art by Matt Stawicki
First Printing: May 2005
Library of Congress Catalog Card Number: 2004116893

9 8 7 6 5 4 3 2 1

US ISBN: 0-7869-3808-0
ISBN-13: 978-0-7869-3808-7
620-96781000-001-EN

U.S., CANADA,
ASIA, PACIFIC, & LATIN AMERICA
Wizards of the Coast, Inc.
P.O. Box 707
Renton, WA 98057-0707
+1-800-324-6496

EUROPEAN HEADQUARTERS
Wizards of the Coast, Belgium
T Hofveld 6d
1702 Groot-Bijgaarden
Belgium
+322 467 3360

Visit our web site at www.wizards.com

TABLE OF CONTENTS

FAERIE IRE

Or, How Zyx Thwarted a
Human Invasion

ERIN TETTENSOR

The Year of the Turret (1360 DR)

Zyx was a nimble dragon. Being only four inches long, his body did not require a great deal of lift to achieve flight, which meant his delicate wings could devote most of their attention to maneuvering. This they did with tireless energy, thrumming at a pace that made them nearly invisible to the naked eye. His tail, meanwhile, was long in proportion to the rest of his body—almost ridiculously so. Acting as an efficient rudder against the air currents, it allowed Zyx to execute sharp changes in direction, darting this way and that with a precision that would make even the most agile hummingbird envious.

All of which was terribly fortunate, for otherwise the yuan-ti would have squashed him like a bug.

"Vermin!" the halfblood hissed, swatting at Zyx with the flat of her scimitar.

"Oops!" sang the faerie dragon merrily as he swept out of the way. "Too slow!"

To drive the insult home, he landed momentarily on the edge of the snakewoman's blade, a taunting smile curling the corners of his mouth.

But his triumph was short-lived. The yuan-ti took another wild swing, and her weapon bit deep into the trunk of a tree. Zyx nearly choked in dismay.

"Clumsy fool!" he cried. He nipped forward and poked the halfblood in the eye. An unimaginative means of attack, perhaps, but the injury to the tree demanded quick retribution. "That yellowwood is several centuries your senior!" he scolded. "Show some respect!"

"I'll show you your own insides, insect!"

She made a grab at the tiny nuisance, but Zyx evaded her with disdainful ease, leaving her clutching empty air.

"Show me, then!" the faerie dragon mocked.

The yuan-ti obligingly charged, and Zyx retreated—but only a short distance. He hovered just out of reach, grinning. And in a sudden flash of inspiration, he winked. It was a master stroke. Enraged beyond all reason, the yuan-ti made a final lunge at her tormentor, crashing through the underbrush with murderous intent.

She never made it. The trap gave way beneath the creature's weight, plunging her through the jungle floor and into the cunningly concealed pit below.

There was a solid *thud*. Branches and leaves tumbled in like an afterthought. Then, for long moments, all was silent. Zyx hovered over the trap, peering into the gloom to ascertain the fate of his victim.

"I hope she's not dead," he muttered. He could not bear the thought of even a single yuan-ti escaping future harassment.

Presently, however, there came a rustling from the pit, and Zyx breathed a relieved sigh. The snakewoman had righted herself, and resumed spitting and cursing as she tried in vain to claw her way out of the trap.

"Good luck!" Zyx called down to her. "I hope the ants aren't too much of a bother. It's that time of year, you know!"

His last barb safely lodged, Zyx left the yuan-ti to the mercy of the jungle and drifted up into the canopy in search of a quiet place to catch his breath. Pestering the evil snakemen was amusing, to be sure, but it was also thoroughly exhausting.

He alit on a large banana leaf, stretching out in the trough to allow the late afternoon sun to warm his scales. It was a luxury he indulged in when he could, for the rainforest surrendered few unbroken hours of sunlight. Soon his eyelids were drooping lazily, blurring his view over the rolling waves of green before him. Nearby, a hawk circled above the treetops, scanning for prey. Even to the bird's keen eyes, Zyx would appear as nothing more than a sunbathing lizard—an appetizing morsel indeed. But the faerie dragon had little to fear. His bliss-inducing breath weapon was enough to keep him safe from even the most ill-intentioned predators, and he had few qualms about using it. As far as Zyx was concerned, the world could use a little more joy.

Still, it was best to be vigilant. The little dragon blinked in an effort to stay awake, forcing himself to focus on the idle drifting of the hawk. His eyes followed the bird as it wheeled to the west, toward the gorge. There the glistening band of ocher that was the River Olung wound its way toward the distant coast of Chult. But something was amiss with the view. A dark tendril rose ominously against the horizon, weaving and swelling like an angry cobra. Frowning, Zyx twisted to his feet and peered into the distance.

"Smoke," he murmured.

It was an uncommon sight. Fires seldom occurred naturally in such a wet climate, and Zyx was not aware of any intelligent species inhabiting the area. He would treat with unalloyed scorn any suggestion that yuan-ti were "intelligent." Zyx was not the kind of dragon to allow something as crude as evidence to interfere with carefully cultivated prejudice.

Wide awake, Zyx abandoned his leaf. Part of his duty as self-appointed guardian of the forest was to investigate unusual occurrences such as these. Thus far, he had acquitted himself admirably in that regard. Why, only last winter he had thwarted an invasion of wayward butterflies who had become disoriented in their annual migration. If Zyx did not look after these things, no one would.

When he came nearer the smoke, there was no mistaking the smell of fresh wood. The dragon curled his nose in disgust. What kind of savage would fell a living tree when there was plenty of deadwood about? A stray yuan-ti, no doubt, for no other creature capable of building a fire lived within a hundred leagues.

Or so Zyx had believed. But as the leaves gave way before him, he was confronted with a sight that drew him up short—a truly horrific sight, one that every forest creature dreads beyond all others. A tremor of shock ran through the faerie dragon, and he landed clumsily on a branch. It could not be. Not here.

No, Zyx thought desperately, this is quite *wrong*.

It was a human.

He had never seen one before, but he knew it the moment he saw it. The way it stalked about the clearing as though it *owned* the place, trampling rare grasses and delicate fungus. The way it attacked a rotting log that was home to millions of tiny creatures, picking it aside like a scab to reveal a great wound in the moss beneath. Zyx averted his gaze in sorrow. How many deaths just then? How many generations of work wasted?

The man paused in his destruction to survey the area with narrowed eyes, the kind of eyes that take brutal stock of their surroundings, slotting everything—animal, vegetable, or mineral—into categories: "useful" or "nuisance." Zyx knew that look. It was not the look of a passing traveler.

His darkest suspicions were confirmed a moment later when the man called out and two more of his pernicious kind appeared, axes slung over their shoulders.

"How's it coming?" the first man called.

"Slowly," replied one of his companions. "Reckon it'll take at least a tenday to widen the path enough to let the wagons through."

"Naw," snorted the third man. "Four days, maybe. Once Ivor and the rest get here, it'll go faster."

The first man grunted, casting a squinted look into the sky, and said, "Better get on with it. Be dark soon."

Taking up a hammer and stake, he scanned the ground with an appraising eye. Zyx realized with horror that the man was erecting a tent.

The little dragon tasted blood. It was only then that he realized he had been biting his tongue. The tip of his tail twitched anxiously, causing the branch beneath him to shudder in sympathy.

This would not do. It would not do at *all*.

Something had to be done.

Fortunately, it did not take long for a plan to blossom, for Zyx's brain was a uniquely fertile place for plots and schemes.

"Don't get comfortable," he growled under his breath, his gaze burning into the interlopers. "You won't be here for long."

"Cirro."

There was no response.

"Cirro!"

As anyone who has ever tried to wake a mist dragon will tell you, it is not an easy task. For such creatures sleep is a sacred rite, an inviolable space, taking its place alongside meditation, rumination, and other places of deep thought. He who wakes a mist dragon does so at his own risk, for who knows what wondrous subconscious revelations he might be interrupting?

Fortunately, Zyx was not troubled with such worries. As far as he was concerned, Cirrothamalan had already experienced rather more epiphanies than was generally advisable for a non-deity.

"Cirro," he said, "I've come to tell you that I'm leaving the forest."

A luminous slit of yellow appeared, and a vertical pupil dilated eagerly. Zyx checked a sigh. He had feared his ploy would work. Though it pained him to admit it, he had the inescapable impression that Cirrothamalan was not always grateful for his company.

"Leaving?" rumbled the mist dragon. He raised his ponderous head. "How tragic. I am sorry to see you go."

"That's very kind of you," Zyx replied, immune to sarcasm. "But perhaps I've exaggerated a little. What I meant to say is that I'm leaving *this part* of the forest—temporarily—because I have urgent business elsewhere."

Cirro's eyelids dropped to half mast. "That's fascinating," he said, his tone suggesting something less than complete fascination. "I am truly grateful you disturbed my sleep to advise me."

"Think nothing of it—we're friends, after all. But actually, I need your help." The little dragon adopted a very serious expression and added, "That is to say, the forest needs your help."

Cirro yawned in a manner not entirely befitting one who has received a call to service, and said, "Go away, Zyx."

"You haven't even heard what I'm going to say," the faerie dragon noted. "Aren't you curious?"

"Have I ever been curious, Zyx? Was I curious when you came to me complaining of rogue butterflies? Was I enthralled by your description of political infighting among the howler monkeys? I have more important things to think about. There are great puzzles in this world that need solving, one of which is why faerie dragons cannot leave anyone in peace."

That said, Cirro lowered his head and curled around himself, signaling the conversation was over.

But Zyx was not one to pick up on subtle cues.

"You'll be interested this time, Cirro," he said. "Humans have moved into the forest."

He should have liked this pronouncement to be followed by a clap of thunder from the heavens.

Had it been, perhaps Cirro would have taken it more seriously. As it was, the mist dragon merely stretched languidly and mumbled, "It was only a matter of time."

"Nonsense!" snapped Zyx. He began to pace nervously on his branch. "They've already made camp, and I heard them talking about bringing wagons in! I'll bet they're here for the trees. I know all about the kinds of things they make out of hardwood. *Ghastly,"* he added with a shudder.

"Mmm," said Cirro. His voice had taken on the thickness of near-sleep.

"And," continued Zyx, pronouncing his next words deliberately, "they're barely a league from your grotto."

Cirro was on his feet so quickly that the breeze knocked Zyx from his perch. The little dragon had to flutter furiously to avoid falling into the river below.

"My grotto?" Cirro roared.

Like most of his kind, Cirrothamalan had a favorite spot for contemplation, a secluded retreat from which he could reflect on the wonderful mysteries of life. The turbid pool itself held little interest for the mist dragon, but the caves beyond were sacred to him. Veiled as they were by a thundering waterfall, the caverns were largely inaccessible to smaller beasts—such as faerie dragons, for example. The grotto was Cirro's sanctuary, jealously guarded. Few forest creatures dared venture near its hallowed banks.

"When the humans find it," Zyx intoned, "they'll claim it for their own. They'll draw water from it. They'll wash their clothes in it. They'll *bathe* in it."

That last image produced equal shivers of disgust from both dragons. Cirro commenced to pace. His great claws sank deep into the clay of the riverbank, sending frogs and dragonflies scattering for their lives.

"All right, faerie dragon," he boomed. "What do you propose?"

"We've got to get rid of them," Zyx said. "Right away."

"Agreed. I'll attack tonight, under cover of darkness. When the rest of them arrive, all they'll find is little pieces of—"

"Er . . . ugh . . . Cirro," Zyx interrupted, grimacing. "That's not quite what I had in mind."

The mist dragon frowned. "What's this?"

"There mustn't be any killing. It's out of the question."

Cirro's scowl deepened. He muttered something unflattering about faerie dragons, but Zyx was unperturbed.

"We only need to scare them," he insisted. The tip of his serpentine tail began to twitch with excitment. "You know, make them think the rainforest is unsafe."

"The rainforest *is* unsafe," Cirro returned. "Have you actually got a plan, faerie dragon, or are you simply talking to hear yourself speak?"

Zyx regarded him with an air of infringed dignity. "Of course I have a plan," he sniffed. "And a good one, too. Watch this."

An army of yuan-ti burst through the trees, scimitars raised and jaws slavering. There were hundreds of them, each one more fearsome-looking than the last. Their fiendish cackles reverberated through the gorge, causing the surrounding trees to erupt with terrified birds. Grinning eagerly, the snakemen advanced toward the dragons. Their leader's eyes fixed hungrily on Cirrothamalan, and it drew a claw across its throat in cruel mockery.

The mist dragon sighed and looked away from his impending doom.

"Yuan-ti don't cackle," he pointed out.

Zyx tilted his head, considering the snakemen with a critical eye before he conceded, "Hmm. Maybe not,"

"And unless I'm much mistaken, they're not usually pink."

"They are *not* pink!" Zyx retorted, scandalized. Then he peered more closely. "A bit rosy, perhaps, but certainly not pink."

"Face it, faerie dragon," Cirro chuckled as the yuan-ti faded from view, "you're terrible at illusions. You won't fool anyone with that nonsense, not even humans."

Zyx pouted. Yet he was forced to admit that the mist dragon was right—he had never been much good at conjuring.

"Still," Zyx said, "it doesn't matter. That wasn't my idea anyway."

Cirro gave him a wry look. "Really."

"No, no, of course not. I was just playing around. My *real* idea has to do with you."

At this, the mist dragon turned his head away slightly, one eye narrowed. "What do you mean?" he asked.

Zyx ignored the skepticism in his friend's voice and said, "You can scare the humans away yourself, Cirro, without hurting them at all. Trust me, I know just the thing. . . ."

———◦◦◦———

The mist crept into the camp like an assassin. It moved slowly at first, coiling leisurely around the abandoned tools and soaking the canvas of the tents. It clung to the waning campfire until nothing remained but defeated wisps of smoke that curled weakly from the damp ashes. At length it stole through the open flaps of the tents where it lingered like a bad dream, enveloping the sleeping forms until the chill became too much to bear and one by one the men opened their eyes.

They awoke to a world of gray. So thick was the fog that they could not see their own hands in front of their faces. They staggered out of the tents, confused, groping in an obscurity no lantern could banish. But the mist did more than tumble benignly through the clearing.

It began at an idle pace, seemingly unthreatening. The fog stirred as though touched by a light breeze, tentacles of mist gently probing the campsite. Though the men could feel no wind on their faces, it was obviously there—for what else could account for the strange motion of the fog? And soon the phantom breeze began to gain in strength, building until it was a veritable gale. Tent flaps fluttered and snapped; the horses screamed and strained against their leads. The fog seemed to take on corporeal form, picking up bits of debris and tossing them recklessly about. The men bent their backs and shielded their eyes as dust and leaves whipped around the camp in a vicious cyclone.

They shouted to each other, but their voices were lost, smothered by the clotted mist. Those sounds that reached their ears told of destruction: the snapping of rope, the rending of fabric. Though they could not see for the impenetrable cloud, the men knew their camp was being devoured.

Then suddenly, inexplicably, it was over. The phantom wind ceased its torment. The fog vanished like steam. Dazed, the men glanced around in utter bewilderment, patting themselves numbly as though expecting to find themselves injured.

Of the camp, little remained but the clearing itself. The tents, the tools—even the horses were gone. Not a trace of debris remained. Were it not for the impressions in the grass, there would be no evidence that the place had been inhabited at all.

"A storm?" spluttered Cirro, outraged. "They called it a *storm?*" Unable to properly express his disgust, he expelled a large puff of vapor.

"I know," Zyx said with real sympathy. "I was disappointed too. If it's any consolation, it was great fun to watch."

Cirro's two-word reply suggested it was of little consolation.

Zyx regarded his friend in the pitying manner of a parent imparting a painful lesson and said, "I'm afraid fog just isn't very scary."

Cirro narrowed his eyes and took a credible snap at the faerie dragon, perhaps to prove that he was indeed capable of being scary.

"I know," Zyx tittered nervously, dancing out of the way. "It was my idea. But don't worry. I've got another one. A better one."

"Not interested," grumbled Cirro. "I will handle this my way, faerie dragon. Enough of your ridiculous schemes."

He opened his great wings and gazed up into the canopy, searching for a gap through which to negotiate his bulk.

Zyx had a sudden vision of appalling carnage, and he landed bravely on the mist dragon's nose.

"Wait a moment. Hear me out," said Zyx. Cirro's eyes crossed as he attempted to focus on the tip of his snout, and Zyx used the distraction to forge ahead. "We've been going about this the wrong way. We've been letting reality get in the way of our planning."

So perplexed was Cirrothamalan by that statement that his eyes crossed even farther.

"I should know better," Zyx continued with a sigh. "I was being far too realistic."

"What *are* you talking about, faerie dragon?"

Zyx smiled patiently and explained, "Let me put it this way. What's the scariest thing in the jungle?"

The mist dragon considered that a moment, then offered, "Woodpeckers?"

Though not the only birds to attempt nesting in the various crooks of Cirro's oft-inert form, woodpeckers were certainly the most painful.

"You're not trying," Zyx frowned. "Think about it from a human's point of view."

With those revised instructions, it didn't take Cirro long to come up with the answer, and his eyes widened with dread.

"The Uluu Thalongh?" he whispered. Even a creature so great as a mist dragon dared not speak the name too loudly.

"The Uluu Thalongh!" Zyx exclaimed with triumph, fear being the exclusive province of the rational.

Cirro succumbed to an involuntary shiver. Of all jungle predators, the Uluu Thalongh inspired the most terror. Though no one—not even the learned Cirrothamalan—could say what the creature truly was, one thing was certain: it was undisputed lord of flesh-eaters, and the very rumor of its proximity was enough to evacuate many miles of rainforest.

"Zyx," Cirro rumbled uncomfortably, "we cannot—"

"Relax. We don't need the *real* Uluu Thalongh. Reality only gets in the way, remember? All we need is for the humans to *believe* the Uluu Thalongh is nearby. That camp will be emptier than a sloth's head in no time!"

Cirro smiled despite himself. It was, he had to admit, a good plan.

"But how do we accomplish it?" asked the mist dragon. "Surely you do not expect the humans to be taken in by one of your ridiculous illusions. The Uluu Thalongh is not known for its rosy complexion."

Zyx ignored the barb. "We don't need illusions," he insisted.

"Oh really? And how do you suggest we evoke the great monster?"

"Impersonation," Zyx replied, as though it was the most obvious thing in the world.

Cirro's expression darkened. "My hearing must be failing

me, faerie dragon. I thought you said 'impersonation.' "

"I did. We'll pretend to be the Uluu Thalongh. Simple."

A little known fact: the axiom about steam coming out of the ears originated with an annoyed mist dragon. A wisp was even then working its way up the side of Cirro's head.

"Simple indeed!" the mist dragon snarled. "As simple as you are! You propose to impersonate a creature that slips inside trees and turns branches into jaws? You must have been dropped on your head as a hatchling!"

"You have no imagination," Zyx sniffed, wounded. "It will work."

"How?"

The little dragon brightened and said, "I thought you'd never ask. Tell me, Cirro, how do you feel about mud?"

———— ∞ ————

A strange keening sound pierced the air. It was at once hollow and sharp, as though someone played upon a cracked wooden pipe. The men winced and covered their ears against the shrill noise, gazing accusingly up at the canopy to identify the offending bird.

But the sound did not emanate from the treetops. Instead it came from deep within the bush, somewhere to the north of the camp. The men peered into the dark recesses of the jungle, but the thick foliage was impenetrable. The piping continued eerily, weaving among the branches like a sinuous tree snake.

"What is it?" Maddock whispered. Something about the sound compelled him to lower his voice.

"It's no bird, that's for sure," said Ivor. He bent to retrieve his axe, and the more experienced of the men followed suit. The jungle was no place to take chances. "And it's getting closer."

Filar grunted and spat on the ground. "Reckon we'd better go check it out."

He pulled his sword from its sheath, turning it over to inspect the edges. The loss of his axe had forced him to use the sword as a tool, and hours of chopping vegetation had left the blade in dismal condition. Still, it would do the job if necessary.

"You men stay here," Ivor instructed the others. "Shout if you see anything."

He gestured at Filar and Maddock, and the three of them left the relative safety of the clearing for the unknown dangers of the brush.

"They're coming!" whispered Zyx with glee.

He was rather proud of his shrill, piping cry, fancying that it sounded a great deal like the bone-chilling call of the Uluu Thalongh. Since neither he nor Cirro had ever heard the bone-chilling call of the Uluu Thalongh, there was no one to disagree with him.

"How close are they?" Cirro wanted to know.

The mist dragon was covered from horn to claw in a thick layer of mud, and was therefore quite unable to see. He had been forced to rely on Zyx's convoluted directions to find the clearing, and considered it nothing shy of a miracle that he had arrived unscathed. Even more impressive, most of the stray branches Zyx had affixed to his body had survived the journey. So far, things were going smoothly.

"They're about a furlong away," Zyx estimated. "That gives you just enough time to get ready. Now remember: think tree."

"Tree," repeated Cirro without much enthusiasm. He drew himself up on his hind legs, propping himself with his tail for additional balance. He felt utterly ridiculous.

Zyx did not help matters, clucking his tongue disapprovingly. "No, no! Your forelegs need to come up. Up! Like branches. There you are."

Cirro had a sudden, pained vision of how he must appear. "If you breathe a word of this to anyone, faerie dragon, I'll swallow you whole."

"Dear Cirro, you're such a joker. Now be quiet. They're almost here. You remember what to do?"

Ivor expected their mysterious quarry to be camouflaged, but he couldn't have guessed how well. If Filar hadn't shouted, he would have walked right past it: an enormous tree, oddly misshapen by strange, grotesque bulges. The tree's appearance was alarming enough, but what caused Filar to cry out—and Ivor to leap back with a curse—was the sudden movement of a branch.

For a brief moment Ivor thought himself imagining things, but no—the branch was definitely reaching for him. Worse, the limb ended in what appeared to be a set of long, sharp teeth. Ivor staggered back in shock, his mind reeling.

All of that was strange enough, but what followed was stranger still. The tree shifted its immense bulk, and there came a crashing sound. Everyone—including the monstrous tree—looked around in confusion. Another crash, and the source of the sound became clear: the smaller branches of the tree were falling off. One by one they tore away from the trunk, plummeting to the ground far below. Filar had to leap back to avoid the leafy bombardment.

Faced with the sudden defection of its appendages, the monster seemed unsure of what to do. It withdrew a few paces, then hovered uncertainly, allowing the men to get a better look at it. Bereft of its treelike appearance, it was little more than an enormous column of mud. But it was a column of mud with eyes, teeth, and claws.

Ivor felt the blood drain from his face as he realized what he was looking at.

"It's . . ." he faltered.

"What?" Maddock prompted, his voice barely above a whisper.

"It's a *mudman!*"

The pronouncement was met with general consternation.

"But there's no such thing as a mudman!" Filar whimpered.

"No?" Ivor gestured wildly with his axe. "What do you call that, then?"

Faced with an incontrovertible argument, Filar conceded the point. As for the mudman, it appeared to be reconsidering its options, for it had drawn back even farther and was engaged in a heated argument with a nearby branch. The creature was obviously quite mad.

"We'll have to kill it," Ivor said in a low voice. "We'll be sending for our families soon, and I'll not have a mudman around my boys."

"Too right," growled Maddock.

Their resolve hardened, the men advanced toward the inattentive creature. They would catch it unawares, and it would all be over before the mudman even knew what hit it.

—❦—

By the time Zyx saw the weapon, it was already too late. The blade caught Cirro in the left haunch, biting easily through the dried mud. The mist dragon howled and wheeled around, his tail very nearly decapitating a large man with an axe. A third man, also with an axe, took a swing at Cirro's foreleg.

"No!" Zyx shrieked, "Stop!"

He was seized with terror. Not for Cirro—the mist dragon was quite capable of scalding the humans to the bone. But that was precisely the problem.

"Cirro, please!" begged the tender-hearted faerie dragon. "Don't hurt them! Oh, this won't do at *all!*" He flitted to and fro like a confused bumblebee, wringing his forefeet in distress. "Think, Zyx, think!"

Below, Cirro unfurled a wing, knocking all three humans to the ground.

"Get them away from me, Zyx!" he snarled. "I'll do what I must!"

To demonstrate the point, the mist dragon slammed his tail into the ground, leaving a deep trough.

This display of strength should have sent any creature into headlong retreat—any sensible creature, that is. But the humans remained stubbornly in place, trading near-misses with the mud-caked dragon. One man hacked continually at Cirro's legs, his pitiful blade finding the occasional tender spot. Another took opportunistic swings with his axe, catching the dragon on the move and thus adding force to his blows.

Cirro kept them at bay as best he could, blowing harmless clouds of steam to obscure their view. But eventually he would lose patience, and when that happened, the steam would become deadly.

There was only one thing to do. Zyx threw himself heroically into the path of the nearest human, preparing to blast the man's face with his bliss-inducing breath. But the faerie dragon's inexperience with humans proved costly, for the graceless creatures were quicker than they appeared. There was a blur of motion, and everything went dark. Zyx was caught.

"Unhand me, you filthy beast!" The tiny creature scowled defiantly at the three faces looming above, its lower jaw jutting forth in an almost comical gesture of bravado.

"What's *this* now?" Maddock muttered.

Even as he asked the question, he cast another wary glance

at the mudman. The monster had withdrawn the moment its ally was captured, but it remained only a few paces away, watchful.

"It's a flying lizard," Ivor declared.

His pronouncement provoked an indignant squeak from the captive.

"Lizard indeed!" said the creature. "I happen to be a faerie dragon, and I'll have you know that it's very bad luck to catch one!"

"Eh?" Ivor blinked. "Faerie dragon?"

At that, Filar let out a loud, expressive groan.

When his companions regarded him with bemused expressions, he explained, "I've heard of them, right enough. My brother up on the coast had a run-in with one last spring. Caused him no end of headache. They spend all day playing practical jokes on whatever poor souls live nearby. Plague a man till he's mad, they will." He shook his head ruefully. "If we live here, we'll never be rid of the little vermin!"

"I say!" objected the diminutive dragon. "Is that kind of language really necessary?"

Ivor ignored it. He hoisted his hand in Filar's direction and asked, "You really think this thing is a faerie dragon?"

Filar shrugged. "It's a talking lizard with wings. What else would it be?"

"Think it'll bother us?"

"Reckon so. It's in its nature."

Ivor cursed violently. "Just our luck, isn't it? Bet there isn't another one of these things for a thousand leagues!" He looked over the little pest in disgust, then opened his hand and shook it free. "Be gone with ye, then," he growled.

The dragon lingered a moment as though it would speak, but wisely thought better of it. Its tiny form darted through the trees and disappeared.

"You're just letting it go?" Maddock cried. He had obviously envisioned a more permanent solution.

With a gesture, Ivor reminded him of the presence of the mudman. "It's a big forest," he said, "and this place don't have much to recommend it."

"Bad company," agreed Filar, "and bad weather besides. If we're gonna rebuild the camp anyway, we might as well find someplace a little more hospitable."

Their perfectly rational concerns had nothing whatever to do with abject fear of the mudman, whose exact nature had been called into question by its unexpected conversion to a quadruped. (Subsequent fireside accounts would identify the monster as the lesser-known but equally fearsome mud*bear*.)

"Move on, then?" suggested Maddock.

"Reckon that's the most reasonable course," said Ivor, with a very reasonable expression.

Thus agreed, the men withdrew from close proximity to the mudman, taking reasonably quick strides back to camp.

"Cirro, I've come to tell you that I'm leaving the forest."

The mist dragon did not so much as open his eyes. "Go away, Zyx," he growled.

It had been nearly a month since the incident with the humans, and Cirro had not heard a peep from the faerie dragon. Only then did he realize how much he'd enjoyed the reprieve.

"I mean it this time," Zyx sighed. "And I just wanted to say that I'm really going to miss you."

Cirro raised his head. He had never heard Zyx sound so earnest. "Is this the truth?" he asked. "Where are you going?"

"The other side of the gorge."

The mist dragon narrowed his eyes and asked, "Is that not where the humans were going?"

Zyx's expression was all innocence. "Someone's got to keep an eye on them," he pointed out.

But Cirrothamalan was no fool. "You can't resist, can you? They are simply too tempting a target!"

A coy smile worked its way across Zyx's snout. "But it was such *fun*," he murmured. His eyes grew unfocused, as though he was reliving a sweet memory.

"I doubt the humans thought it was much fun," Cirro noted.

The faerie dragon overlooked that observation with his usual blitheness. "It will be a grand adventure," he said. "But I shall miss you, my friend."

It seemed Zyx was in earnest after all. Cirro rose to his feet, and with due ceremony offered the traditional farewell of his kind.

"Good-bye, Zyx. May the mysteries of life unfold themselves to you."

As the tiny dragon flitted away, Cirro felt a peculiar weight in his stomach, as though he had swallowed a large stone. Was it possible? Might he actually miss the little pest?

"I'll come back to visit someday!" Zyx piped as he disappeared from view.

The stone in Cirro's stomach vanished, replaced by an ill-tempered growl. He might have guessed. One was never truly rid of a faerie dragon. They were as clinging as a burr, as nagging as a conscience. He could name several diseases that were easier to be rid of. Still, some part of him welcomed such constants in life. And when Zyx returned, as he no doubt would, some part of Cirro would welcome the faerie dragon too.

THE WOMAN WHO
DREW DRAGONS

ROSEMARY JONES

The Year of the Helm (1362 DR)

Of course, if that female painter hadn't shown up about the same time that Guerner called for more drinks, the tavernkeeper Varney might not have pursued his great idea about dragons. At least, that was what Varney said later. Mrs. Varney just said, "Well, isn't that like Varney, trying to blame somebody else for his troubles."

It all started with Varney's customers, as Varney pointed out to Mrs. Varney. Those customers, a group of regulars, were having one of their endless nightly debates about the habits of dragons and their own fortitude during encounters with the scaly beasts.

"So I just twitched the string like this, and up leaps that black dragon. Thought his whole cave was infested by snakes, and he lets out this roar and races away. Leaving me in possession of all his treasure," said the gnome Silvenestri Silver, wriggling a piece of twine across the table.

In the middle of winter, in the dark days that marked the end of one year and the beginning of the next, Silver spent most of his time in his favorite tavern, the Dragon Defeated, telling tales of his past exploits as a treasure-stealer. When the roads dried out and warmer weather came, he'd be away to a bigger city to look for work. Sembian cities held certain perils for a professional treasure-hunter (like rival claimants to his prizes and unkind people who whined that he'd cheated them of their share), so Silver preferred to wait out winter in Halfknot, the small town with a mixed population of humans, dwarves, and gnomes where nothing much ever happened.

Varney and his wife scrubbed the tables, moving around the group of listeners gathered around the gnome and his string. Mrs. Varney wished that they'd all go home and whispered to Varney that it was time to shoo everyone out the door. But Varney disagreed. Winter was too slow a time for the Dragon Defeated and its owner to lose any chance of an extra purchase.

Looking over the group arguing about dragons, Varney knew the order wouldn't come from the dwarf, Badger Bates. The dwarf would nurse his one drink all night unless someone else paid. If the human, Wyrmbait Nix, hadn't lost all his coin to Silver in one of their numerous bets, he might buy something to eat. The big man was always hungry and not too fussy about Mrs. Varney's cooking. Of course, His Honor, Grangy Guerner, part-time magistrate and full-time ratcatcher, always had plenty of jingle in his pocket, but he rarely lingered in the tavern for any length of time.

"Dragons aren't afraid of snakes," said the dwarf Badger Bates, taking up the thread of his never-ending dispute with Silver about which of them knew the most about the dragons.

He pointed one dirty finger at the gnome sitting across from him. "All I'm saying is that proof is proof. I've never seen any proof of your story except a snip of dirty twine. Now folks know when I tell about Malaeragoth, I'm going show them proof of my words. I've got my scale, don't I?"

Bates tapped the iron box sitting beside his plate. The dwarf worked in the local foundry but had once dug gardens and built fountains for the wizard Uvalkhur the Undaunted. When certain rival wizards murdered the old man in his own home, Malaeragoth, the sapphire dragon and sometimes steed of Uvalkhur, suddenly appeared before the thieving wizards ransacking the mansion and revenged his former master. Almost one hundred years had passed since the day that Malaeragoth tore apart the manor to play cat-and-mouse games with the murderers, but the ferocity of his vengeance remained a favorite tale in Sembia. Of all those who'd occupied the manor that day, only Badger Bates had escaped with his life. And from that day to the present, no more had been seen of the sapphire dragon.

"And besides, the last time that you told that story about the black dragon, you said you cast an illusion of one snake crawling across his den," argued Bates. "Now when I talk about Malacragoth—"

"One snake, ten snakes, what does it matter?" Silver said, cutting off Bates's last sentence. "You're missing the point. What I'm trying to say is that it pays, and pays well if you're hunting someone else's treasure, to know who you're stealing from. Dragons are no different from people. Know their habits, know where they keep their loot, and know how to trick them. That dragon—and I never said that he was the usual sort of black dragon—that dragon had what the wizard called a *pho-bee-a*. Couldn't abide snakes in any form. And when he saw a snake, or thought he saw one, he ran."

"I am the last person alive to have actually seen Malaeragoth and I can produce my proof anytime I want," Bates persisted, flipping open the lid of his iron box. The shimmering sapphire scale inside shone like an evening star in the tavern's dim light. "Besides, Malaeragoth wasn't one of your commonplace black dragons that any reprobate gnome illusionist could trick," finished Bates in a huff.

"I paid good gold for information about that black dragon," snarled Silver, "and more for a great snake illusion. That's what made it possible for me to defeat that dragon—and a lesser gnome couldn't have done it. You may have been clever enough to pick up that scale, after you crawled out of whatever hole that you hid in, but avoiding Malaeragoth isn't the same as tricking a dragon in his own lair!"

"Humph," said Badger Bates. "Proof is proof, and I still don't see anything on the table."

"I've got the scars from my encounters, and nobody asks me to plop those on the table when I tell my stories," said Wyrmbait Nix. "But scars or no scars, I still believe the gnome. As for putting things down on the table, Silver pays for his fair share of the drinks, which is more than you've ever done, Badger," continued Nix, who made his living capturing baby dragons for wizards' menageries. He spent his winter months in town, offering to show any lady in the tavern his scars, including the terrific bite mark left on his leg by a baby blue dragon. "And neither of you has spent day after day crawling through dark dank holes after those nasty-tempered wyrmlings!"

"Yeah, well, they don't call you Wyrmbait for nothing," said Silver. "But I'd rather steal a treasure and keep a whole skin, than carry around a bag of hissing, wiggling baby dragons nipping at my fingers. Nasty way to make a living, Nix, nasty."

"Baby bites," scoffed Bates. "Why that's nothing compared to the fury of Malaeragoth. He ripped Uvalkhur's roof off with one swipe of his claws. He hunted Uvalkhur's killers through the hallways like one of Guerner's terriers after rats. I saw him, and that's more than either of you have ever seen—a great old dragon like that, fighting with all his strength!"

The ratcatcher Guerner suddenly spoke up. "Well, I've never seen a dragon, and I've never wanted to see one. Catching rats is enough vermin for me. But I like hearing your stories, makes these winter nights pass quicker. I'll stand you a drink all round for your tales. Hey, Varney, draw us four more cups," he said to the tavernkeeper.

Varney smirked at Mrs. Varney. He'd been right and she'd been wrong, it was worth staying open a little longer.

The chink of Guerner's coin dropping into his box sparked Varney's big idea, or "another one of Varney's big ideas" as Mrs. Varney would say in later years to friends and relations. Middle of the tenday, middle of the winter, was such a lonely time for a tavernkeeper's coin box in Sembia. It had been another lousy winter for trade. There'd been talk of odd trouble in odd places, ghosts in the forests and suchlike. In a small town like Halfknot, where Varney ran the Dragon Defeated, people relied on travelers for their extra coin. And when the gods, elves, Zhentarim, and who knew what else kept disrupting trade, well, then, it meant everyone got very nervous and hoarded what gold they had.

But with the Year of Maidens passed and the Year of the Helm begun, Varney wanted to encourage customers to stop saving and start spending at the Dragon Defeated. Advertising Mrs. Varney's meat pies as being made from the best berrygobblers hadn't done the trick. In fact, some unkind bard had started a song about "Mrs. Varney's Rat Pies."

As Varney served Guerner's round, a woman blew through the tavern's door with a cold, wet wind and an offer to repaint the Dragon Defeated's sign. Varney just knew that her offer was all that was needed to start his great idea attracting a little cash to his tavern.

Small and fair-haired, the painter's skin held that ruddy brown tinge of a wanderer who spent most of her time outdoors. Spots of color sprayed across her hands, the marks of her trade.

"I was heading east," the painter said, "but the roads are rivers of mud and I'm tired of slipping and falling every third step. So I'm stopping in Halfknot until the roads dry out. I'm painting signs for the baker, the butcher, and the hostler. I'll do yours too in return for a few meals."

Varney promised as many meat pies as the painter could eat.

The next morning, Varney, the painter, and Mrs. Varney discussed a new design for the Dragon Defeated's well-weathered sign. The current placard depicted a group of men attacking a rearing white dragon.

"I noticed your sign when I first came to town," said the painter, standing underneath it, ignoring the rain dripping on her head and down her neck. "That dragon is simply awful. The neck is all wrong, the head's too small, and those wings! They look like a bird's wings, not a dragon's!"

"Can you add a princess, dear?" asked Mrs. Varney, who was a sentimental soul. "You know, one of those girls all dressed in fine silks with a little tiny crown perched on top of her curls, being rescued by the lads? Like in the stories my granny told."

"Well," said the painter. "I don't know as much about princesses as I do about dragons, but I can draw one. What else?"

"Can you make the chaps in the sign look like those three over there?" asked Varney, pointing a thumb at Silver, Bates, and Nix, who were walking down the street. The gnome, the dwarf, and the human were still arguing about who knew more about dragons.

The painter looked them over. "Don't you want something better? I'm not sure that they'll attract the customers."

"I want it to look just like them," said Varney. "I've got an idea about those three."

Once the repainted sign was flapping in the gusts of winter wind, Varney nailed another smaller sign next to his door advertising free beer on the slowest night of the tenday in return for a good dragon story.

Much to the town's surprise, Varney lived up to his promise. Every storyteller got one free beer—small and a bit watered, but free. Also, Varney had every listener and storyteller put a coin or a button or a packet of pins in a cup. At the end of the evening, the best story was awarded the cup, with the tavern's own "dragon defeaters" Silver, Nix, and Bates acting as judges. Of course, food and additional beer were charged at Varney's usual rates, and the winner most often stood the company an extra round, all of which meant that Varney's coin box started to fill up very nicely.

So Varney's idea worked, as Varney liked to tell friends and relations in later years. More people came to the Dragon Defeated, just to hear a story well told, and after a few tendays, as the weather improved and travel became easier, the promise of a free beer and the possibility of winning a cup of coins and buttons spread up and down the roads, drawing more out-of-towners and regulars from other taverns. All sorts of strange folk began to appear at the Dragon Defeated to compete with their story.

Silver, Nix, and Bates took to strutting around town because of their positions as "dragon experts." The dwarf even promised to give Malaeragoth's sapphire scale to the first person who managed to astound all three judges.

On the night of the "unfortunate incident," as Varney described it in later years, the Dragon Defeated was packed with a lively, hard-drinking crowd of humans, dwarves, and gnomes. A human fighter with well-oiled leather armor and a really big sword slung across his back finished his tale of hand-to-claw combat with a green dragon with a thump of his fist on his chest. The audience looked between him and the judges, waiting to hear what the trio thought.

"Well," said Nix, cleaning his teeth with an ivory toothpick, "if you'd lunged a bit more and ducked less, you could have finished the fight in half the time. If you're going to go hunting dragons, you can't be afraid of being nipped on the arm or leg. Bites heal. Look at my scars. Besides, we heard something similar from a man from Triel last tenday, didn't we boys?"

"Yup, I don't think that story is worth even a button," said Bates, who was known throughout Halfknot as a dwarf so cheap that he wouldn't give away the time of day for free. There was a running side bet going at the Dragon Defeated that no one would ever get Malaeragoth's sapphire scale from the dwarf. "Besides, I like to see a bit of proof, I do. Anyone can tell a fancy story, but not everyone can produce solid evidence."

"I think the whole thing showed a lack of finesse," Silver said, washing his fingers in a porcelain bowl. "With a little bit of guile," added the gnome, using his embroidered hankie to dry off his fingertips, "he could have had the head off that creature and been out of the forest without even pulling that really big sword out of its scabbard. If he'd studied his dragons before he went, he'd have known how to handle them. Everyone knows that you're most likely to find green dragons there and those type of dragons are cross-eyed and easy to confuse."

"You're wrong," said the sign painter, sitting in the corner nearest the fire and eating one of Mrs. Varney's meat pies. "A green dragon is not that easy to kill and they're never cross-eyed."

A number of heads turned to stare at the woman. She smiled slightly at the three dragon experts and continued to eat her pie with calm, deliberate bites.

"What do you know about greens, missy?" said Nix.

"I've painted a hundred or so, and I've never seen a single crossed eye," she replied, saying more than she'd said in all the previous tendays. Behind her table, her large pack leaned against the wall. The roads outside were dry, she was dressed for traveling, and she'd come for one last meal before leaving town. Being on her way out of Halfknot, she obviously didn't care who she offended that night. Or, at least, that was Mrs. Varney's explanation of the subsequent events.

"What do you mean, madam, that you've painted greens?" said Silver.

"I draw dragons," said the woman. "My name, by the way, is Petra. The dragons sometimes call me Ossalurkarif, but I prefer Petra. I definitely prefer Petra to 'missy' or 'madam.'"

"Lady Petra," said Silver, leaping up on his table so everyone could see him, then making an elaborate bow, "my apologies for these repeated questions, but what do you know about dragons?"

"More than you do." Petra sighed and pushed her pie aside. "I've sat and listened for all these tendays. And your tales are all very pretty and well-told. But not one of you has really looked at the dragons that you say that you've met. You've fought them, you've killed them, you've stolen from them, and once or twice, you've even had a conversation with one. But none of you have ever noticed much more than if a dragon is green, red, or blue."

She reached behind her and pulled a number of long metal and oiled canvas tubes out of her pack.

"I draw dragons," she said again. "Somebody has to. We live in a realm filled with dragons, but what does anyone really know? Your wizards talk of *Draco Mystere,* but what good is reading the words of others compared to actual field study? Why you won't find in books whether a red adult has one or two phalanges or the color of a bronze hatchling's tongue. But I can show you that! And I can prove greens don't have crossed eyes."

Petra opened one of the tubes and drew out a number of tightly rolled parchments. As she spread them across her table, people stood up to get a better look, causing the gnomes to join Silver on the tabletop so they could see over the heads of the humans. The dwarves just muscled themselves to the front of the crowd. As the sound of "oohs" and "aahs" rose from the crowd, Varney stopped pouring beer and boosted himself up on the bar to see Petra's drawings.

Filling every inch of the vellum were dozens and dozens of drawings of green dragons. There were greens in flight, rearing up to peer over treetops, curled around a clutch of eggs, and resting with chins across crossed claws, looking like tabby cats asleep in the sun.

"Look there," said Petra, pointing at the head of a green dragon with eyes deep-set under a row of hornlets and crest fully extended. "Perfectly normal eyes. Not a sign of crossing."

"Well," said Silver finally. "I guess I got my dragons a little mixed up. It's the whites that have crossed eyes."

"No," said Petra, pulling another tube from her pack and twisting it open. "Whites have beautiful eyes. Much more variation in eye colors than other dragons, in fact, probably because of the white scales. I've seen whites with blue eyes, green eyes, and the most wonderful shade of amber. The one with amber eyes was a very old dragon whose scales had gone a lovely shade of cream, with just a slight tint of azure on the belly. He said that all his brothers had amber eyes, but none of his sisters, who tended to have lavender or violet eyes."

"You talk to dragons?" said Nix, managing to sound both intrigued and disbelieving at the same time. "You've spoken with white dragons?"

"The polite ones," answered Petra with a shrug. "If I'm painting a big portrait. It can take hours sometimes and they do get so bored posing. I guess that's why I like doing the little sketches more, like the ones of the greens. There I'm just drawing them quickly as they go about their lives. It seems less intrusive somehow. Dragons are very sensitive about such things."

"So how many kinds of dragons have you drawn?" challenged Nix. "I've captured more than three different species in my time. I could show the bites on my leg from a blue, and the one on my arm from a green, and the one from a red wyrmling on my—"

"Not in front of the ladies," cried Froedegra, the black-smith's daughter, who knew very well where the little red dragon had bit Nix and never wanted to see that scar again.

"Thank you, but you don't need to show me anything," said Petra. "I know the bite of one dragon from another. I've drawn copper dragons on the High Moor, red dragons playing in a volcano's fire, gold dragons reading scrolls in labyrinths, white dragons sliding through snow and ice, bronze dragons being ridden by wizards on battlefields, blue dragons burrowing beneath hot sands, and black dragons flying above the salt marshes, where the world is neither sea nor land, but a bit of both. I've walked all the Realms from end to end, just to draw dragons."

As she recited her catalog of dragons, Petra pulled scroll tube after scroll tube from her pack. Dragons crawled, walked, swam, flew, dug, ran, stretched, fought, and slept in the dozens of drawings spread across all the tables of the tavern. More dragons in more colors than anyone had ever seen before. Silver and Nix were silenced.

But Badger Bates was moved to speak, because he knew that if he displayed the awe that the others showed, he'd lose Malaeragoth's sapphire scale. And Bates never gave up anything without a battle.

"There's no sapphire dragon here," he said, surveying the drawings that littered the tavern. "There's one that I've seen that you have not: Malaeragoth in his rage! I saw him that day he ripped up the wizard's killers, and nobody has seen him since."

"Malaeragoth! That dragon is dangerous to draw," said Petra, frowning at the name. "I painted him once and only once, as he paced through his cold caverns, but he caught sight of my painting in his scrying mirror and sent a servant to steal the picture from me."

"Easy to say, hard to prove," answered Bates. "I don't believe you. That old dragon has been gone for a hundred years. There's many here who know that I'm the last alive to see him."

Petra shook her blond head at the dwarf's taunt and began to gather up her pictures, rolling them tightly and packing them back into their protective tubes.

"Malaeragoth served Uvalkhur in Sembia many years ago," continued Bates, "and I was digging a fountain for the wizard's garden when thieves snuck in and murdered the master in his own place. And I can give you proof that I was there that day, for here's Malaeragoth's own scale," said the dwarf, banging his iron box down on the table and flipping open the lid.

"I never said that you were a liar, though you were more than rude to call me one," answered Petra in the same calm voice that she had used to tell Nix and Silver that they knew nothing about green dragons' eyes. "Malaeragoth's scale that may well be. It's off an old dragon, and a sapphire too. The color and the size are evidence of that. But if you've seen Malaeragoth's rage than you know that the sapphire dragon is a dragon best left sleeping. I wouldn't go shouting his name and boasting of my knowledge quite so loud. It's not for nothing that he's taken to calling himself the Unseen Dragon."

"Well," said Silver, determined to regain his status as dragon expert before the crowd, "Badger's not a complete fool. Proof is proof, as he likes to say. You could have drawn your pictures from the stories that you've heard here. You've been listening to us all winter long. How do we know that you've seen these beasts with your own eyes?"

"Because I only draw what I have seen and all my dragons are true in every detail," answered Petra, and her voice went a little higher at being questioned by the gnome as well as the dwarf. "And if you had any brains behind your eyes, you'd give me that cup that sits on the bar. For I've shown you more of dragons tonight than any tale told here this winter!"

Bates sucked in his breath and blew it out again. "Show me Malaeragoth," he said, "and I'll give you Malaeragoth's sapphire scale and double the coins in the cup as well."

The tavern crowd gasped. The sapphire scale might be rare, but coin out of Bates's purse was something even rarer.

"Done!" said Petra, for like most painters, she never could resist a bet. "I'll draw Malaeragoth as I last saw him, old and wily, and as fond of magic as any wizard! But he's a large dragon and I need a large space to paint." She looked around the room and walked over to the north wall. Mrs. Varney had whitewashed the plaster only a few days before. Petra looked at Varney, still sitting on the top of his bar, and asked, "May I paint the dragon here?"

Varney agreed, thinking that a mural of the sapphire dragon would draw the drinkers just as much as any story. And that, as Mrs. Varney would say in later years, was just typical of Varney's foolishness.

Petra called for raw eggs and clean water to mix her paints. Varney brought the ingredients, totaling the cost in his mind and determined to add it as "extras" to her tab. From her pack, Petra pulled out her paint box with its jars of powdered pigments and its multitude of brushes. She grabbed a stick from the fireplace and sketched the outline of Malaeragoth upon the wall. In her drawing, the dragon was frozen in midstep, facing a floating mirror.

Petra mixed the colors on the lid of her paintbox, which unhinged to become a separate tray holding five colors and three brushes. At first, she painted with a broad brush, tipped with oxhair, and laid down large strokes of a deep sea blue.

Then she painted with a smaller brush, tipped with fox fur, the finer details of Malaeragoth's scales, claws, ears, and nose in ultramarine and turquoise. Last, she took up a tiny brush, tipped with squirrel hair, to add minute dots of lapis and gold dust to the dragon's form. Malaeragoth twinkled like a jewel upon the wall, and the sapphire scale in Bates' box shown with the same blue light. Looking closely at Malaeragoth's long throat, the crowd could even see where a single scale had dropped away and been replaced by a newer, lighter blue scale.

Petra painted very fast, something that she had learned from trying to draw pictures of dragons in flight, but dawn light was showing at the windows before she was done. Her audience stretched and shook some sleeping gnomes awake as she cleaned her brushes with quick economical moves.

Nix and Silver shoved and pushed other people aside to take a closer look at the dragon, but Bates remained in his chair, clutching his iron box in one white-knuckled hand.

While the crowd admired the vibrant sapphire dragon, Petra mixed new colors in her box lid and painted a smaller picture within the frame of the painted mirror. But no one except Varney looked at Malaeragoth's mirror, painted as floating before the dragon. In the painted mirror, Varney saw his own tavern with himself counting coins into his coin box behind the bar and others craning to look at a woman painting upon the wall a sapphire dragon looking at them. It was, thought Varney, a very clever conceit and he felt very pleased about the new mural decorating the wall of the Dragon Defeated. Unlike the sign creaking in the wind outside, he wouldn't even have to pay the painter in kind for the new decoration of his tavern.

"Well," said Petra to Bates as she worked on the picture in the mirror, "is that not Malaeragoth to the life?"

The dwarf had not moved, nor spoken, nor slept for the entire night. Instead, he'd sat on a stool watching the painter with his face growing redder and redder as she got closer to finishing her portrait of the sapphire dragon. Looking at the black anger in his scowl, Nix and Silver knew that the dwarf had lost his bet, but they winked at each other, sure that Bates would find a way to wiggle out of paying.

"Not to the life," said the dwarf after a long, long pause. "I'm an old dwarf and I know what I know. I'm not going to be tricked by some woman."

The crowd murmured their disapproval. "Why it's a fine picture," said Nix, "you can almost see the beast breathe!"

"Still," added Silver for mischief's sake, "the dwarf doesn't lie. What's wrong with the painting, Badger?"

"Malaeragoth had eyes," said Bates pointing to two empty holes in the dragon's head where Petra had not laid a speck of paint upon the plaster. "If she'd really seen him, she'd know what color they were."

"As green as unripe plums when he's content, as bright as summer lightning when he's angry," answered Petra.

"Show me!" challenged the dwarf.

"Best not," said Petra, packing up her paints and all her brushes except one tiny brush tipped with golden hair. "Better that you should pay me as you promised and leave Malaeragoth as he stands. Leave his eyes blind. The old wyrm doesn't like people spying on him. And" she added in an angry undertone, "I don't like people trying to weasel out of a bet."

"If you can finish it, and finish it right," said Bates, "I'll pay. But not a penny before that, and not the cup either. Don't you lads agree?"

"Well," said Nix, who had a tingle in his big toe that reminded him of the time that a red hatchling had bitten him to the bone, "I think the lass has done a very fine job. It's definitely not your ordinary blue dragon. It's a sapphire as sure as anything, and who's to say it's not Malaeragoth."

"I do!" shouted Bates. "I'm the last living person to see that dragon and only I know what his eyes look like!"

Since Silver loved to make trouble, he sided with the dwarf. "An unfinished painting is like a tale without an end. We've never given the cup away to any story that didn't have a proper ending. Varney, what do you say?"

Varney made another mistake at that moment by saying, "I say that you're the judges. If you don't think it's worthy of the cup, the cup and the coins stay here. Not a single button for the lady. And you, Miss Petra the Painter, owe me for your drinks and those eggs and water for your paints."

Petra flushed as red as Bates. "Have it your way," she muttered, loud enough for Nix to hear and remember afterward. "I warned you. But it's your wall. And your lives."

She picked up the little brush tipped with golden hair and pulled a silk-wrapped jar out of the side pocket of her pack. She unscrewed the ivory lid of the jar and dipped the brush into it. Something sparkled on the tip of the brush but nobody could say for sure what color was the paint. With quick, deft strokes, Petra filled in the eyes of the dragon.

The dragon's eyes were beautiful, iridescent as pearls and green as new plums, and they sparkled in the pale winter sunlight shining through the cracks of the tavern's shutters. The play of shadow and light upon the dragon's head made the eyes look alive, thought Varney.

"I'll take my payment now," said Petra, grabbing the cup off the bar and tipping the coins and buttons into her pack. She was heading toward the door as she talked.

To everyone's amazement, Bates did not protest. The dwarf let out a long, loud sigh.

"Yup," he said. "It's Malaeragoth!" And he added in a stubborn, angry tone, "But it's not a very good likeness! He was much uglier than that."

At the sound of its name, the painted dragon blinked and took a long, hard look into the painted mirror that floated in front of it. Varney stared at the painted mirror too. He saw the crowd within the mirror turn, and shove, and move in a swell of mixing painted colors, pushing away from the painted dragon staring at them with a malevolent gaze.

Varney saw his own painted jaw drop open in surprise. His painted wife rushed to his side. And he felt Mrs. Varney's hard grip upon his arm.

"Run, you old fool, *run!*" she shrieked.

On the wall, Malaeragoth's painted lips curled back from long, gleaming fangs.

"It moved!" cried Nix, diving for a window and tearing at the shutter as he spoke, years of dragon hunting propelling him away from possible danger.

Silver followed close upon his heels.

"No," said Badger Bates, stubborn and argumentative to the last, "it can't move. It's just a picture."

But even as Bates spoke, the painted dragon coiled off the wall, leaving gaping holes in the plaster behind him. Stones and plaster crashed and ricocheted through the screaming, running crowd. Varney shoved Mrs. Varney behind the heavy wooden bar and threw himself over her.

"Ooof," said Mrs. Varney.

"Hush," said Varney.

The painting crumbled slowly like a dam dissolving before raging flood water. Plaster and stones, flecked with a blue rainbow of painted colors, washed across the floor.

Chairs and tables snapped like twigs beneath the dragon's great weight as he advanced into the room. Malaeragoth lashed his tail free of the painting and the roof beams cracked as he rose to his full height, pushing up against them. Malaeragoth roared, a psionic blast that blew through the crowd like a storm wind through a flock of birds. The sheer force of Malaeragoth's cry buckled the remaining walls and blew out the shutters. Nix and Silver leaped through the open window and ran as fast as they could, never stopping until they reached the edge of town.

But Badger Bates stood firm, rooted by the sheer shock

of seeing the sapphire dragon again and frozen by the fury of knowing that he was not the last living person to witness Malaeragoth's fabled rage.

And Malaeragoth fell upon Badger Bates, crushing him beneath sapphire scales. The dragon raised itself off the dead dwarf, roared once more, and vanished as suddenly as it had appeared.

—— ❧ ——

When the dust cleared from the collapse of the north wall and the subsequent fall of the Dragon Defeated's roof, Varney and Mrs. Varney crawled out from their hiding place behind the bar and began to pick through the ruins.

Once assured that the sapphire dragon was gone, Nix and Silver, being very thankful to still be alive, returned to help them.

"Well," said Silver, rummaging through Badger's flattened remains as any good thief would, "there's nothing of value here." He slipped his former friend's purse into his own pocket and blew the dust of the crushed iron box and Malaeragoth's sapphire scale off his hands. "What have you got there, Nix?"

"It's the sign," said Nix. He called to the tavernkeeper trying to dig out his squashed coin box from the rubble. "Hey, Varney, do you want this?"

The sign's paint had been scraped away in several places, leaving the rearing white dragon without a head, showing only two of the three adventurers, and depicting just the remains of the painted dwarf's left boot. But the princess, with a tiny crown perched on top of her golden curls, was still smiling valiantly at her rescuers.

"Aww," said Nix, "it's a terrible shame that it's so ruined. It was a grand picture. Maybe you could have the painter woman paint it again. She said she was sorry for what happened, but

Bates shouldn't have tried to cheat on a bet."

Varney shuddered. "Not her. I'll have nothing more to do with a woman who draws dragons," he said. "She's off to the east, says she wants to study landwyrms."

Varney took the sign from Nix and stared at it for a few minutes.

"I have an idea," Varney said, getting more and more enthusiastic as he talked. "I'll cut it down and just save the princess. We could call the new place something like the Royal Rescue and hire a bard to sing tales of royal ladies in love. Everybody likes a good love story in the springtime. Stories about princesses are much safer than letting people draw dragons on a wall."

But that princess idea, as Mrs. Varney would say in later years to friends and relations, was just the start of another of Varney's disasters.

THE HUNTING GAME

ERIK SCOTT DE BIE

Flamerule, the Year of the Wave (1364 DR)

The caravan rolled along, the wagons creaking, the men coughing and cursing, and the horses whinnying, just as it had for miles and miles before across the Heartlands. The road to Baldur's Gate would be a long one, one that many of the gruff caravan guards had seen many times before. They were familiar with it, familiar enough to watch gullies, turns, stands of trees, and boulders that made up familiar ambush spots.

The scouts were so preoccupied with watching for trouble at their flanks, front, or rear, such that few paid attention to a dark shape in the sky.

Few except Alin Cateln.

Looking out the window, idly plucking at his harp as the wagon in which he rode jostled on, the young bard wondered absently if it was a wisp of cloud or some high-flying night bird. The trip had passed so uneventfully that he was eager to make up distractions for himself on this, the sixth day out of Hill's Edge. His seat tossed him up and down, but still it was more comfortable than a saddle.

"Say, what's that, do you reckon?" he asked the driver.

The gruff-faced man looked at the sky. "What?"

"That shape right there," Alin said, pointing.

"There? The only thing that ain't cloud?" he asked, and Alin nodded. "That'd be Selûne, boy, on her nightly walk."

Alin rolled his eyes. Of course the man had not seen it. Just like that, the shape—if it had even existed outside his imagination—vanished.

The stopover in Hill's Edge had been entirely too long and torturous, for the warm Flamerule nights—especially in the hot Year of the Wave—had kept joviality and company outside the inns and taverns where he had needed to play for his lodging and meals. Dashing young men with songs on their tongues and blushing maidens with flaxen or dusky hair and faces tanned golden by the sun . . . too bad Alin had been trapped indoors.

The wagon gave a shake and disrupted his reverie. Tossing the dark hair that fell in spikes across his face, Alin plucked a sour note on his harp. Ever since that day when his father had sent him away for failing at the Cormyrean academy, Alin had always needed to sing for his supper, or for rides with caravans, and not make merry.

Even on the road, he had to compete with another, much more practiced minstrel: an adventuring bard by the name of Tannin, who traveled with the caravan along with his adventuring companions. The caravanners would surely put Alin off soon—he only hoped they waited until Triel.

There came shouts from outside, but he ignored them. Surely it was just another arguing match between two of the caravan guards.

Unbidden, the words of a song came to his lips, and he strummed a few notes on the harp.

"I walk the road both winding and true," he sang. "It leads to friends both old and new."

Alin was in the midst of remembering the third line when the front half of the wagon vanished in a flash of burning crimson fury. The force of the blast threw him back, shattering open the shutters on the wagon window as his body flew out. Immolated by flames spawned from the Nine Hells themselves, Alin screamed in pain and terror. Through the darkness, he could see only one thing—the flash of a terrible, dark eye wreathed in crackling flame.

Then he saw nothing.

∗∞∞∗

When light came back into the world, Alin was aware of a sensation of softness surrounding his body. He wondered, for a moment, if he had made it to the Great Wheel and if he would see his mistress Tymora any instant.

Then, after a few happy breaths, Alin realized he was hungry—in fact, he was starving. A brief look around told him he was not quite in Brightwater yet. Instead, Alin was merely tucked under thick blankets and staring up at the ceiling of a bedroom.

He tried to rise, but his head exploded in lancing pain. At first, Alin was afraid his head had come free of his body, but he soon realized—by feeling with his fingers—that it was still attached to his neck.

What a terrible dream, Alin thought.

Finally, after many abortive attempts, Alin managed to lever himself out of bed. He was nude but he was not cold. The window, open to the night air, let in a pleasant breeze. The room was simple, bare, and small, with only a bed and a chair for furniture. His light tunic, indigo-dyed vest, and leather breeches, neatly folded, sat on the chair. Alin picked them up and inhaled their scent—not flowery, but clean.

For a moment, as he dressed, Alin wondered if it was all just a dream. Then he heard voices. The joyous sounds of a tavern rose to meet him from down a flight of stairs.

Still rubbing his head but smiling, Alin went down.

— ❧❦❧ —

The atmosphere in the common room of Triel's Singing Wind Inn was on the somber side, though travelers still raised tankards and mugs in toasts to companions long gone and new friends made. Several spoke in hushed voices about a dragon attack, but Alin didn't know if it was for real, or just the ale talking. The rafters were smoke-stained and the air was thick with the scent of pipes, spilled ale, and unwashed bodies. A bard strummed on a harp and sung a tawdry ballad of gallant but stupid knights and the lusty barmaids who loved them.

Alin inhaled deeply and felt his lungs burn. He loved every moment of it.

Over in the corner, Alin glimpsed an unusual pair—a hulking man in dark leathers with a greataxe standing by the table and a thin woman in silks and robes who must have been half the man's size—sharing a quiet drink. He did not have time to see more, as a meaty hand came from the side to catch his shoulder.

"Hey, look who's up!" a friendly voice said.

Alin turned. Beside him was a hefty man in a gold and white tunic. His skin was fair, his hair gold, and he wore a thick mustache.

"I'm sorry, have we met?" asked Alin, who didn't know the face.

"If by 'met,' ye mean 'hauled yer half-dead carcass from the burning wreck of a caravan and healed ye while Thard carried ye back 'ere,' then aye, we've met," the man said. "After the dragon, ye're lucky to be alive—thank the Morninglord for young bones!"

It came back to Alin in a flash: the caravan, the flames, and the burning eye. Apparently, it had *not* all been a dream.

"You . . . you saved my life?" Alin asked. "How can I repay you?"

"Well, yer name would be a good start," the man said. He took Alin's hand. "Mine be Delkin Snowdawn, Morning Brother of Lathander, o' Luskan. And who might ye be?"

"A-Alin," the young bard managed through teeth clenched against the pain in his hand. Delkin's grasp was certainly a firm one. When the priest finally released his hand, Alin put it behind his back and rubbed it. "Alin Cateln, of Tilverton."

"Ah, a Cormyrean," Delkin said. "Good wine there—some o' the best."

Alin nodded dumbly. He was about to speak again when Delkin seized him about the waist and pulled him along.

"Ye've got to meet me friends, the other Moor Runners," he boomed. "And, seeing as how ye're awake, let me get ye a drink to put ye back to sleep."

Alin blinked, and the priest laughed and added, "Ah, I just be kiddin' with ye."

"Moor Runners?" Alin asked. That sounded familiar.

"Won quite a name for ourselves in the Evermoors, killing trolls," Delkin replied. "Though that be quite a while back, the name just stuck, ye know. Come o'er here."

Alin could not refuse as the priest half carried him over to the mismatched pair he had seen before.

"Thard and Inri," Delkin introduced, indicating the hulking man and the slight woman in turn.

"My lord, my lady," Alin said with a low bow.

The man was even bigger close up. The woman was a petite elf maid, with hair like gold and a complexion to match. The two completely ignored Alin.

He stood there a moment, uncertain, and looked at Delkin, but the priest was already gone. He turned back to the companions. His mind racing fast, Alin did the only thing he could do: he searched for clues as to what he should say. His eye caught on the design etched in the blade of the greataxe.

"The blades of Tempus, emblazoned upon a swift steed," he said. "That means you are a warrior of the Sky Ponies, correct? Such a heavy axe—you must be a strong warrior."

The hulking man looked at him curiously and asked, "Aye, what of it?" His voice was rough and deep.

The bard turned to the elf maid next. "And you, fair lady, by your garb I make you to be a sorceress—shifting veils that change colors in the light, to reflect the chaos that is your magic, am I right?" he asked.

She looked at him for the first time, and her eyes were startlingly pink and red in hue.

"And your gaze, like the sunrise . . ." Alin began. "It reminds me of a ballad. 'Ah, many a time I've spent, on soft-packed ground with my dear lassie, watching the golden jewel climb lazily, my arm around her, gazing more into her eyes than the rise . . .'"

By the time Delkin brought him the promised drink, Alin was sitting with the two, rattling on and on about his journeys, art, and life story. Thard wore a soft, proud smile, and even Inri's eyes were dancing.

"Ye make friends quick," Delkin praised him as he passed tankards of ale around the table. The barbarian took his tankard and drained it off in one gulp.

"Your companions are fine adventurers," Alin said. "I was merely listening to their stories—they are the ones worthy of praise, not I."

"Mayhap," Delkin said. He eyed Inri suspiciously, and the elf maid's eyes twitched toward him. "Though they be having ulterior motives. . . ."

Alin's brow wrinkled and he asked, "What ulterior motives?"

The Moor Runners looked at one another.

"I had doubted it before," Inri said. If moonlight could dance, Alin thought, it might have been her voice. "But not now. We wish to have you join us."

"As our skald . . . er, bard," Thard rumbled.

Delkin nodded and smiled broadly.

Alin was stunned. "But, what, why?" he asked. "You . . . you just met me, and now you want me to be part of your band?"

Delkin wrapped his arm around Alin. "Ye see, Alven—" he began.

"Alin," the bard corrected him.

"Right. Our bard, Tannin . . . well, he . . . ah, *departed* at the caravan, and we're looking for a replacement."

Alin's suspicions were confirmed—the Moor Runners were the adventurers who had been with the caravan.

"A replacement?" asked Alin. "And you want *me?*"

"That be yer trade, aye?" replied the priest. "We heard ye sing along the road, and—"

"I'd love to come with you!" Alin shouted, startling the Moor Runners. None had expected such a reply, and so quickly, but none protested.

"Good," Thard rumbled. "Been needin' a good tune, e'er since Tannin was killed."

"Killed?" asked Alin.

An unhappy Delkin flinched and glowered at Thard.

"In the dragon attack," Inri explained.

"Aye, wretched beast took us by surprise," Delkin mused. "Poor Tannin . . . 'Tis a risky line of work, adventuring and all. . . ." He looked at Alin. "Er, not that ye'll be in any danger."

Alin realized he should have been terrified, but instead he felt excitement rushing through him.

"A dragon?" Alin asked. "You can kill such a creature, right?"

The Moor Runners looked at one another, dubious.

Finally Delkin shrugged and said, "Aye, definitely. Ah, well ... mayhap. Well, ah, not actually, no. Well, what we really need ..."

Just then, the doors of the Wind swung open and crashed loudly against the interior walls. The heads of the inn's patrons, as though pulled by invisible reins, jerked toward the disturbance, and more than a few breaths caught.

The fiery-haired woman who entered the common room was tall, slim, and stunning. Black leather and plate in the Thayan style, complete with spikes like talons, wrapped her muscular frame. A black half-cape fell from one shoulder and a sheathed, curved sword was thrust through her belt of dark reptile skin. A silver ring in the shape of a winged dragon swallowing its own tail gleamed from her right hand. A spiked gauntlet covered her left. Her pale face was lean and sharp, and her eyes—gleaming dark orbs—had a hungry look to them.

"Who be the beauty, I wonder?" Delkin said.

Inri looked sharply at him, then turned wary eyes back on the stranger. Alin said nothing. He just sat there, stunned.

The silence lasted only a moment before the woman spoke. Her voice was powerful, almost husky, and easily caught the attention of all who heard.

"I understand you've a dragon about," she said.

"Aye? What of it?" a one-eyed patron scoffed.

"I'm looking for a few brave souls who'll help me dispose of the beast," the woman replied. "I need a tracker and a mage, if possible."

"Help *ye?*" another man asked. Alin recognized him as a snide caravanner. "Some lass in ridiculous ..."

He trailed off when a sliver of metal appeared at his throat. A gasp ran through the common room. No one had seen the woman so much as move, much less draw her blade. The man trembled, his mouth hanging open.

"Ryla Dragonclaw," she said from between clenched teeth. "Remember it."

The man quivered in fear under the intensity of her gaze.

"The Dragonslayer!" Alin blurted. His voice sounded blasphemously loud in the awed stillness.

Ryla's eyes flicked to him and she sheathed her sword with a flourish. Leaving a relieved caravanner behind her, Ryla walked toward the Moor Runners, her step smooth and confident.

"You know me," she said to Alin, her words meant only for him.

He tried to stammer out a response, but no words would come. Her direct speech and her burning gaze thrilled and stunned him. Struck dumb, the bard could only look at that vision of loveliness, her hair painting a crimson corona around her sensuous face.

"Well met, Lady Dragonclaw," Delkin started.

"Just Ryla," the dragonslayer said. "I am no lady, nor a knight."

The priest shrugged and went on, "Ryla, then. I be Delkin Snowdawn, captain o' the Moor Runners. This is Alin Catalan—"

"Cateln," Alin breathed.

"Right," Delkin said. "Alin Catalan of Tilverton—" he gestured to Inri and Thard—"and these be—"

"Ah, adventurers," she interrupted the priest, continuing to speak to the bard.

The two other Moor Runners narrowed their eyes. Ryla looked directly at Alin and mouthed his name, as though turning it over on her tongue. A shiver of thrill passed down his spine.

"Just what I need," the strange woman added.

Inri looked at Ryla, then at Delkin, but it was Alin who spoke. "To slay your dragon?" he asked with unmasked excitement.

"Tharas'kalagram," Ryla replied. "Yes. A red wyrm I've followed this far. I know where he's headed, and I need some brave and . . ." She looked Alin up and down. Her eyes were burning. *"Hearty* adventurers to help me kill him."

As she stared at Alin, she licked her lips ever so slightly, so only he could notice.

"My apologies, dragonslayer," Delkin said, taking the prompt from Inri. "We're a bit occupied at the moment replacing our bard, and we can't be bothered to—"

"We'll do it!" Alin said.

The other Moor Runners looked at him with expressions ranging from the shock on Delkin's face, to the surprise registering through Thard's features, and the horrified disdain in Inri's eyes.

Ryla's ruby lips curled up in the vestiges of a smile.

"Rest well, then, brave sir bard," she said. "We leave at dawn, for the Forest of Wyrms."

"Who gave you the right to speak for us?" Inri asked as soon as Alin came out of the inn, rubbing his eyes in the bright sunlight.

"What?" asked Alin as he finished securing the cuffs of his tunic. "I thought. . ."

The Moor Runners were all saddled and ready before Alin, who was unused to rising at first light. Atop a giant black stallion, Thard was a giant in furs and boiled leather. On a white mare next to him, Inri rode sidesaddle, clad in green and silver silks. In scale mail and a white tabard with the sunrise of Lathander, the priest Delkin looked nervous on his dun. With a whistle from her rider, Delkin's steed stepped in front of Inri's mare and the priest spoke to calm the sorceress.

"Alkin, I'm all for dragon slaying, but can we really trust this heroine o' yers?"

Alin didn't get a chance to correct him as Inri spoke up. "She wears a magical ring—and that is all. Would a dragon-slayer really be so naked of magic?'

Thard nodded. Even though the Uthgardt people didn't make extensive use of magic, he had to agree. "Something seems wrong."

"Maybe she's just ... amazing," the bard argued. He patted Neb, his strong Cormyrean steed. He was pleased the horse had survived the dragon's attack. "Thayan armor is renowned, and a katana—a Kara-Turan blade—*is* the finest sword ever made. Mayhap she doesn't need magic."

The Moor Runners were all about to protest, but something silenced them. Alin felt a presence behind him.

"Mayhap I don't," offered Ryla's sultry voice.

Striding up to them, the dragonslayer was radiant. The dark armor made a striking contrast with her milky skin and her hair seemed afire in the sunrise. Her eyes were fixed on Alin. He lost himself again in those smoldering eyes.

After a moment, Delkin cleared his throat. "You have no horse, Lady?" he asked.

"I've always preferred to carry myself," Ryla said without breaking the gaze she shared with the bard. She paused, but only for a breath before adding, "On my own two feet."

Delkin grinned, but saw—from a look at his companions—that lightening the mood was a lost cause.

"We shall outpace you for certain," Inri said. "Unless you run as fast as you draw steel."

Ryla looked away and fixed her deadly gaze on the elf maid, who met it, but soon shrank back, seeming to grow smaller on her steed. Thard fingered his axe, and a slight smile crossed Ryla's face.

"You can ride with me," Alin offered, startling all.

They all looked at him—Inri in disbelief, Ryla with a slightly bemused smile.

"As you wish," Inri said.

She turned to the north, muttering something under her breath in Elvish, and urged her steed into a trot. The mount gave a snort but started walking, and Thard's steed followed. Delkin shrugged and turned as well.

Ryla looked up at Alin with thanks written on her pale features and offered a playfully dainty hand. He pulled her up, and was startled at her grip—it was more powerful than that of Captain Agatan, the strongest soldier he had ever known. She mounted behind him and wrapped her arms gently around his waist. His face flushed, but he would not turn and let her see.

"Hold tight," he murmured.

"Always," replied Ryla. Her whisper, so close in his ear, startled and excited him.

The journey to the Forest of Wyrms took most of the day, with short breaks for meals and walking the horses. During the entire ride, Ryla had pressed her body close against Alin, and when they had walked the horses, she'd stayed close to him. It didn't seem she was doing it intentionally—indeed, Ryla hardly seemed aware of either her proximity or her effect on the bard—but Alin hardly cared. He could feel the soft swell of her slim stomach juxtaposed against the cool steel of her armor. The odd duality was thrilling.

"What is it you've got there?" the bard asked Delkin, trying to get his mind off the beautiful dragonslayer. He had wondered about Delkin's saddlebags all morning.

"Oh, ye mean these?" the cleric asked, unbuckling and lifting one of the flaps. Contained in the saddlebags were thick, heavy pots and pans, spoons, ladles, and other cooking utensils. "There ain't nothing beats a good meal on the road, I always say."

"You're a cook?" Alin asked, eyeing Delkin's ample belly.

The sturdy priest laughed. "No, no," said Delkin. "I'm more an eater than a cooker. But Thard's a cook to rival the finest in Waterdeep. He'll be cookin' dinner this e'en . . . ye'll see what I be meaning."

They broke for a highsun meal among a stand of boulders. Delkin broke out the trail rations and began dividing them, but Ryla declined the hardtack and dried fruit, saying she was not hungry. None of the Moor Runners protested. They fell to their meal while she went around one of the boulders.

After a few minutes of biting the hardened bread, Alin found he was not hungry either. Or, at least, not for trail rations. Rather, he hungered and thirsted for Ryla's presence. He excused himself and followed the dragonslayer. His exit drew glances ranging from the bemused, in Delkin's case, to the suspicious, in Inri's. Alin climbed the small mountain of giant rocks in search of a certain fiery-haired warrior.

It didn't take the bard long to find Ryla. The beautiful dragonslayer was perched on the highest boulder, gazing all around, like a queen surveying her lands. She was turned away from his approach, and her blade lay across her lap. As the sunlight played along the katana's length, it almost seemed that the crimson dragon etched on the steel was alive and dancing.

"Looking for our quarry?" Alin asked.

Ryla leaped to her feet and spun, blade up and ready. The bard, startled, stumbled back toward the edge of the boulder. He teetered on one foot and fought to keep his balance.

He realized Ryla was laughing. The woman had sheathed her katana and extended a hand to help him. He took it, and she pulled him up with seemingly little effort.

"You could say that," she replied. "Though, really, I'm just looking."

Almost the same instant Alin realized she was still holding his hand, Ryla let him go and moved away. She took up her position on the rock again, one leg bent close to her chest. Her hair shimmered in the sunlight.

Breath was hard to come by for the bard, though he knew he would have to remember to breathe or he would pass out on his feet.

"Lady Dragonclaw?" Alin asked.

"Just Ryla," replied the dragonslayer. She glanced at him to accentuate her point. "I'm no lady."

"Oh, aye. I remember." Alin felt warmth rising in him at the familiarity. "Ryla ... You must tell me about your travels—your exploits. I collect stories, and you're famous, after all."

"There's not much to tell." Ryla looked away and said, "I hunt dragons. 'Tis a game, nothing more."

"A game?"

A smile played across Ryla's fine features. Alin felt self conscious and looked away.

She said, "To me, 'tis a game, as surely as you skip rocks over water or fought with wooden swords as a child. Some hunt foxes, some boars. I hunt dragons. A hunting game."

Alin drank in her words for a moment before he realized she had stopped.

"But ..." he said, "but surely there is more!" He looked back, and she was smiling mischievously. "Like, ah, how many have you slain? How do you seem so young when your legend was told in my father's day? You are no elf maid! Why do you vanish for years at a time and return in the tales? Whence your armor, or your sword? Are they of some great epic make—a master smith, or an archmage?"

"Nothing so fancy," replied Ryla. "As to how many, surely you can count." Alin had noticed the twelve spikes on her armor before, but he finally realized what they were: dragon claws. "And 'tis not polite to ask a lady her age."

"I thought you were no lady," returned Alin.

Ryla gave him a devious smile. "Some secrets I'll keep," she said. "Except to observe that those stories you mention were probably told in your grandfather's day, not your father's."

Alin's eyes opened wide in surprise, but the dragonslayer's lips moved no more. He left her to her surveying and climbed back down, his mind roiling.

⸻ ⟡ ⸻

The sun was dipping in the east. The Moor Runners had been traveling over flat plains for a long while, and they were about to ride over a rise when they heard a bird's cry from above. Inri waved them to stop. The sorceress put out her arm and gave a fey whistle. In a moment, a black raven swooped down and landed on her bracer. Then the bird began speaking to Inri in perfect Elvish.

"Her familiar," Delkin explained.

Ryla gave a snort.

The raven finished and Inri nodded. At her short command, the bird squawked and flew off.

Inri turned to the Moor Runners and said, "Anthas says there is a war party of orcs encamped immediately to the north—a score or more of them."

Delkin nodded and said, "Aye, then, we'll break here and camp."

The Moor Runners swung down from their horses and began unstrapping their saddlebags. Alin dismounted and offered his hand up to Ryla. The dragonslayer, however, did not notice.

With a suspicious look on her fine features, she glared at Inri from atop Alin's steed, and asked, "Why are we stopping?"

"It wouldn't make sense to waste our energy on a score of orcs," Delkin explained as he unrolled his travel tent. "They're not hurting anyone at the moment—let them be for now."

"They're vermin," argued Ryla with a hiss. "They should be destroyed."

"But we're hunting a dragon," reminded Alin. "Not orcs."

The dragonslayer regarded him with a venomous stare. He could see her temper flaring again.

"I hadn't forgotten," she said as she pulled the reins from his hand. "Don't make camp just yet. I'll be right back."

With that, she wheeled to the north and kicked Neb into a gallop. Fiery hair and black half-cape streaming behind her, she flew over the plains toward the orc camp.

"Morninglord's heel!" shouted Delkin.

The Moor Runners dropped their gear and scrambled to mount and follow. Deprived of his horse and pack, Alin began running after Ryla. Of course, the horse easily outdistanced him. As soon as he got to the top of the hill, he stopped and his jaw dropped in shock.

A hundred yards away, Ryla had just reached the orc encampment, where there were considerably more than a score of orcs. There were perhaps three-dozen of the creatures, all with weapons close to hand. They leaped up with shouts of alarm but Ryla didn't even hesitate. The flame-haired woman pounced from the charging Neb, steel flashing in her hands, and slammed her feet into the first orc to rise. She rode him down and fell onto the others with blade and fist.

Logic told Alin that she was hopelessly overmatched, but Ryla didn't hesitate for a heartbeat. She laid into the orcs with her blade, slashing left and right. Everywhere her blade fell, dead and dying orcs tumbled down, and her fist slapped weapons aside and knocked more of the creatures from their feet. Blades struck her armor but she shrugged them off without pause.

Alin felt a song of battle coming to his lips, unbidden, and he sang as loud as he could, praying Ryla could hear him and take heart from his song.

In short order, though, he realized the ballad was not meant to encourage her. Rather, it merely praised her ferocity. There was no grace or finesse to her fighting, only sheer brutality and phenomenal strength.

After a single verse had been sung and a dozen orcs felled, the other Moor Runners arrived and stared at the woman tearing through the orcs like an incarnation of fury.

"By the dawn. . . ." Delkin breathed.

Ryla slashed down, disemboweling a yelping orc on her right, and knocked a berserker down on her left with a punch. An orc stepped on her katana blade, held it pinned, and raised its greataxe over its head with a deep war cry. Ryla roared right back, jerked the blade up with a pulse of her mighty shoulders, throwing the orc off its feet into the air, and cut the hapless creature in two as it fell to the ground. Then she spun and caught a high slash from behind.

Neb, who had been left unmolested by the orcs who were more intent on the wild woman attacking them, had circled around and soon trotted to a stop next to the loudly singing bard.

Alin's ballad cut off as he realized Inri was casting a spell. Tongues of flame curled and licked around her silvery bracers and condensed between her hands into a bead of crimson. Alin's eyes went wide—he had seen war wizards sling fire before—and moved to stop her, but Thard held him back. Alin realized he could not break Inri's concentration, or the spell might go awry and explode in the midst of the Moor Runners.

He watched, helpless, as the elf maid opened her eyes and threw toward the battle, where the last of the orcs had surrounded Ryla. An inferno burst in the camp, and Alin averted his eyes. He could hardly hear the screams over the dull roar of the flames.

When he looked back, the camp was a smoldering ruin. His heart fell—he thought Ryla killed for sure—but then he saw movement.

Delkin motioned Alin to mount his waiting horse then he

led the Moor Runners down the hill toward the blackened encampment.

Tapping her blade against her boot, Ryla was waiting for them. The fire had seared the blood from the katana blade and her skin, but had not blackened either. It seemed the flame had done nothing except purify her.

"You're alive!" the bard gasped in relief.

As Alin came closer, however, he saw that her legs were trembling. He leaped from his saddle and rushed to her. Weak, Ryla collapsed on his shoulder. She felt surprisingly light, almost frail in his arms.

"Didn't think . . . I could . . . handle it, eh?" Ryla asked, her breath short. She held up her right hand. The silver dragon ring glowed fiercely.

"Your ring blocks fire?" asked the bard.

Ryla gave a weak laugh. "Something . . . like that," she replied.

As Alin helped her mount Neb, Ryla flashed a look at Inri . . . a little smile that set the elf maid bristling as though at a thinly veiled threat.

━━━✑⟋⟍✑━━━

The Moor Runners set up camp a mile outside the Forest of Wyrms. At a distance, the forest looked peaceful, almost inviting. The towering redwoods were spread out enough to accommodate several men walking abreast, and rose majestically into the sky. Alin could not help singing a soft ballad about the place that he'd learned in Cormyr. The Moor Runners seemed comforted by his voice—except for Ryla, whose expression was unreadable.

"A bold and epic tale will be our deeds, or a dark and tragic one will be our deaths," Alin sang. He felt a little thrill run through him, and he hesitated to begin another verse.

"Restrain yer enthusiasm," Delkin said with a clap on the

shoulder that startled Alin out of his tune. The bard looked at the priest in shock, but Delkin smiled. "And get yeself some rest. We've got a big day ahead of us tomorrow." He gestured at Alin's rapier. "I haven't even asked. Ye know how to use that thing?"

"Ah . . . of course!" Alin said. "I've taken lessons since I could walk, and—"

"Good," the cleric rumbled. "Ye might need it tomorrow."

"Tomorrow?"

"There be dragons 'ere, boy," Delkin said. "Hope ye paid attention at those lessons, though them beasts don't take to fencing much."

The priest rumbled with laughter and walked back to where Thard was cooking, a dozen paces away.

Alin smiled. He pulled his harp out of his saddlebags and unwrapped it carefully. Easing it into its accustomed position against the calluses inside his arm, he strummed a few notes on the strings. He wondered if he might spend a few hours that evening working on the new lay he was composing: *The Ballad of Dragonclaw*.

"Eyes like fire, atop a golden spire . . ." he sang. "Surveying the land, queen of the hunting game . . ."

He stopped himself. He had not meant to sing those words. It was just something Ryla had said, words that were running through his mind. The hunting game . . .

"A dangerous game," he breathed.

"I can't eat this!" Ryla's angry voice came. "It's practically raw."

Alin turned his head just in time to see Ryla hurl a haunch of venison in Thard's face. The barbarian barely caught the seared meat before it smacked into his nose. Sizzling juices still came off the meat, however, spattering his skin, beard, and fur coat.

" 'Ware, ye wench!" he roared, as though castigating an impulsive child who was throwing a tantrum. He slapped the meat aside and into the dust.

Delkin tried to save the venison but his fingers were too clumsy and he dropped it.

"Justiciar's hand!" the priest cursed. "It's ruined!"

Delkin rounded on Ryla and the Moor Runners fell silent. From the looks on their faces, Alin guessed that he had just discovered how one went about making the normally ebullient cleric furious: wasted food. Putting his hands on his hips, he gazed death at the dragonslayer.

Ryla was not about to back down. She drew herself up even taller than her intimidating frame should have allowed and faced the broad-shouldered priest. Her pursed lips said nothing but Alin could see them trembling a tiny bit. He got the distinct sense, however, that it was not from fear.

Delkin seemed to have composed himself, though Alin could see his hands trembling. " 'Twas cooked in the Uthgardt style," he rumbled. "Perfectly seasoned, lovingly handled. Thard is a master cook, and ye have insulted him. Apologize." It was not a request.

"It wasn't cooked enough," Ryla retorted with a dismissive wave. "Your master cook is a master fool."

" 'Twas well done—half burned, even, just as ye asked!" Delkin roared. "Apologize!"

"I refuse," responded Ryla.

"Ye insult all o' us!" Delkin shouted. "Apologize!"

"No."

There was silence. The four adventurers stared at the dragonslayer in varying degress of shock. Thard's gaze was stony, Inri's suspicious, and Delkin's outright furious. Alin looked at Ryla with sympathy, and he could not keep the longing out of his gaze.

The dragonslayer looked around at the four faces and found nothing that pleased her in any of the gazes. Her lip curled up in a self-righteous sneer.

"Is *this* what passes for heroism these days?" she asked. "Rudeness? Discourtesy? Suspicion?" She looked at Delkin,

Thard, and Inri respectively as she spat those three words. "Are all of you adventurers *this* unwelcoming to those who would call you friend?"

There was no response. The Moor Runners looked at her with wide eyes, but no one spoke. Alin gaped. Thard brooded. Delkin flushed. Inri just looked at Ryla with a baleful glare.

Ryla made a dismissive sound in her throat then said, "Pathetic—"

With that, she turned on her heel and stormed out of the campsite toward the trees.

The three Moor Runners looked at Alin, dumbfounded.

"She'll get over it," the bard assured them. "She's not *really* angry."

"I hope a dragon eats every one of you!" the dragonslayer shouted back, rage hot in her voice.

The Moor Runners, all but Inri suitably chagrined, sent helpless looks the bard's way.

"Ye go and talk to the lass," suggested Delkin with downcast eyes. "She be in no mood for any o' us."

Before the suggestion even passed the cleric's lips, Alin was already following the dragonslayer.

She walked only a short way before picking up the pace, and even began running. The bard followed without hesitation, clutching his deep indigo cloak against the night's chill. She was making excellent time, and his talents had never exactly *run* to run*ning*.

Alin decided to file that joke away for future use.

In a few minutes, Ryla passed between the tall redwoods at the edge of the Forest of Wyrms and Alin pulled up short, perhaps a hundred yards behind her.

He reached into his tunic and drew out a silver coin on a leather thong. Then he gave a short prayer. "Lady Luck, for the love I bear thee, don't let a dragon pounce on me!"

He kissed the symbol and jogged toward the wood. Clouds

came over the moon, so he pulled out a sphere of glass and strummed a high note on his harp. With the touch of his bardic magic—little more than a cantrip of power—the large marble began to glow with a soft, red-white radiance akin to a torch.

He came upon Ryla in a small grove near the edge of the forest. Her katana discarded, she was punching one of the trees with her spiked gauntlet, taking off chunks of reddish wood with each left-handed strike. The bard watched for a moment, awed at her strength, and cleared his throat.

Ryla stopped punching the tree and leaned against it, her back to him, as though the strength had gone out of her.

He took a step forward and said, "Ryla . . ."

She turned, her eyes burning. Her features were luminous and almost feral under Selûne's glow. Water had stained her cheeks and seemed to gleam crimson in his magelight.

"What do you know?" she demanded. "What gives you the right to judge me?"

"I'm not judging you," Alin said.

"Then why are you here?" pressed Ryla.

"I . . ." The bard trailed off. How could he speak, when she was so beautiful in the moonlight? Somehow, he managed, "I only thought I'd ask you . . . about my ballad."

"A ballad?" Ryla looked intrigued. "What ballad?"

She took a step toward him.

"Ah! A-about you," he stammered. "The ballad of—of Dragonclaw."

"A song about me?" Ryla said, one scarlet eyebrow rising.

As she walked toward him, her hands deftly unbuckled the black breastplate she wore and slid it over her head. It fell to the ground, revealing her gray undershirt—an undershirt soaked with sweat and clinging tightly to her skin.

Alin swallowed. It had grown even harder to think coherently.

"Ah, yes . . . a ballad."

She stepped within reach, unbuckled her black leather skirt, and stepped out of it.

"Wri-written b-by me." Alin stuttered. He felt warm all over.

"Tell me, good sir bard," Ryla purred. He had had no idea she could sound like that. She raised her right hand and ran the back of her fingers down his cheek. Her touch sent tremors through his body. "Is there anyone . . . special, back home, waiting for her dark-haired, blue-eyed hero to come home a dragonslayer?"

She stepped closer and stared into his eyes.

"N-no," Alin said.

Ryla pressed her body against his, and chills shot through him. He could see tiny flecks of what he thought was crimson in her eyes. She was so beautiful. . . .

"Though I . . . I've always loved . . . the lady Alusair . . . from afar."

"A princess, eh?" Ryla murmured. She pressed her lips against his cheek and her breasts against his chest. "I can hardly compete."

"Oh, it's just—" she kissed his neck and ear—"a boy's fantasy."

"A fantasy. . . ." she whispered.

She pushed him down, and Alin fell on his rump. One foot on either side of him, Ryla towered over him. She pulled the tunic over her head and stood in the moonlight in only her boots and ring. Her hair was a fiery cascade and her flawless skin sparkled. She put her hands on her hips. The movement only emphasized her curves.

"Who is your princess now?" she asked with a lusty smile.

"Y-you are," the bard stammered.

"Perfect answer."

Then Ryla slid down onto him, and Alin lost all ability to think.

He didn't need to.

"What's new with ye, boy?" Delkin asked Alin, clapping him hard on the shoulder.

The bard didn't even notice. They were deep in the Forest of Wyrms, one of the most dangerous places in Faerûn, with certain death all around, but he hardly thought about it. His star-struck eyes were fixed on Ryla's smooth shoulders as she strode ahead of them, her black half-cape shifting in the light breeze, and her hair a scarlet cascade.

"Oh, nothing," the bard replied. "Just musing over a dream I had last night."

The dragonslayer's face, by chance, half turned to him. An errant strand of hair fell across her face. Alin felt warm all over.

"Several times, last night," he added.

"By the looks of yer musing, it must've been a good 'un," the priest said with a snicker. Then Delkin's expression turned serious. "Don't let it distract ye. There be dragons 'ere, and ye needs be on yer guard. What can ye tell us o' this place?"

Shaking his head to clear it of his daydreams, Alin pursed his lips. He recalled all the stories he had ever heard of the Western Heartlands and the Forest of Wyrms.

"It's said green dragons have claimed this place," explained Alin. "And for good reason. The beasts infest the forest as thickly as jackrabbits."

"Keep yer eyes open," said Delkin with a nod.

Alin nodded. He looked at the other Moor Runners as they picked through the dense helmthorn brush, trying not to be stabbed by needles that were as long as a man's hand. Scanning the ground in front of them, Thard was impassive as always, but his hand was on the axe at his belt. Ryla followed close behind him, ready to draw her blade at a moment's notice. Only Inri's attention seemed not focused on the task at hand. Instead, she watched Ryla's every move with suspicion, and more than once Alin caught her hand moving through the gestures of a spell.

"What's with Inri?" the bard asked Delkin.

Delkin wore a bemused smile when he turned to Alin and said, "Oh, Madam Sorceress isn't too happy she's no longer the on'y lass around us Moor Runners anymore. Women kin be competitive, if'n ye know what I mean. At least she 'as Thard."

Alin's mind filled in the details. "Is that all?" pressed Alin.

"An' she be suspicious," the priest admitted. "Lady Dragonclaw's magic be concealed."

Alin raised a finger to his lips in thought.

"Aye, a mystery," agreed Delkin. He looked up at the front of the group. "Lady Dragonclaw, ye're sure our dragon's here? I haven't seen or heard anything."

"My apologies, but you're a priest, not a scout," Ryla said, not bothering to correct him regarding her name. "And yes. I saw him land here, and he hasn't left since the attack on the caravan."

Reassured, the Moor Runners continued on, looking all around, all the time. Alin pressed all his senses into service, using the techniques he had learned from his master to extend his hearing into the surrounding trees.

Thus, he was startled when Inri appeared at his side, seemingly from nowhere.

"Is she not suspicious?" the elf asked. "How could she have seen this Tharas'kalagram land here, when she was near Triel with the rest of us?"

Alin turned a scowl to her. "Find someone else to listen to your suspicions," he said. "Focus on the task ahead."

"Quiet you two," Ryla said. "I hear something."

"What is it?" Delkin asked.

Ryla turned to him and said, "A dragon."

At that moment, a huge green wyrm burst from the trees

with a roar, not ten paces from the dragonslayer. The beast was at least forty feet long and muscles pulsed along its entire serpentine body. Fiery eyes glared death down upon the five adventurers, and putrid green spittle dripped from its dagger-like fangs. Delkin shouted, raising his symbol of Lathander high, even as Thard drew his axe and Inri prepared a spell.

The creature rose up above them, its jaws opening wide. Alin would not have been surprised to see two cows from back home fit between those jaws.

"Tempus!" Thard shouted, swinging his greataxe with shattering force against its foreleg.

The dragon screeched as several of its scales caved in and green blood sprayed the barbarian.

It lashed out at him with its other claw, an attack he barely ducked. The sword-length talons slashed a nearby tree in two. Thard kept rolling, for the fangs were not far behind.

Standing behind Delkin, Inri finished her chant and pointed over his shoulder, sending a bolt of lightning at the beast. It slammed into the dragon's chest, causing the huge body to spasm with electricity. Enraged, the beast breathed in and its chest bulged.

"Dragonbreath!" Delkin shouted, then immediately fell into a chant to Lathander.

The shout jarred Alin, who realized he had been watching open-mouthed as the dragon attacked, unable to respond as quickly as his fellows. His first order of business was to shut his gaping mouth, then he dived behind the priest.

At that instant, the creature exhaled, and a vast spray of corrosive green gas fell upon them. Alin screamed, for he saw choking, burning death coming for him, but the gas didn't sear his flesh. Instead, it billowed and raged around them, pushed aside by a shimmering golden shield surrounding Delkin's holy symbol.

"Ha ha!" came Ryla's shout.

The dragonslayer flew out of a nearby tree and drove her

katana deep into the crown of the dragon's head. The wyrm shook and roared, but Ryla held on, wrapped her legs around its forehead, and pulled the katana out, only to plunge the blade into it again and again.

Thard came at the dragon's body again, swinging and hewing its green scales with his axe. He again went for the wound he'd made on the beast's leg, and more blood flew. The dragon, distracted with Ryla, made only half-hearted attempts to pull its injured claw away. Meanwhile, it pawed at its head with the other talons.

Alin felt a surge of triumph and leaped to his feet. Harp in hand, he plucked a discordant note and sent a wave of disharmony toward the dragon. The sound struck the creature and it recoiled for the barest of instants, keeping it from knocking Ryla from its head.

The dragonslayer screeched again and sliced her katana into one of the wyrm's eyes. The dragon roared and shook its head frantically, throwing her off. She flew, limbs spiraling wildly, over fifty feet through the air. She landed on her face a dozen paces away from Alin.

"Ryla!" Alin shouted, running from the circle of the priest's power.

"Alin, no!" snapped Delkin, dropping his shield as his concentration broke.

Thard may have been fast, but he was not fast enough to dodge the dragon's bulk as the creature lunged into their midst, barreling the hulking barbarian aside like a discarded child's toy. As Alin leaped at Ryla to cover her body with his own, a sweeping tail struck him in the midsection, launching him through the air. As he flew, he heard the screams of the other Moor Runners.

Then he slammed against a great redwood, and he heard nothing at all.

⟲∽⟳

When he woke, a soft hand was touching his forehead. At first, he tried to kiss it, but then he realized it was not Ryla but Inri who was waking him.

"We were all knocked cold, but Ryla killed the beast," Inri said before he could ask.

He sat up at once, a hundred questions on his lips, but Inri cut them off with a silent command to follow as she started away. The bard stood, finding his body aching but whole, and made his way after the sorceress. She mercifully slowed her walk to allow him to follow.

When they arrived back at the spot where the dragon had come upon them, Alin was chilled to the bone. Thard peeked from beneath a bloody bandage across his forehead and leaned heavily on a long shovel. Arms crossed, Ryla seemed unhurt—causing Alin's heart to leap—but wore a grim frown. Even Inri had not escaped unscathed; she wore one arm in an improvised sling.

It was the fifth member of their party who caused Alin's breath to catch.

Delkin lay half buried in a shallow grave. His face, burned black by the dragon's breath, was unrecognizable—Alin could only tell it was him by the honey-gold curls.

With a strangled cry, Alin dropped to his knees by the priest's grave.

"Don't touch him!" Inri shouted. "The acid will burn your flesh as well."

Alin might have ignored her and reached for his friend, but Thard caught him in time. As it was, he merely wept into the barbarian's strong arm.

Ryla gave an exasperated sigh. "I told you we didn't have time to bury him," she said. "The night is coming, and when the dragon wakes—"

"For pity's sake," Inri begged. "Just a few more minutes."

The dragonslayer rolled her eyes but shrugged in acceptance.

Alin stood and walked toward her. He looked at Ryla with a shocked expression, and she flashed him a seductive smile. When he gave no response, she turned and pointed.

Just up the path, a bloody ruin decorated the small clearing: the remains of the green dragon. Dozens of tree trunks lay snapped and splintered on the ground. Some trees even lay pulled up by the roots. Blood and bits of dragonflesh spattered the trees that were left standing a sickly green color. The creature looked as though it had been torn in half lengthwise, and huge gashes had torn its thick carapace to ribbons. Many of its exposed bones were splintered, as though some great force had thrown it against those broken trees.

Alin's thoughts leaped to Ryla—he had known the dragon-slayer was strong, but how strong was she?

The bard looked back, a question in his eyes, and Ryla smiled.

"And I know where its lair is," she said.

The dragon's lair was huge, a yawning cave bored in the side of a small volcano. Two rotting green dragon carcasses lay outside, grim watchguards that delivered a dark message to any brave or foolish enough to enter. The bodies were fresh, and assailed the cave with a foul odor.

"At least he won't smell us," Alin observed to no one in particular.

Ryla smiled and waved the party of four forward. Thard, axe in hand, took point, with the dragonslayer and Inri following close behind. Alin, rapier drawn, took up the rear, but he didn't know how effective he would be in an attack. His sword seemed woefully inadequate compared to the others' weapons.

Entering the place was a shock, for the cave's darkness was much warmer than the light outside. The adventurers could see nothing in the blackness, and Alin recast his light spell. The light extended only a few feet in every direction, and the darkness pressed upon it like a living, breathing foe. Unrecognizable bones and bits of arms and armor littered the wide tunnel. The occasional snap of bones or metallic rustle of armor was the only sound. No rats, spiders, or other vermin scuttled by their feet. Alin suspected that few living creatures would survive long in the lair of a dragon.

They didn't have far to go through the oppressive blackness to reach Tharas'kalagram's inner lair. Less than a hundred paces in, they came upon a glowing cavern. Peering over the lip of a higher ledge, the four could see a gargantuan serpentine beast slumbering amidst piles of gold and gems. The horde was huge, a treasure out of a bard's epic tale. Gold and silver sparkled and dazzled, threatening to blind any who looked upon it at the wrong angle. The dragon that slept upon it was even larger, at least double the size of the green wyrm that had attacked them in the forest.

"Good, he's asleep," Ryla whispered. "Let's go."

With that, she disappeared into the forest of stalagmites.

"Ryla?" Alin asked. "Ryla!"

He slapped a hand over his mouth to stifle his shout when they all heard a rumbling sound from below. They didn't have time to look over the edge, though, as another earth-shaking snore came up from the lair.

"She gives us no strategy?" Inri asked. "What . . . ?"

Ryla reappeared from behind the stalagmites, an irritated expression on her face.

"All right, all right," she growled. "Thard, you strike from hiding, then run—that rocky outcropping there." She pointed down in the dragon's lair toward a smaller tunnel and fallen boulders that would provide cover. "Inri, you stay up here and hit the beast with all the magic you can muster. Alin, help Inri."

"What about you?" the bard asked.

The end of Ryla's mouth turned up in a smile. "Once Thard hits him, Kalag—the dragon—will awaken. When it attacks him, that's when I go on top of it and take out its eyes. When the dragon is blinded, we have the advantage."

Thard and Alin nodded. Only Inri looked unconvinced.

"Magical protections?" she prompted, as though reminding a youngster.

A flicker of something passed over Ryla's face, but it was gone before Alin could read her features.

"If you must," she said in apparent exasperation.

"Thard will need the most," Inri said.

She began casting spells upon the barbarian, keeping her voice low. Alin did the same, ransacking his brain for spells he knew that might help the man. Finally, he settled on one of his most powerful charms—a spell of invisibility.

Inri nodded as he cast it, as though grateful.

"Take this spell too," said the sorceress. "It will allow us to converse without speaking."

She chanted a few arcane syllables under her breath, and a silvery radiance fell over them. Ryla flinched but grudgingly remained in the aura of radiance.

Gods! Alin said through the bond.

Yes, came Inri's voice in his mind. *Try not to fill our minds with meaningless exclamations, though.*

Instead of shutting his mouth, Alin emptied his mind, suitably chastened.

When they were finished, Thard picked Inri up so they could share a kiss. Cheeks flaming from embarrassment at the passionate feelings he felt through the mental bond, Alin stole a longing glance at Ryla, but the dragonslayer looked preoccupied with planning. He could also feel no thoughts coming from her—perhaps she knew how to hide her thoughts from others, even with Inri's spell. He turned away before she could read *his* thoughts.

The Moor Runners took up their places, Thard heading

down closer and Ryla disappearing up the wall. Excitement shivered down Alin's spine as he waited. Thard looked like a hero of legend, picking his way between stalagmites as effortlessly as though they were tree trunks. All the while, he kept his eyes fixed upon the dragon's slumbering form and his hand on his axe handle.

Is it asleep? Inri asked Thard.

They could feel the barbarian's mental confirmation.

Alin clutched his rapier hilt firmly but dared not draw it, for he feared the sound it would make. Besides, he reminded himself, such a tiny blade would be nigh useless against the colossal dragon that awaited them. He called to mind his bardic tricks and the magic that would summon them, but even there he could do little but conjure dancing lights or perform feats of legerdemain. Once again, he felt useless in a fight, but he didn't feel out of place. Rather, he was there to bear witness to the epic battle sure to unfold—he would write it into *The Ballad of Dragonclaw* and—

Then they heard Thard's confusion in their minds. *Wait, this is not the beast that attacked the caravan.*

What? asked Alin. He could feel Inri's confusion and suspicion as well.

The scars are different.

At that moment, the dragon's eyes opened and its gaze fixed on Thard. Crimson, fiery death filled its mouth and its eyes were burning with terrible laughter.

"Tempus!" the barbarian shouted, throwing himself forward.

Through the mental link, they felt more than saw his scorching doom.

"No!" Inri screamed. "Ryla!"

She began a spell of escape.

But then the words stopped as a blade protruded through her chest and blood leaked from her lips. Ryla slid the katana out and spun the elf around. Inri blinked, too stunned even to gasp in pain, and the dragonslayer took her head off with a backhand slash. The headless body tumbled over the ledge, and down into the dragon's lair.

Alin looked up at Ryla with absolute confusion. The dragonslayer smiled and planted a kiss on his forehead. Then she made her way down toward the dragon, stripping off her armor piece by piece as she went. When she reached the bottom, she stood before the beast with only the silver ring on her right hand.

The dragon growled and pulled back, as though to pounce, but Ryla laughed. Laughed!

"Oh, come now Kalag," she said. "Surely you recognize me."

"You broke the rules, Rylatar'ralah'tyma," the dragon growled.

Alin's limbs froze at the mighty sound, but his hair rose for an entirely different reason. The name—Rylatar—he had heard that name before.

The dragon continued, "You're not allowed to change. The rules—"

"Are *our* rules, anyway," she countered with a dismissive wave. Then Ryla ran her hands down her arms and over her beautiful, bare skin. "Really Kalag, you'd rather I were horribly scarred by some lowly green's acid gas? My beautiful body. . . ."

The wyrm scoffed. "You're hideous as it is," he hissed.

A lovely pout appeared on Ryla's lips. "You don't like the ring?" she asked, holding it up as though modeling it for him. The silver sparkled in the firelight.

The dragon's lips pulled back in a sneer.

Ryla shrugged and said, "Fine."

She slipped the ring off her finger, and the bard watched with a mixture of horror and wonder as her body rippled and grew, her skin sloughing off and revealing crimson scales and deep indigo wings. Her head lengthened and her sparkling white teeth became fangs. Within a breath, Ryla had grown to the size and shape of the other dragon. Her red scales sparkled in the firelight.

"Eyes like fire, atop a golden spire," Alin found himself singing under his breath.

His mind seemed far away. As it stretched and snapped, he was vaguely aware that he had lost something.

"A thought occurred to me, about the age," Ryla growled. "We should assume elf bodies in the future . . . just so we don't seem too young."

" 'We'?" Kalag asked.

"Oh, yes," Ryla said. Her talon held out the tiny silver ring to the other dragon. "I'm done being the hunter—time for me to be the hunted. I found you, now it's your turn to hunt me."

The dragon looked at the ring and asked, "Why do you do it? The adventurers? Why?"

Ryla rumbled, as though with mirth. "I enjoy the deception," she said. "And I brought you meat. What are you complaining about?'

"I wonder, sometimes, if you're not fond of them," Kalag growled.

"I'm not fond of anything," retorted Ryla.

"Sharp death in hand, whose passion knows no name . . ." Alin sang as he felt reason fleeing.

He fought the desire to babble incoherently, but it wasn't for fear that the dragons would hear him, but only because it would disrupt his song.

"Then you won't object when I eat the little bard who's hiding up there," reasoned Kalag.

"Actually, I would object," Ryla replied.

Kalag shot her a look that could only be a dragon's form of jealousy, and Alin would have shivered if he had maintained his sanity. Instead, he chuckled.

Ryla caught the glare and said, "I propose a new hunting

game: one where we're the hunters, he's the hunted, and he gets a head start."

Alin's ears pricked and shivers of terror shot down his spine. His shattered mind hardly registered the threat, though. It was too busy putting words to his music, music twisted by madness.

"Mercy? From you, Rylatar?" Kalag smiled. "Very well then. How much of a head start?"

"Oh, five years will suffice," she said. "The lives of dragons are long—it will be but a summer's day to us, but a lifetime of fear for him."

"This bard must be special, to warrant such treatment."

At the notion, Ryla scoffed—an action that sent flame lancing out to melt a stalagmite.

"If you must know," she said. "It's because he's composing a very nice ballad. This way, he'll have time to finish it."

"Ruling her land, queen of the hunting game!" the maddened bard sang with a smile as he climbed to his feet.

Then came the most hideous sound he had ever heard—and would always hear as he ran—booming and thunderous, but dark and mocking:

A dragon's laugh.

THE ROAD HOME

HARLEY STROH

21 Marpenoth, the Year of the Shield (1367 DR)

Worthless band o' cutthroats, scoundrels, and knaves," the dwarf spat, climbing atop a scarred oak table. His hard eyes searched the war weary faces of the crowded inn. "Who among you slakes his thirst with blood and fills his belly with battle? Who in all of Moradin's creation has so little fear of death?

"The Company of the Chimera!" the dwarf bellowed, answering his own query with a triumphant roar. "The finest company of rogues ever to cast dice with the Gods of War!"

The common room erupted with cheers that shook sawdust from the ceiling. Flagons were raised high and naked blades flashed in the smokey light of fat-lamps. For two tendays the Company of the Chimera had occupied the Inn of the Seven Silvers, cowing the locals until none dared to pass the inn's double doors. Hired to guard over the Sembian waystation and twenty miles of the Dawnpost highway, the mercenaries had done more damage and caused more terror than any brigands in memory.

"Join us, dragon-tribe girl!" Tombli stabbed a blistered finger toward the long-limbed barbarian sitting by an open window. "Or are the women of the North as icy as their winters?"

Clad in tanned pelts and an oiled sealskin cape, Saskia was immune to the frosty draft that had driven her companions close to the crackling hearth. With pale white skin and crystal blue eyes, she might have been cunningly carved from ice herself, were it not for the raven black hair that spilled to the middle of her back. A notched sword rested against her shoulder, the barbarian's only companion. She surveyed the company, their noses red with drink, their bellies soft and full.

"Keep your toasts," Saskia said. "I'll take my drink with warriors."

"If the copper-counting lords of Sembia choose to pay our band to watch over their packs of ratty bondsmen, then I say let them pay!" Tombli dropped from the table. "We've earned our season's keep and not a Chimera has fallen."

"Your peace is killing us, little man."

Tombli loosened the jeweled dagger at his waist, the symbol of his devotion to Abbathor, the dwarf god of greed and avarice.

"As captain of the company, I command you to drink."

The barbarian wrapped her arms around her bastard sword and pulled the hood of her cape down over her eyes.

Snarling, Tombli stole a brand from the crackling fire. He kicked the door of the inn open wide and cast the log into the darkness. It spun to a flaming halt in the center of the road.

Tombli slammed a flagon onto the table before Saskia and challenged, "Drink or fight."

A chill breeze cut through the room and Saskia's eyes flashed from beneath the trim of her hood. The inn erupted with cheers and catcalls when the barbarian pushed the flagon away.

Saskia rose slowly and stretched like a cat, her lips pulled into a grim smile. Wagers were made and grimy coins changed hands. By the time the barbarian had shed her cloak and tied her sleeves up, every warrior sober enough to walk had stumbled outside. Laying her sword to the side, Saskia strode out into the street to drunken shouts and wild applause.

A biting pain erupted from the back of Saskia's thigh. The barbarian fell to her knees in surprise, a war dart buried deep in her leg. Tombli stood silhouetted in the doorway, another dart readied to throw.

"Civilization is making you slow," Tombli laughed. "Half a year ago, it would have been impossible to hit you. Now I'd have to try to miss."

He drew back his arm to throw again.

Cursing, Saskia flung herself to the ground. A dart hissed past, but she was prone, with no way of dodging the others that were sure to follow. With a swipe of her hand, Saskia hurled a scattering of gravel at the dwarf. It was a desperate move. Nothing could distract the dwarf lord's trained arm.

Tombli's laughter was cut short when a pebble exploded against his chest in a flash that lit up the night. The dwarf staggered back, momentarily stunned. Saskia was equally surprised, but a life spent hunting beasts on the wild tundra had trained her to seize every opportunity, no matter how improbable. Saskia's vision went red and she sprang at Tombli, roaring like a tiger. The pair fell back inside the inn, Saskia's fierce blows raining down on Tombli's face.

It took half a dozen Chimeras to pull her off the dwarf. Tombli sat up slowly, his face pulped and bloodied.

"Hold her down," he mumbled through a swollen lip. Tombli

tore a tankard out of the hands of the nearest Chimera and stumbled forward until he stood above the barbarian. His beard was soaked with blood and his forge-hardened face grimaced in pain.

"To the Company of the Chimera!" Tombli shouted, raising the tankard high. The company echoed the dwarf's toast with sullen murmurs. Gripping Saskia's hair in his fist, he emptied the tankard over her head. "To the Company of the Chimera. Many heads, one purpose."

------ ∞ ------

"Lie still," Grummond ordered, his greasy hands working the tip of the dart from Saskia's leg. The company's surgeon was a smashed nose half-orc who had seen more battle with his one good eye than all the rest of the company together.

"Fightin' the captain," Grummond scoffed. Pressing his hands to either side of the wound, Grummond leaned into her leg and sank his teeth into the tip of the dart. With a jerk of his head he tore the dart loose and spat it onto the floor. "Were you half drunk or half daft?"

"The dwarf thinks too highly of himself," Saskia said, "and he's guiled you all into fearing him."

"Tombli's a war-caster o' Abbathor. Nothing but trouble, that one." The half-orc poured a rust colored syrup over the ragged wound and gave her thigh a slap. "His father was an exile o' the Rift Clans, his mother a duergar princess. Ain't no dwarfhold gonna adopt a half-gray bastard. Tombli's been takin' that pain out on the world ever since."

"If he's such an almighty priest, how come you do all our healing?"

"Not every priest's a healer," Grummond said, his one good eye on the door. "But if'n you hate him so much, why stay with the Chimeras?"

Saskia shrugged. "A wolf needs a pack, an Uthgardt needs a tribe. It is the way of things."

Grummond studied her. He had known many barbarians, but there was something different about Saskia. The North-lander had no mirth to match her melancholy. She didn't fight out of bitterness, like Tombli, or greed, like the company. Instead it was as if a war-worm had curled up inside her belly, giving her a hunger for battle that refused to be sated. The only challenge worthy of her respect would be the one that killed her. Anything less merited only disdain and scorn.

Grummond turned to put away his oils and salves and said, "So how'd you witch up that bit o' magic?"

"What do you mean?"

"The flash, the boom!" Grummond laughed. "I lost a pair o' gold crowns to that pretty little trick."

"I don't know what you're talking about," Saskia growled, something ancient and cruel flashing in her blue eyes.

"All right," Grummond held up his hands in defense. "Didn't mean nothin' by it. You know who your friends are."

A shout went up from the common room.

"Gruumsh's blood," the half-orc swore. "What now?"

Tombli leaned into the room, jerked a thumb at Saskia, and said, "Get up and put some civilized clothes on. I need your eyes."

———— ❧ ————

A band of trappers had ridden into the waystation. The company gathered to meet them, crowding around the men and their heavy iron cage. By the time Saskia had limped outside Tombli was already engaged in a shouting match with a swarthy Calishite, trying to drive down the trapper's price by bluff and bluster.

The man's armor was brutally torn in several places and a long bandage wrapped the length of his leg. Whatever was in the cage had given the trapper and his fellows a hard time of it.

Saskia eased through the crowd then stopped short.

The trappers had caught a dragon.

Saskia had seen images of drakes before. She had seen the likenesses of great wyrms inked onto scraped hides, carved from ivory and wood, gilded in gold and silver, and painted on cavern walls. But the miniature dragon, no larger than a cat, had something every representation had lacked. Like an exotic sword polished to a razor's edge, the dragon was *beautiful*.

Long lines of sinewy muscle tensed and corded beneath glossy scales the color of wine. A pair of sharp horns curled above dark eyes that flashed violet, framing a savage maw filled with needle-sharp teeth. Its delicate wings strained anxiously against the tight confines of the cage, and the body ended in a serpentine tail tipped with a single ivory barb.

Tombli whispered from Saskia's elbow, "What in the Nine Hells *is* it?"

Saskia struggled to translate the Uthgardt word to Common, but the best she could manage was a vulgar approximation of: "A pseudodragon."

Tombli snorted. "A *sort-of-dragon?*" He spun back on the Calishite and shouted, "Cheating son of a djinni! One hundred golden lions and not a falcon more!"

While Tombli and the Calishite fell back into vicious bargaining, Saskia knelt before the cage. The wyrm's gemstone eyes were timeless, utterly indifferent to the concerns of man. Its scaled kin had reigned long before the press of cities and farms, and would exist long after the last eldritch tower crumbled to dust.

Free me, sister.

Saskia flinched. She hadn't heard Uthgardt spoken since she had fled her home. The dragon hissed with impatience. Again the words leaped into her mind.

Free me!

As a girl Saskia had been plagued by dreams in which entire flights of great wyrms filled the skies. Worse, her dreams had worked tiny miracles on the world around her. When Saskia had nightmares, lights danced across the northern skies, sentries reported watch fires flaring blue and red, and rusting blades were made bright. The tribe's aging shaman, terrified of what he couldn't explain, declared her visions to be portents of evil and did everything in his power to purge her of the wicked taint. But every ritual and ceremony failed and in the end Saskia was branded a witch, damned by an untapped potential she couldn't control.

Free me!

"No," Saskia said, her voice a fierce whisper. Her eyes narrowed to shards of ice and her words slipped into Uthgardt. *"I sacrificed fortunes to your troves, swore my spirit to your totem and placed my body upon your altar."* She spat on the ground. *"Your kin denied me."*

Before Saskia could stand, the dragon's long tail shot between the bars of the cage. It struck once, as delicate as a lover's caress, slashing a crimson arc across her cheek.

Saskia fell backward, her blood flaring as the dragon's poison charged through her veins. The weight of her own body bore down upon her like a coat of wet furs. Her head lolled weakly and her fingers went numb. As the sky darkened, her ears were filled with the thunder of a roaring drum.

Once more the voice leaped unbidden into her mind.

We did not deny you. You denied us.

Saskia slept and as she slept, she remembered.

She was standing on a steep slope, knee deep in drifting snow. Before her rose a towering chain of granite peaks that stretched to the sky.

The Spine of the World.

Behind her the mountains fell away through rolling clouds of snow and blowing ice. A relentless wind hammered her body, threatening to pluck her from the mountain and hurl her into the whirling white abyss. Her cheeks were black with frost, her fingers and toes were numb with cold, and her eyes burned from days of seeing nothing but endless expanses of white.

Kicking and punching holds into the slope, Saskia continued her climb.

A tenday ago the elders of her village had given her a choice: leave the tribe forever or submit to the Trial of the Dragon. Saskia had chosen the trial: to travel alone through the wilderness, without weapons or provisions, to the summit of the Uthgarheis, the lonely peak that ruled the Spine of the World. There, atop all of creation, she would be met and judged by the spirit totem of her tribe.

Uthgar had favored her early in the trial, sending a goblin war band tripping and snorting across her path. It had been easy enough to ambush their scouts. Armed with a goblin waraxe Saskia was able to kill a snowbound caribou, taking its hide for warmth and smoking its fatty meat for rations. Arriving at the base of the Uthgarheis, she rested for a day then started her climb along the rocky southern ridge.

That was two days ago.

She hadn't slept since beginning the climb. The caribou hide was frozen stiff around her, and her bundle of smoked meat had begun to dwindle. Still she pressed on, climbing ridge after icebound ridge. To give up was to accept that she was a witch, a corrupt soul given over to wickedness and evil. Saskia knew that couldn't be true, and meeting with the elder spirit would prove it.

On the third day she summited the slender pinnacle of rock that crowned the Uthgarheis. Delirious with exhaustion and triumph, she crawled before the shelter of a fallen cairn and collapsed, too tired to see if the Elder Spirit was waiting for her.

The howl of a thousand starving wolves woke her from her sleep. Sitting up, Saskia looked to the north. A dark storm rolled toward her, sliding across the sky like a black avalanche. Shards of blowing ice cut her cheeks and day turned to night.

The first gusts tore away her meager shelter. Shouting a war cry, Saskia raised her axe high and buried it into the rocky ground. She held on with the last of her strength and cried to the Great Worm for mercy.

Saskia had thought she had survived the Great Worm's Trial.

It hadn't begun.

Eight days later Saskia stumbled back into camp, frozen in body and numb in soul. The Great Worm never came. She slept for days, slipping in and out of a delirious fever that made her skin hot to the touch. When the fever finally broke, the tribe's shaman came to her tent and told of her the Great Worm's death. The Elder Spirit had been killed by a company of villains only two days after she began her quest. They had gutted his lair, taken his hide like savages, and carried away the dragon's wealth on the backs of slaves and mules.

Her trial had been in vain. Like a foolish child wishing on falling stars, her passionate prayers had gone unheard.

The next morning Saskia left for the south, swearing never to return.

Saskia stretched out on the ground, her long limbs sore from inaction. Dawn would be coming soon, but sleep eluded the barbarian. Left in its place was the anxious exhaustion so common to the cities of man. Of all the curses visited on civilized folk, that was the worst: to go through their waking hours half asleep and their sleeping hours half awake.

Saskia's dreams had returned. Nightmares of massive golden drakes that blotted out the sun with their blinding wings, silk-scaled terrors the color of soot, white dragons that drove winter's hoarfrost before them. The dragons swooped out of the northlands like a winged plague, storming the walled cities of man and laying waste to all in their path.

At one point in every dream, the largest and oldest dragon, his scales mottled with age, would beckon to her with a single claw, his clouded eyes smoldering like the embers of a dying fire. Then two words would thunder inside her mind: *Join us*.

Even the memory was enough to make her start. Yes, Saskia thought, sleep could wait.

Saskia exhaled hard and she gazed longingly into the clear sky. Hunting with her father she had learned to track the stars as they made their course across the heavens, but entire tendays passed without her noting the changes of Selûne. She had come south hoping to outrun her curse, but all she had lost were the things she valued most. Saskia knew she couldn't stay with the Chimeras any longer, but where *was* a barbarian to go after being cast out of her tribe?

The crash of metal broke the night's fragile peace. Saskia pulled herself up and followed the muffled ringing back to its source.

Tombli was in the stables, waging a one-sided battle against the caged pseudodragon. He rained blows down upon the cage with a war club, his drunken laughter filling the night.

"Dance, mighty wyrm!" Tombli commanded. "Earn your keep!"

The pseudodragon's barbed tail had been amputated the day after it attacked Saskia. It was defenseless before the dwarf's cruelty.

Saskia slipped silently into the dark shadows of a stall.

The dwarf took the key from his belt, jangling it just out of the dragon's reach.

"Come on, pretty thing. Show me a little wrath.

"No?" Tombli asked with disappointment. Unable to fit the ring back onto his belt, the drunk dwarf cast it aside and traded the club for his jeweled dagger. "Worthless lizard. Better to sell your vitals to the mages and tan your hide for my boots."

The barbarian stepped from the shadows, bringing both fists down on Tombli in a blow that would have felled an ox. The dwarf staggered two steps backward then lashed out blindly with his blade, the dagger cutting a glowing green line in the darkness. Grummond had warned Saskia of Tombli's wicked blade, a serpentine dirk that wept poison, but the barbarian hadn't believed such a thing was possible.

The dwarf regained his balance and charged her with a roar. Saskia plucked the club from the ground and broke it against the dwarf's head as he rushed passed. Tombli fell to one knee, then pulled himself back up, his hard black eyes aflame with rage.

Saskia settled into a crouch and readied herself for another charge.

Growling a prayer, Tombli drew a short rod of iron from a pouch and stabbed his dagger toward the sky. He was answered with a resounding crack that shook the air. Saskia fell to the ground, every muscle in her body contracted into painful knots.

"Think to fight me, barbarian?" Tombli spat out a mouthful of blood. "You and the wyrm are one and the same: feeble pets, without tooth or guile."

Finally the pseudodragon came alive, hurling itself at the bars of its cage with all the fury of a true drake. The cage crashed to the ground, but the stout bars held.

"Gnash all you like, lizard," Tombli snorted. "Those bars are enchanted cold iron, and the finest turn-picks in Sembia would think twice before trying *that* lock."

Saskia strained in vain against the dwarf's spell. Tombli saw the frustration rising in her blue eyes and began to chuckle.

"Grim spell, isn't it? No one ever forgets their first time. I like to follow it with something I call 'Abbathor's Flowering.'" The dwarf whispered a soft prayer and laid the tip of his dagger against the bare skin of her neck. A shock shot through her body, tracing blue lines of lightning along the veins under her skin. Her veins pulsed once, twice, then burst through the surface of her skin.

Saskia tried to scream but her jaw was clenched shut. Frustrated by her helplessness she could only moan incoherently, tears mixing with the blood running down her face.

"You fear the pain."

She could feel the dwarf's excited breath on her lips.

"You don't have to say it," Tombli whispered. "I can see it in your eyes."

Defiant rage erupted from Saskia's proud heart. What did that vile dwarf know of pain? Pain taught her people what it meant to be alive. From birth to death, pain was the single constant in the life of an Uthgardt warrior. It wasn't the pain she feared, but so pathetic an end, slaughtered like a pig by a southern priest.

"Watch closely, dragon. It's been years since I've had the pleasure of skinning a woman alive."

Tombli's threats fell upon deaf ears. Filled with self-loathing, she was beyond the reach of his grubby, blistered fingers. Saskia had come south seeking escape, but like the dragon, she found herself in a cage. Worse, hers was one of her own choosing, and she would die in it.

Free me!

Saskia's soul flared. Years of frustration and denial were erased in a single moment, eclipsed by her rage. She commanded the universe and it leaped to obey.

The key lifted from the ground, held by an invisible hand.

Delicately, but without hesitation, it drifted into the lock and gave the softest of turns. Tombli looked up, his blistered face wrinkled with confusion, just in time to see the cage door swing open.

The drake exploded into motion, distilling days and nights of torment into a whirlwind of fangs and claws. Tombli swung his dagger this way and that, but to no avail. The dragon spun around the dwarf like a dizzying cloud of razors, laying open Tombli like a butcher slicing ham.

Crying in terror, Tombli buried his ragged face in his hands and charged for the door of the stables. The pseudodragon lashed out once with its stump of a tail and caught Tombli's heavy boot, spilling the dwarf into the moldy hay. Tombli fought to his knees with a choking wail and scrambled from the stables and into the darkness.

The pseudodragon settled on Saskia's hip, fastidiously licking the blood from its claws. Inch by painful inch, Saskia's muscles began to unknot, and soon she found she was able to stand.

Greetings, mistress. I am the Wyrm Aeristhax, heir apparent to the mighty Akilskyls, Wyrm of Renown.

"A witch," Saskia said, her voice a mix of despair and disgust. "I'm a witch."

Witch, sorceress, wizling, bruja, hag . . . a thousand words for a thousand tribes of man. Deny the Blessing as it suits you; we will have more pressing issues soon enough.

The dragon examined its claws.

Really, you southern women think too much. It's a wonder you have time for life at all.

Saskia started to correct the dragon then stopped. Perhaps she was a witch; what of it? Unless she found some weapons, and quickly, she would be a dead witch. The Company of the Chimera was a hundred strong and had allies throughout the heart of Sembia and all the Dales. Saskia smiled openly at the thought of a running battle with an entire mercenary company. It was the sort of feat that only a barbarian could hope to pull off.

At the back of the stables were two crates of weapons, cast-offs and rejects from the company's cache. Saskia rummaged through the crates, discarding the weak and delicate, finally settling on a stout shortspear and a brace of heavy throwing daggers.

Aeristhax flew to her shoulder, growling softly.

The mountain-born has raised the alarm.

Saskia nodded and together the pair slipped outside.

Dawn was coming quickly, the village awakening with the crack of drover whips. Saskia cut two horses from the corral, not troubling with a saddle or reins, simply tying on halters. She was almost finished when a voice called for her to stop.

Saskia turned to see Grummond standing on the edge of the corral. The healer wore a coat of burnished chain mail and carried an orc's recurve bow. A handful of black-shafted war arrows were thrust into the ground at his feet.

"You nearly killed the captain," said Grummond as he knocked an arrow and took aim. A dozen other Chimeras fell in line behind him. "We can't let you go."

Saskia swung easily onto the back of the first horse. She was answered with the sharp snap of a bowstring. Aeristhax hissed in anger as the arrow cut its way toward them.

Saskia waved her hand the way another woman might have batted at a fly. Intuitive sorcery, pent up for years, coursed through her, directing the weft and warp of the Weave. The arrow ricocheted off an invisible wall and shot into the sky, tracing a long black arc through the dawn.

Saskia howled in triumph and raised her spear high, her body crackling with power. The Chimeras broke into a charge then skidded to a stop. The barbarian was glowing with an unearthly blue radiance. Grummond waved them back, his bow forgotten.

Aeristhax gave a coughing hiss and took to wing. Saskia kicked hard at her mount and the horses leaped into a gallop, following the dragon north to freedom.

Night came peacefully to Tassledale. Aeristhax hunted in long, lazy circles on the last winds of the fading day, while Saskia made camp on the rocky crest of a hill overlooking the village of Archtassel. She had ridden until the horses could go no farther. The mounts rested, grazing on the meager autumn grasses. The lights of Archtassel slowly winked to life as mothers called their children home and farmers made their way back from the fields.

Surveying their peaceful tranquility, Saskia understood why dragons rampaged through such lands. Like every living thing, civilizations were meant to rise and fall. Ripe fruit was meant to be plucked.

But thoughts of conquest could wait for the morrow.

Saskia knelt on the ground before a pile of twigs and dead wood. At a word the fire sprang to life, the wood cracking and popping as mundane flames settled in, a trail of sweet smelling smoke curling into the chill night air. Saskia warmed herself at the fire's side and whittled a stick into a skewer while she waited for Aeris to return with dinner.

Above her the Five Wanderers shone brightly, twinkling as they made their chaotic way across the heavens. Saskia looked up from her fire and measured their progress.

HOW BURLMARR SAVED THE UNSEEN PROTECTOR

Kameron M. Franklin

Uktar, the Year of the Gauntlet (1369 DR)

It would probably be the last caravan to Leilon before winter brought snow to the passes of the Sword Mountains. Burlmarr hovered over the circled wagons, listening to the gnomes as they sat around the campfire discussing the weather. Or, at least that's what he imagined they were discussing. He couldn't actually hear their voices, but he could see their lips move, and he knew what time of year it was, so that seemed like the logical thing they would be talking about.

The fire had nearly burned itself down to glowing coals when the traders finally turned in. A solitary gnome tossed another log on the embers and crouched down to stoke the flames back to life with a few long breaths. He stood up, stretched, and spent a moment gazing at the night sky before trundling over to a wagon and lifting a crossbow from the back. After loading it, the gnome began an inspection of the wagon circle, keeping one eye on the shadows that occupied the rocky terrain around them.

Burlmarr made his own rounds, tirelessly floating back and forth over the camp. The mountains were far from safe. Orc raiders or marauding monsters often made their way through the passes from the north, looking for anything that would provide enough sustenance to last them through the harsh conditions of the coming months. The caravan would be an irresistible target.

Movement in the shadows up the mountainside to the north of the campsite caught Burlmarr's attention. He swept the terrain with eyes that could see well beyond a thousand feet, and easily spotted the source of the disturbance a few hundred yards away. In black and white vision that ignored the lack of light, he saw a warband of orcs making its way toward the sleeping gnomes. With a thought, Burlmarr glided up to meet them and get a better look.

He could count about fifty of them as he got closer, creeping from the boulders and outcroppings that dotted that side of the pass. They wore piecemeal armor of stiff hide and metal scales, some with crude helmets covering their porcine heads and others only unkempt masses of gray dreadlocks. Even so poorly armed, there were more than enough to overwhelm the caravan, but not a number that would give Burlmarr any trouble. It would probably be best if he confronted them away from the gnomes' campsite. The only thing left was to decide on the best tactics to use. That's when he noticed the hill giant bringing up the rear.

The brute stood about ten feet tall, but would probably have been at least six inches taller where it not stooped over enough that its thick, powerful arms hung past its knees. The giant wore a patchwork of hides, some with the fur still on it. As the brute strode down the mountain, it was picking up boulders with one hand and stacking them in the crook of its other arm.

As mighty as he was, Burlmarr could not be everywhere at once. The orcs were spread too far apart for him to eliminate in one attack, and he had to stop the giant before it was close enough to hurl those rocks onto the unsuspecting caravan.

Burlmarr's foreclaws materialized first. Then he was looking down at the orcs past his blunt snout covered in scales and whiskers of faded white and deep gold. He opened wide and shot a cone of flame into the midst of the warband. The fire swept through the rear ranks of the orcs and raced over the hill giant, consuming them in its hunger. Burlmarr turned to face the remaining orcs, only to see them running wildly down the mountain toward the camp. He cursed himself for a fool. Of course the survivors would panic and run when he appeared in their midst. He had to act fast. The orcs would reach the gnomes in seconds.

Burlmarr stretched out his right foreclaw and spoke.

"Svent throden ghiks mirth kruhkxiss!"

A thick bolt of electricity lanced out from a claw and struck the nearest orc then arced to the next, and the next, and the next, until the twenty or so remaining raiders all lay motionless on the mountainside, smoke wafting from charred holes in their torsos. The gnomes were safe.

Burlmarr wept as he melted back into the blackness of the night.

"Mother!"

Burlmarr barely got the word out before he retched again, though this time he was able to lean over the bed enough that the remaining contents of his stomach spilled onto the floor instead of the bed sheets. Dizzy and weak, he swooned and nearly toppled out of the bed, but his mother appeared just in time to lay him back against the pillows.

"Oh, my poor boy, just look at you."

"I'm sorry, Mother. I didn't mean to make a mess. My head just hurts so bad."

"Did you have another one of those dreams?"

Burlmarr nodded slightly, hoping to avoid making the throbbing worse. It was the third night in a row he'd had the dream, which was always a little different. Mostly a different location, though once he could hear instead of see. He knew they were all the same dream because in every one, he was a dragon. The same dragon, he was pretty sure.

And there were always gnomes. Gnomes from the village. Gnomes he knew.

"Well, we can't have you sleeping in soiled linens," his mother said.

She helped him out of bed and walked him over to the hearth, where she lowered him to the floor. After wrapping a blanket around him, she rolled up the bed sheets and used them to clean the mess. Burlmarr's eyelids began to droop, so he lay down before the glowing embers in the fireplace and drifted off to sleep before his mother could finish making the bed with fresh sheets.

——•∛•——

The caravan arrived in Leilon just before supper time. After unloading the ore they brought and purchasing winter supplies for the village, the gnomes made their way to the Knight's Goblet to get a late meal. The tavern catered to travelers, and was known for its roast boar served with thick slices of nutty-flavored bread. It was quiet in the common room as the gnomes sat at their table eating. Trade was slow that time of year. Most merchant companies had stopped sending their caravans through the passes for fear of getting caught in a mountain storm.

"There was something going on up in the mountains last night, I tell you," one of the gnomes insisted through a mouthful of boar and bread. "Fire and lightning was flashing all over the place."

"Would you stop with this, already," another of the gnomes groaned. "It was nothing more than a storm."

"How could it have been a storm if there weren't no clouds in the sky," the first gnome protested. "Besides, I'm pretty sure I saw him."

"Who?"

"You know. The Unseen Protector."

The whole table went silent as everyone stopped eating to stare at the gnome. Then they broke out in raucous laughter.

"That's nothing but a fireside story told to children by the village elders."

"I did see him." The gnome's face was flushed and his voice was defensive. "A great gold dragon, just like the stories say."

"If it was the *Unseen* Protector," one of the others blurted out between guffaws, "then how did you see him?"

The gnomes slapped the table and held their bellies as laughter overtook them again. The lone gnome stood up, his face a mixture of fury and embarrassment, and left the table.

Daikon had heard enough as well. From his vantage at a nearby table, his back to the gnomes, he was just another human and had been able to eavesdrop on the entire conversation without drawing attention to himself. It was time to report back on his success.

His hooded cloak wrapped tightly around him, Daikon left the warmth and light of the inn's common room and walked out into the dark street, his breath a puff of white before him in the chill night air. It was a brisk walk to the camp in the hills outside of town where his men waited. Thoughts of power kept him warm. The Archmage Arcane had been vague in his promises, but Daikon had enough ambition to fill in the blanks himself.

He nodded to his bodyguards as he emerged from the shadows at the camp's perimeter. His assistant slept under the cart that had been used to haul the bribe they'd taken to gain the hill giant's help. That would have to be retrieved before some scavengers stumbled upon it, or the Archmage Arcane would be displeased. Daikon made a mental note not to bring it up just yet.

Rummaging through his pack in the rear of the cart, Daikon removed a gray lump of stone. He crawled into the back of the cart, the stone cupped in his hands. With a deep, steadying breath, Daikon closed his eyes and envisioned a frail, withered man, his frame bent with old age.

This is Daikon. The hill giant's forces attacked the caravan and were destroyed by what the gnomes called their 'Unseen Protector.' You were right.

Of course I was right, came the surly reply. *Now quit wasting my time. I don't want to hear from you again until you have confirmed the Protector's identity.*

Daikon kept his mind clear until he returned the stone to its place in his backpack. It didn't hurt to be safe. Only when it was tucked away did he once again ponder why the Archmage Arcane had sent him on his mission. What was so important that not even the archmage's closest aides could be trusted? Why had he been chosen, summoned from the Sea Tower in the middle of the night then teleported to the small town of Leilon as soon as he'd agreed?

There were rumors that Arklem Greeth was preparing to step down, that a successor would be named. Perhaps the mission was a test of his loyalty and ability. Not that Daikon expected to be named archmage so soon, but there would definitely be some shifting of positions once the new Archmage Arcane was pronounced.

With a smug smile, Daikon hopped out of the cart and kicked his assistant. It was time to make some plans.

The gnomes woke up early, ate a quick breakfast, and moved their wagons out before most of Leilon stirred. The past night's mirth was replaced with an air of expectation and urgency. Everyone couldn't wait to get home.

As the caravan climbed the mountain trail, the golden touch of the morning sun on the snow caps kept everyone's spirits light and cheerful. They stopped for lunch near where they had camped the last night on the trail. There were no charred remains left on the mountainside. One of them mentioned that the Unseen Protector must have removed all the bodies and even the gnome who swore he had seen the battle laughed.

Laughter turned to gurgles, blood spilling from his mouth, when a crossbow bolt pierced his throat. Another bolt sunk into the chest of the gnome across from him, followed by a missile of colored light that smote the gnome to the left.

The remaining gnome sprinted for his wagon, desperately wishing the Unseen Protector was real and would suddenly appear. He dived underneath and curled up in a ball next to one of the wheels, shaking in fear.

"Come out, little friend," a voice called from somewhere out of sight. "We want to talk."

The gnome didn't move, but his eyes darted back and forth trying to locate the source of the voice. It sounded very familiar, but he couldn't quite place it. If it was a friend, he needed to warn them about the ambushers.

"You should find a place to hide," he called out, "we were just ambushed. They ... they killed everyone else. The attackers could still be around."

"We took care of them. You have nothing to worry about. Come, talk."

"A-all right," the gnome stammered as he crawled out from under the wagon. "I'm coming out."

Daikon's bodyguard dumped the last gnome beside the rest, lining them up in a row and rolling them onto their backs. Daikon returned from where they had left their cart and waved for everyone to gather around the bodies.

"Now that we have all the information we need to locate Ieirithymbul, along with the names and daily routines of enough gnomes who live there, it's time for the final act that will make our infiltration of the village possible."

Daikon opened the bag he had gone to retrieve and pulled out a silver pendant with a crystal embedded in its center. He held it in front of them and they leaned in to get a closer look. The crystal was so clear he knew they could see their own reflections.

"I have three others like this," Daikon continued. "They were crafted by the Brotherhood and provided for us by the Archmage Arcane so that we could complete this task for him. When the wearer puts on the pendant, his form is altered to that which he first envisions in his mind. He keeps that form as long as he wears the pendant.

"When I give you your pendant, I want you to first spend a few moments concentrating on one of these." Daikon nudged the dead gnome nearest him. "Once you have the image firmly in your mind, put the pendant on."

When he was sure they understood, Daikon handed each a pendant and assigned them a gnome to study. He let the others go first to be sure they did it right. Each stood over their particular gnome for a few moments before slowly fastening the pendant around their necks. As they did, their forms shimmered and shrank until they resembled the gnome lying at their feet. After his assistant's transformation was complete, Daikon placed the final pendant around his neck and underwent his own.

"All right, we're finished with these," he said, motioning

to the bodies. "Dump them in a ravine or something where they won't be found, along with our cart. Then let's load up in their wagons and get moving. It's still a few days ride until we get to the village."

——◦∞◦——

Burlmarr sat on a stool, hunkered over a spinning grinding wheel. He held the rough piece of quartz in his hands against the wheel to remove waste and give it the general shape one of the older apprentices used to practice the facet cuts Master Thintagast taught. He paused for a moment to allow Ambrythynn, a fellow apprentice who was furiously pumping the pedal that powered the grinder, to stop for a breath and pour water over the wheel. Through a window in the far wall, Burlmarr could see townsfolk passing by under the bright sun. It wasn't easy keeping his thoughts on the task at hand.

The caravan should be returning from Leilon any day now. Will everything be ready for the celebration in time?

"I know I'll be ready," Burlmarr replied, keeping his eye on the quartz as the wheel wore it down. "I just hope I don't get sick again."

"Ready for what?" Ambrythynn asked between breaths.

"You asked me if I would be ready for the party the elders are going to throw when the caravan returns."

"I did not."

"Yes, you did. I heard . . ." Burlmarr looked up to see Ambrythynn's brow furrowed and the corner of his mouth turned up in a way that said he had no idea what Burlmarr was talking about. "Never mind."

I'm going to ask Lissa to marry me. I've already spoken to her father, and he's agreed to help build us a house if I complete my apprenticeship by next Greengrass.

"By Greengrass?" Burlmarr couldn't keep the incredulity from his voice. "Don't you think that's a little soon, considering we both just started with Master Thintagast this past summer? Besides, I thought you had your eye on Maree Blimthalloon?"

"What are you talking about?"

"Ha, ha. That's a good joke, trying to make me think I'm hearing things. Don't worry, I won't tell Maree."

"Tell Maree what?"

"That you like Lissa Boavartarr."

"I don't. Who told you that?"

"You did, just now."

"I did not."

"It was funny the first time, Ambrythynn, but the act is getting old." Burlmarr sat up and rubbed his temples with the hand not holding the quartz. "I'm starting to get a headache and I want to get this done before we have to go home, so let's just get back to work."

"Fine." Ambrythynn frowned, but went back to pumping the pedal.

Halbrondell, your goat got into my cabbages, again! I've just about had it with that beast. I'm of half a mind to take it to the butcher as payment for the damages!

Burlmarr's head seemed to explode and the room spun like a child's toy. He crashed to the floor wretching.

"Burlmarr? Master Thintagast, something's wrong with Burlmarr!"

The voice sounded like Ambrythynn's, but it was very distant, and getting farther away. The pain in Burlmarr's head was unrelenting, and he slipped into unconsciousness.

When Burlmarr awoke, he found himself lying in a cot with Goodwife Thintagast seated at his side. Master Thintagast leaned over her shoulder, and all the apprentices crowded around behind him.

"Don't try to get up yet," Goodwife Thintagast said, gently

pushing Burlmarr back down as he atempted to sit up. "You had a nasty fall, there. Fortunately, it seems your head was just as hard as the floor."

Several snickers escaped from some of the apprentices.

"All right, everyone back to the shop," Master Thintagast prodded. "Looks like young Burlmarr is going to live. As for you," he said turning back to Burlmarr, "why don't you head home for the day."

He smiled warmly and nodded before following the other apprentices.

———∞———

Once he had proved to Goodwife Thintagast that he could stand on his own two feet for more than a few seconds, Burlmarr was sent on his way. He took the walk home slowly, stopping to sit when he felt out of breath or light-headed. It gave him time to consider what was happening to him.

The episodes had started almost a month ago, with increasing frequency as his fortieth birthday approached. For a moment, he wondered if it was some sort of family disease or curse, but all the relatives he could think of had lived long, healthy lives. He decided he would ask his mother, though, just to be sure.

As he neared his home, Burlmarr realized he'd never before fallen sick during the day. Most of the time it was at night, following particularly vivid dreams. Dreams about a dragon. About being a dragon.

———∞———

Palarandusk hovered over the village green in the semisolid, invisible form that had kept him alive and active well past the years even dragons considered the twilight of life. That was, in part, a result of the many experiments he had been subjected to while enslaved to the Netherese sorcerer Mileirigath. But even that powerful magic was beginning to fail and he had, as of yet, been unable to recreate the combination of spells that originally altered him, his vast knowledge of the arcane, and the many tomes he had taken with him when the Empire of Netheril fell notwithstanding. Some stop-gap measures had been discovered, but most of those never worked more than once. One or two even had unexpected side effects. Well aware that any day may be his last, he remained diligent in his guardianship of the gnomes of Ieirithymbul.

The caravan had just arrived and the gnomes were gathering to help unload the provisions brought from Leilon. He was glad to see that everyone had made it back safely, though he regretted not having been able to escort them home. Unfortunately, some aggressive Forgebar dwarves had needed persuading that their intentions for Ieirithymbul and its mines were misguided. It would take the dwarves months to recover and find their way back to the surface.

By the time he made it back to the caravan, they were only a day out from the village. So Palarandusk returned to drift amongst his beloved children, eavesdropping on their plans, their dreams, and their quarrels. It made the sacrifices worthwhile to think he played a part in shaping their lives. Protecting the little village may not be as glorious as his days of defending Neverwinter, but the intimacy he had with the gnomes of Ieirithymbul was much more satisfying. He knew their names, watched many grow up, wept for their losses, and celebrated their successes alongside them.

It was the celebrations and feasts that he enjoyed the most. During those times, the normally taciturn gnomes opened themselves up to reveal their zest for life, and Palarandusk would bask in the energy like a lizard on a rock at highsun. For that reason, he was looking forward to the celebration that would take place the following night. He had listened in on the elders' plans. It would be a typical feast, like all the past ones the gnomes threw when the last caravan returned before the snows blocked the passes, but Palarandusk would enjoy himself no less. There would be plenty to see.

⚬⚭⚬

Burlmarr sat at the edge of the green, watching the dancers spin around the crackling bonfire in the center of the celebration area. He felt dizzy and flushed, though he hadn't touched a drop of the ale provided by Master Brimmloch for the festivities. It was likely the sickness. He had gotten his hopes up that he could make it through the party—there had been no episodes the day before—but he should have known better. He lowered his head into his hands, his temples throbbing. Perhaps it was time to go home.

He stood up, and suddenly he could see the entire village green, but from above, as though he was a bird flying overhead in the night sky. The sudden change in perspective overwhelmed Burlmarr and he lurched forward, stumbling a few steps before losing his balance and plopping to the ground.

Burlmarr squeezed his eyes shut. He could still see the green from above, but without the conflicting information from his own vantage, the vertigo quickly passed. He remained seated, however, rooted to the spot by fear and uncertainty.

What was happening to him? It was almost as if he were seeing through someone else's eyes.

In his mind, he watched as those eyes drifted across the green, pausing occasionally to focus on a pair dancing, or some animated discussion that Burlmarr couldn't hear. Then he watched as the eyes got closer and closer to a young gnome huddled on the ground, his hands covering his face. Burlmarr moved his hand to reach an itch, and the gnome in his mind's eye did the same.

Burlmarr gasped. The eyes were looking right at him. He was watching himself!

Struck by an impulse, Burlmarr rose unsteadily to his feet and swept his arm out in front and above him. He touched nothing, but the motion of his arm slowed momentarily at the arc of its swing, as though the air in that area was congealing. A wave of nausea swept over him, and he thought he heard someone grunt. Burlmarr sat back down, trembling.

"Who's there?"

"Can you see me, little one?" The question whispered in his ear like a gentle rumble.

"N-no. But I can see me. I mean, even though I have my eyes closed, I can still see, but it's like I'm seeing what somebody else sees." Excitement and terror had taken hold of Burlmarr's voice. The words rushed out like the waters of a swollen river over its banks. "Except now I'm not only seeing things, but I'm hearing voices, too. I'm starting to think I may be drunk, even though I didn't have any ale. Or maybe this is a fever dream. I've been really sick lately."

"No, little one, you are neither intoxicated nor ill. I can assure you that I am very real, but this would not be the appropriate place to prove that. Can you still see what I am seeing?"

Burlmarr nodded as the view shifted to look away from the green and out into the night.

"Good. Use my eyes to follow me. I would like to talk with you for a bit and learn more."

In his mind, Burlmarr moved between buildings, making his way toward the edge of the village, but he hadn't taken a step. The excitement that had been pumping through Burlmarr's veins suddenly crashed against a dam of caution. What was he doing, prepared to wander out of the village in the middle of the night after some disembodied voice? What if the voice belonged to some creature that was trying to lure him away so it could feast on his heart?

But Burlmarr knew it was no soul-sucking, flesh-eating monster he was being asked to follow. No, the whole thing was too much like his dreams. He didn't know how, but he was sure he was seeing through the eyes of a dragon. And in the back of his mind, the childhood stories the village elders told whispered to him a hope of who that dragon might be.

Flushed once more with excitement, Burlmarr walked after the voice. His steps were hesitant and awkward. It was disorienting to use another's eyes. His legs were distrustful of the sensory information, their movements jerky like a puppet on strings. When the view in his mind halted a few yards ahead of him, Burlmarr had to resist the urge to stop, continuing forward until he appeared in the picture in his mind.

Soon, they left behind the sounds of the village and its celebration. Buildings were replaced by sparsely wooded hills, the pale moon bathing the terrain in its cold light.

They began to climb up into the treeline when Burlmarr's vision went black.

"I-I can't see," Burlmarr said.

He strained his ears, trying to capture some sound that would indicate his companion had not continued on and left him, but all he heard was the night breeze amongst the trees.

"Open your eyes."

Burlmarr cried out, jumping backward and losing his balance. His arms flailed and his eyes popped open to see the stars in the sky as he fell on his rear.

"I am sorry, little one. I did not mean to startle you."

"That's . . . that's all right. What happened?"

"I would guess that the link between our senses was broken somehow."

"Right. Of course." Burlmarr felt his cheeks burn with embarrassment. "So, what do we do now?"

"I suppose we could introduce ourselves," the voice replied. Burlmarr thought he detected a note of amusement.

"All right. I guess I'll go first. My name is Burlmarr. I'm a gnome from the village of Ieirithymbul, but you already knew that. Um, I'm apprenticed to Master Thintagast. I live with my mother and father. I have . . ."

"That is quite enough," the voice chuckled, a deep rumbling that gently rattled Burlmarr. "There will be plenty of time for me to learn your life's story. For now, it is enough that we know each others' names."

"But I don't know yours."

"Oh, I think you do. Or at least you know one of them. Do you really have no idea who I am?"

"Well, I have a guess, but I can hardly believe that it would actually be you."

"Would you like to know for sure? Would you like see who you are truly speaking with?"

Burlmarr opened his mouth to shout yes, but his voice got stuck in his throat and all he could do was vigorously nod his head.

"Very well," the voice said, and a blunt snout twice the size of Burlmarr's head appeared not six feet away, long, tubular whiskers of gold and white trailing from a scaly jaw. Two eyes of molten gold winked into existence, glowing from underneath a pair of horns that swept back to a long, sinewy neck. Twin frills ran down the length of the neck from the back of the dragon's head to just above its thickly corded shoulders. Great wings, oversized replicas of the neck frills, sprouted from its shoulders to sweep back along the length of its body to the tip of its tail. The dragon's form swamped Burlmarr's field of vision, blotting out the countryside, but Burlmarr was not afraid. No gnome of Ieirithymbul could ever fear the majestic creature that stood before him.

"I am Palarandusk, once called the Sun Dragon." The wyrm's lips parted in a toothy smile that conveyed a sense of warmth and friendship. "You know me as the Unseen Protector."

Elder Gromann plodded home. Revelers were still about, but he was tired, and he hadn't seen his wife in a while. Kaylindrra was probably already in bed, waiting for him, and she didn't like sleeping alone.

There were no lights on when he entered, though the moonlight was more than enough for his eyes to see by. However, once he closed the door, even that was taken away. Fortunately, Gromann knew the layout of his house well enough that it made no difference.

"Kaylin, dear, I'm home," he called out softly, making his way back to the bedroom.

There was no answer. Perhaps she was already asleep. His eyes were starting to adjust to the darkness as he turned the corner into the room. He paused. Two dark shapes stood at the far side of the bed. A third dark mass lay at the head of the bed.

"Kaylindrra?"

A pair of hands grabbed Gromann's right arm and jerked him into the room. Four small globes of green-white light sprang to life across the bed, revealing the four gnomes who drove the caravan: Drom, Merem, Furnis, and Sudo. Drom sat on the bed next to Kaylindrra, his hand over her mouth and a knife resting against her neck. Her eyes were wide and darting wildly.

"What is going on? In the name of Garl Glittergold, if this is some kind of prank. . . ."

"Oh, it's no prank, old man," Merem said. The glow from the lights cast eerie shadows across his face and made the tone of his skin seem sickly. "And we are not who you think."

Merem lifted a crystal amulet, which Gromann just then noticed, from around his neck. As he did so, his form seemed to distort and grow, until a human towered there, wrapped in a hooded cloak.

"Wh-what do you want?"

"You are going to show us where we can find the lair of this dragon you call the Unseen Protector."

"I don't know what you're talking about. That's just a bed-time story told to children."

Kaylindrra squealed from behind her captor's hand as he pressed the knife against her skin hard enough to draw a drop of blood.

"Don't test my patience. We know there is a dragon that protects your caravans, your village. And we know that in your stories, the dragon has revealed himself to the elders. If the dragon is real, then perhaps that is true as well.

"In fact, I'm willing to bet your little woman's life that it is. What do you say? Am I right, and you'll take us on a late night stroll? Or does your wife die?"

"No, no. You're right," Gromann pleaded. "I can lead you to him. Just don't hurt her. Don't hurt my Kaylin."

"Tie her up," the man who had been Merem said to the one who looked like Drom. He hung the crystal amulet around his neck once more and quickly turned back into Merem. "We don't want anybody to know what we're about just yet."

Gromann watched through teary eyes as Kaylin was bound to the bed and gagged. Then the false Merem pushed him out of the room.

"Is there a back door out of this place?" He asked as the rest of the false gnomes filed out behind him. Gromann nodded and led them out of his house through the kitchen.

They made their way quietly through the village with only the night stars as witness. The festivities were all but over and no one was out and about so far from the green. Gromann led them out of the valley and up into the foot-hills of Felrenden, desperately trying to remember where the ancient gold dragon had revealed himself, several years past. There was a cleft with an old statue of marble inside. . . .

After a couple hours of searching, the man disguised as Merem jerked Gromann to a halt.

"Are we going to get there soon, old man? I hope you're not trying to stall or something."

"Please, it was a long time ago. I'm trying to remember. I'm not even sure if this is his only lair."

"Well, hurry up. This is taking too long."

He let Gromann go and they started walking again. A few minutes later, and Gromann thought he recognized an out-cropping of rock.

"I think this is it," the elder exclaimed.

Excitement stirred within his breast at a sudden thought. If the Unseen Protector did show himself, if Gromann had found his lair, it seemed likely the gold would make short work of the men. Gromann quickly hid his grin.

"This? It's nothing but an overhang with some odd bits of art and other trinkets laying around." The false Merem did not sound convinced. "What are you trying to pull, old man?"

"The Unseen Protector has no need for a home like mere mortals. He is invisible and without form, appearing only when he is ready to strike." Gromann couldn't help but slip into his storyteller voice.

"Save your fireside showmanship for the children," Merem snorted. "All right, let's get set up," he ordered the others. "I'll summon the Archmage Arcane."

He removed the crystal amulet and was once again human. From a pouch on his belt, he produced a small stone and stood silently for a moment, holding it in the palm of his hand. Then he returned it to his pouch and took a few steps backward.

A brilliant white light flashed into existence where the man had stood. It began to expand in an oval until it was seven feet tall, energy crackling at its edges. Once its growth stabilized, a foot emerged, followed by a knee, and the rest of a heavily armored man. Not two seconds after, a form bent with age hobbled out, his bald crown ringed by long, white hair leading the way. A handful of other humans brought up the rear, dressed in a similar fashion as the one who had summoned them. The portal closed with another flash.

"You have done well, Daikon," the old man said as he directed the others to begin setting up some strange rods around the cleft.

"Thank you, Master."

"Now, who do we have here?" The old man came to stand before Gromann. Bent over as he was, he stood only a little taller than the gnome.

"I am Froga Gromann, elder of Ieirithymbul." Gromann straightened, pride in his voice.

"So you are, so you are." He patted Gromann's head patronizingly then turned back to the others and said, "Are we ready? Daikon, please position the bait. Quickly, now. The dragon should be arriving any minute. I made sure our arrival was suitably announced."

Daikon dragged Gromann a few feet until they were in the middle of the circle of rods that had been planted into the ground. He used the amulet again to transform into Merem and drew a dagger from his belt.

"Night, night, old one."

He swung the hilt at Gromman's head and everything went black.

Palarandusk drifted, invisible and intangible, up the hillside toward where he had seen the flash of light. The little one, Burlmarr, should have been home in bed by then. An interesting gnome, that one. Palarandusk would have to keep his eye on him.

As he climbed into the foothills, the dragon realized he was nearing one of his many stashes of treasure that were hidden around the valley of Felrenden. Then he saw the two gnomes huddled at the base of an outcropping. He surged forward, worry growing in his heart. One of the gnomes looked hurt.

When he was within a few feet, Palarandusk slowly materialized his head. One of the gnomes shrieked. The other, older gnome lay motionless. Palarandusk could see a large bruise forming on the side of his head. Was that Elder Gromann?

"Do not be afraid, little one," said the dragon. "Are you hurt?"

"Y-yes," the young gnome stammered, "I-I mean, no. I'm fine, but Elder Gromann is hurt. I came to find him when his wife said he hadn't come home from the celebration."

"What was that flash of light?"

"I don't know. I just got here myself and found Elder Gromann lying on the ground. I can't get him to wake up. Can you help us?"

"Let me see what I can do."

Palarandusk moved forward and began to materialize fully. A scent in the air stopped him. There were men about. Palarandusk had been the target of adventurers seeking trophies before. Perhaps the elder had been kidnapped by them to use as bait. In which case, he had walked right into their trap. In fact, he then noticed the rods spaced at intervals around the outcropping.

"Fool, it is too late. There will be no escape." The young gnome had become a human wrapped in a hooded cloak, slinking toward the edge of the ring.

"Erans ne!" another voice cried out to Palarandusk's left.

The dragon whirled to face it. Recognizing the command phrase, he began to dematerialize. Arcs of energy shot toward him from the ends of the rods, each arc a different color. As they neared the dragon, rather than striking him, they encircled him from his snout to the tip of his tail. He was suddenly solid again, and he couldn't move.

"Welcome, great Palarandusk." The old man who had shouted the Draconic words came forward to stand in front of the dragon at the perimeter of the snare. "You have been bound in an anti-magic stasis field. You are immobile, cut off from the Weave. You are mine. I could kill you, if I wished.

"Fortunately, you have something I need. I know that you possess magic from the fallen Empire of Netheril. I know you have used that magic to prolong your life. As you can see, I am not exactly young anymore." The man chuckled at his own joke. "In exchange for the magic you used, I will set you free."

Burlmarr tiptoed into his home. It was a few hours before sunrise, and he'd hear no end of it if he woke his parents. He slipped off his shoes and trousers and snuggled under the covers. There was too much to think about to fall right to sleep, however. He had spent the last few hours—he had lost track of just how long—talking with the Unseen Protector. He still couldn't believe he had spoken with a dragon, let alone a childhood-story-come-true.

The subject of their conversation had been just as amazing. Palarandusk had questioned him extensively about his sickness and his ability to apparently link to the dragon's senses of sight and hearing. After casting several spells, it had been determined that the ability was not magical in nature. Palarandusk knew of some individuals who had learned to manifest mental powers through a regimen of strict discipline that took months, even years of subconscious scrutiny and introspection. That Burlmarr did so without such training meant he was likely some sort of "wilder." The sickness was probably a symptom of his inability to control the power, a result of overtaxing his mind. It would lessen—and eventually go away, Burlmarr hoped—as his mastery over the ability grew.

That still left the reason of why Palarandusk was the target of the link. It might have been because of the place the Unseen Protector held in the subconscious of Ieirithymbul, but the dragon had never been more than bedtime tales to Burlmarr. Palarandusk felt it was more likely connected to the various spells that sustained him. Perhaps one or more of them were natural attractants of mental energy.

Burlmarr yawned and rolled onto his side. All his thinking had finally exhausted his mind. His eyes were dry and his eyelids heavy. He quit trying to keep them open.

No sooner were his eyes closed than he began to dream. He was up in the hills surrounding the valley the gnomes called home. It was night, but the area was lit by arcs of multi-colored energy. The arcs held him trapped, staring straight into the face of a bent old man.

Burlmarr sat bolt upright in bed. It wasn't a dream. Palarandusk was in trouble. He leaped out of bed and pulled his pants on. His mother rushed into his room as he was fastening the laces of his shoes.

"Is everything all right? Are you sick, Burlmarr?"

"I'm fine, Mother. I have to go."

"But it's the middle of the night."

"I'm sorry. A friend's in trouble. I'll explain later."

He brushed past her and raced out the door.

As Burlmarr climbed out of the valley, his pace began to slow, allowing his thoughts to catch up with his actions. Questions crept forward from the back of his mind. How was he going to find Palarandusk? He hadn't recognized anything in the quick view he got from the dragon's perspective. What was he going to do when he got there? He was no great hero, like Ardabad, Braeder, or Pheldaer. He could barely control what little power he did have. If something was powerful enough to capture the great dragon, what hope did he have against it?

Burlmarr shook his head, trying to break free from the doubts. It didn't matter. Palarandusk was his friend. He would find a way to help.

At least locating the dragon wouldn't really be a problem. Burlamarr could see a flickering, multi-colored light in the distance already. It was probably the energy that held Palarandusk.

After another hour of walking and climbing, Burlmarr ducked behind a boulder only a few yards away from Palarandusk and his captors. He couldn't tell if the dragon was in any sort of pain, but he knew he probably didn't have long to think of something. He had to disrupt the arcs of energy.

A rod shooting forth an arc of red energy stood just a short distance from where Burlmarr hid. Next to it, though, was an armored man with a greatsword strapped to his back. He was facing away from Burlmarr, but the gnome knew there was no way he could reach the rod without being seen. If only there was some way he could distract the man. Burlmarr considered one of the minor illusions he could create, but he didn't want to draw anyone else's attention with sounds or light.

At his wit's end, Burlmarr sat back and growled in frustration. He didn't come all that way just to be useless. He would think of something if he had to beat his head against the boulder until the sun came up.

That was it. He would use his head. If he had the ability to link with someone else's senses, perhaps he could temporarily shut those senses down. All he needed was a few seconds in which to race out and tear up the rod.

Not sure exactly how to proceed, Burlmarr focused on the armored man and reached out with his mind. He was surprised when he actually touched something. It was like a bundle of emotions and memories. The sensation almost overwhelmed Burlmarr and he pulled back instinctively.

Taking a deep breath, he probed again, and found another bundle. As soon as he touched it, he could smell sweat mixed with metal, feel the weight of steel plates on his shoulders, and hear the crackling of energy. Smiling with success, Burlmarr imagined each and every one of those senses shut off, and the sensations disappeared. He realized then that the emotions and memories were no longer there, either. It was as if the man's entire brain had shut down.

Without a moment to waste, Burlmarr sprinted for the rod and yanked it out of the ground with all his might. The arc of red energy sputtered and went out.

Burlmarr stood basking in his triumph, the rod held aloft. From the corner of his eye, he caught movement and turned. There was a sharp crack and Burlmarr fell backward to the ground, the rod in his hands cleanly cloven in two. The armored man had shaken off whatever Burlmarr had done to him, drawn his sword, and swung at the gnome. Only the fact that he had been holding the rod above his head when he turned had saved him, the stout shaft deflecting the blade.

The armored man advanced on Burlmarr, and the gnome scrambled backward on the ground. In two long strides, the man was on the gnome and thrust his sword through Burlmarr's stomach, pinning him to the dirt. Burlmarr screamed in agony, blood flecking his lips.

From behind him, he heard Palarandusk roar. A huge shadow enveloped him, and he saw the dragon's jaws snap over the armored man, biting him in two. A chant began to Burlmarr's right and he turned his head to see the bent old man waving a staff before him.

"I don't think so," said the dragon. "I've had enough of your magic tonight."

Palarandusk began speaking rapidly in his own tongue. He finished first and a funnel of whirling wind appeared above the old man. It quickly descended upon him, beating him to the ground. When it finally touched down, it picked the old wizard up and swung him around inside its funnel, finally flinging him screaming into the night. Palarandusk then charged off in another direction, and Burlmarr heard shrieks that were silenced by the *whoosh* of flames.

Burlmarr's feet grew cold and he made an attempt to pull the blade from his midsection, but his strength was gone. He laid back, coughing up more blood. The stars in the night sky were growing dim, though Burlmarr was sure it was still a few hours before dawn. He blinked, and a scaly paw appeared above him. It grasped the sword hilt between its claws and removed the weapon. Another paw gently scooped up the gnome and brought him face to face with Palarandusk.

"I am sorry, little one. I would not have wished harm to come to you even if it meant my death." Tears where forming in the dragon's eyes. "I have no magic that would heal you. All I can do is promise that your sacrifice will not be forgotten. May Garl Glittergold give you a place of honor in the Golden Hills."

Burlmarr smiled at his friend, and closed his eyes.

A TALL TALE

J.L. COLLINS

The Year of the Tankard (1370 DR)

Flickering torches mounted on a pair of poles were the only guide for their eyes as they approached the decrepit barn. Once used for storage for the remote lumber camp, it had become home to old, worn out equipment, hay, and as refuge once a year for a peculiar traveling caravan.

They approached in silence, their voices having fallen in unsure expectation of what might await them inside. Myth, legend, rumors, each they knew well enough, but would they actually see what lived only in their imaginations? In their nightmares? The forest was quiet, and though their feet knew the paths and treeswell , their pace slowed, expectation turning to hesitation leading only to doubt, and fear.

The peeling paint and warped wood walls, once

comforting reminders of seasons past, had become as eerie as the walls of a crumbled keep, with secrets etched into every stone. More than once they looked over their shoulders for eyes that were not there. They knew it was foolishness to expect to find anyone else in their isolated home, yet on that night they did not feel alone at all. . . .

✦⟨∞⟩✦

"I've seen a dragon!" exclaimed Nollo, an excited grin evident on his young face.

The three other boys, along with the half-elf girl, exchanged looks ranging from amusement to irritation at the claim. McDodd, as expected, was the first to voice his disbelief.

"The closest thing you've seen to a dragon, wagon-boy, is a sand snake bitin' you in your rear when you dropped your breeches to wet the sand!" The biggest of the boys, McDodd often used his size to intimidate the others into agreeing with him. It rarely worked.

Craster giggled, and though he was as small and skinny as Nollo he was filthy compared to the young boy's groomed appearance. His laugh regularly followed McDodd's biting remarks. Nollo frowned at McDodd's rebuttal. Though a few years younger, he did not back down from the larger boy's taunts.

"I have too seen a dragon. I even fed it! And they're called wyrms!" Nollo bit back the rest of his reply, as though realizing he might be saying too much.

McDodd inhaled, preparing another sarcastic remark when Kirsk held up his hand, causing the bigger boy to exhale sharply.

"What? You think he's actually tellin' the truth? He's as big a liar as his father," McDodd said.

He couldn't resist challenging Kirsk's attempt to silence him. Though physically bigger, McDodd stopped short of intimidating him into agreement, as Kirsk's quiet confidence unnerved the braggart. Kirsk glanced at the half-elf girl Syndar, catching her gaze with his deep blue, nearly black eyes, before turning back to Nollo.

"Tell us about your dragon, Nollo, and what you fed it." Kirsk's words were spoken with a gentle encouragement.

Nollo smiled and said, "I gave it deer meat, and some fish left over from my father's cooking pot. It was really hungry, so I stole another fish from the bucket, feeding it to him whole. His teeth were so big, he bit it in half and swallowed both bites at once!"

Nollo used his fingers to mimic the gaping jaws of his dinner companion.

McDodd could not hold back. "That's the stupidest thing I've ever heard, and Craster says a lot of stupid things."

Craster started laughing at McDodd's comment then sheepishly scratched the back of his neck with his black fingernails. He looked the beggar in his tattered breeches and patchwork tunic.

McDodd continued, "Everyone knows dragons eat cows, horses, and elves. Especially elves." His mouth turned into a cruel smile as he leered at Syndar.

She met McDodd's gaze evenly and said, "The only stupid one McDodd is you. A dragon wouldn't even eat you because you're so stupid. Dragons eat wild animals that roam too close to their lair. They even raid the occasional orchard if they want some sweet fruit. My mother told me about dragons from a book she keeps." Syndar spoke with the voice of a girl trying to be a woman, surrounded by boys who were not yet men. Kirsk smiled as she stuck her tongue out at McDodd who was shaking his head.

"Explain to me again why we let her up in our tree? Fruit? Is she saying dragons eat fruit? I think elves have fruit between their ears. It rots, becoming soft and mushy." McDodd gestured to his ear as he spoke. "Your mother won't know, she left the elven kingdoms to come live in a stupid boring lumber camp. I doubt she even owns a book. What good are books in a lumber camp? Next you're going to say that she's still teachin' you magic too, right?"

"She is you dullard! One day I'll turn you into toad and you'll beg me to turn you back, but I won't, because all I'll hear is some stupid frog and I'll kick you into a puddle and forget all about you."

Syndar's face turned an angry pink, and though blessed with the ageless beauty and grace of her elf mother, she already demonstrated the temper and strong-willed nature of her human father.

Kirsk intervened. "Leave it be, McDodd. If Syndar says she knows magic, then one day she'll show us. Nollo is our guest in the tree, let him finish his story."

Kirsk waited for McDodd to press the issue, but the bully relented, glaring before punching Nollo in the arm.

"You heard 'im. So what else did your dragon eat? Some of those stupid animals your father tries passing off as monsters? He should be arrested."

Nollo rubbed his arm. "No, he curled up and went to sleep."

Kirsk's curiosity got the better of him. "Nollo, dragons don't usually eat fish fed to them by humans. Why didn't the dragon didn't eat you instead?"

"Because he was caged," Nollo said. "I wouldn't feed a dragon if it wasn't caged. That's stupid."

His reply was so immediate, Kirsk almost believed him.

Craster laughed again, prompting McDodd to punch him.

"A cage?" McDodd pressed. "I doubt you saw a dragon in a cage. They happen to be as big as a castle and fly so high you can't see them."

McDodd waited for the boy's reply then looked surprised when Syndar supported the braggart.

"Nollo, that's a tall tale and you know it," she said. "Dragons are too strong. If they can carry a horse and rider into the air, they could break out of a cage pretty easy."

She smiled at the young boy, as if to encourage his story while keeping him honest.

Nollo sighed, staring out as a warm breeze wafted through the framed window of the tree house. A lantern on the floor cast shadows along the wall.

"You can keep them in cages if they're small enough," Nollo replied, his voice so quiet the others almost missed it.

"What do you mean small enough?" Kirsk persisted. "You mean like a *baby* dragon?"

Nollo glanced up, nervous, nodding slowly.

Kirsk smiled and asked, "Where is this baby dragon then?"

Nollo pulled a knife from the pocket of his soft breeches. Elegantly dressed with his embroidered shirt, he wiped some dirt from his polished boots and notched the wood by his feet.

"Not 'posed to say," he said. "My pappy would get mad."

McDodd opened his mouth, but Syndar spoke first. "Was it one of the carnivals back east? You said your father took you 'round the southern edge of the desert. My mother says tribes of men and wandering tent cities live within sight of the sands. Is that where you saw it?"

Nollo shook his head in silent disagreement, stabbing at the floor of the tree house.

To the surprise of all, Craster uttered their unspoken question: "You sayin' yer pappy got a caged dragon up in that barn?"

Nollo looked up too quickly, his expression betraying him.

"Who told you that?" the boy asked. "There's no dragon, I just . . . I saw one once. You're lying!"

Kirsk reached out a calloused hand to Nollo's shoulder and said, "It's all right Nollo, we know what's in the barn. Every year you and your father spend a tenday restocking for the journey west toward the Sword Coast. Every year we share tales, and every year you tell us about the beasts, wizards, and barbarians you encounter. We don't care if it's true, we just like your stories. It's better than listening to McDodd burp and break wind everyday, for sure."

Both Syndar and Craster laughed, causing the bigger boy to turn red, threatening Kirsk with a punch. Craster switched sides and encouraged the fight.

"Yeah, knock 'im, McDodd. Knock his teeth in!"

Syndar rolled her eyes, and Kirsk sat motionless, familiar with the bully's threats.

"One day, Kirsk," McDodd threatened even as he lowered his arm. "One day you'll get what's coming."

Ignoring the bully, Kirsk regarded Nollo and said, "Tell us about the barn. Your father must have something special if you aren't supposed to tell anyone. What is it? A talking bird? You swore once you had a talking bird, but when we went to see it, he just pooped in Craster's hair. That was funny, only because Craster did all the talking."

Syndar giggled at the familiar story, and McDodd punched Craster in the arm just because.

"Nothin' special. Just . . . animals," Nollo mumbled, looking out the window.

McDodd finally found a target for his frustration. "Ha! Just like the time you told us you had a beholder—a floating eye sack that could turn us to stone. 'Cept when we arrived, it wasn't floating, or wavin' its eyes around. Just some pumpkins that grew into a giant pumpkin, with a rotted hole for a mouth, and stems you swore were once eye stalks. Last year, you swore your pap had a drow girl in a cage. Syndar was so scared she wouldn't go into the barn. She believed you, but I knew better. Funny how the evil dark elf was actually Grapper's daughter covered in dirt and soot. A chimney sweep's daughter paid to pretend she was drow. Your pappy is so cheap, he didn't even give her fake ears!"

McDodd laughed with Craster joining in. "Yeh, yer pap is cheap! And stupid!"

Nollo flushed red, his embarrassment becoming anger at the taunts.

"You're all just stupid tree-cutters!" Nollo shouted. "You wouldn't know a dwarf from a gnome from a halfling. I *have* fed a dragon. I did it tonight. And I said they're called *wyrms!*"

He stopped his outburst, seeing looks of surprise from the four local youth. They had never heard him so angry before.

"I . . . I should go," Nollo said. "My pappy is mad if I'm late two nights in a row."

As he started for the rope ladder hanging from the side of the tree house, Kirsk's gentle hand paused him.

"Do you really have a baby dragon in the barn?"

Nollo stammered out his reply. "Y-yes."

"Well, I give the kid respect," said McDodd. "Three lies in three years, and each bigger than the last."

Kirsk looked back to Syndar, who voiced everyone's thoughts: "Let's go see it."

Nollo shook his head and said, "No! I promised my pappy I wouldn't tell. It's his big surprise for carnival this year. Every year he gets mad when no one comes to see his animals, so he said he'll get something so special, they'll beg him to stay and run the show all year long. Please, I won't be able to sit for a month if he finds out."

The others looked to each other as McDodd said, "I'll go, just to prove what a liar you are."

Nollo looked to Kirsk, his expression changing as a new thought emerged.

"If he thinks I'm a liar, then I'll prove him wrong. 'Cept you all have to pay a coin each to see it. Two if you want a touch." Nollo grinned, secure in the knowledge his father couldn't be sore if he turned profit like he was taught to.

Craster whined, "I ain't got no coins."

McDodd punched him, right in the same spot, and said, "Yer stupid. We ain't payin' no coins to see a lizard in a cage. I'll bet you it's a lizard with wings of cloth, 'cause his pap is stupid and cheap."

Craster winced as he rubbed his arm. "Yeh, stupid and cheap."

Kirsk shared a secret smile with Syndar before gesturing to the open night before them.

"Here's the deal Nollo," he said. "You take us to the barn, and show us your dragon. We'll pay you a coin each if we agree it's real." McDodd started to swear but Syndar pinched him as Kirsk finished, "In fact, if you have any fish left, I'll pay an extra coin to feed it myself. Is that fair, O carnival master?"

Nollo smiled at the title, swinging onto the ladder. "Sure is! Better count your fingers though, you might not have them all when you're done!"

The young boy nimbly climbed down as Kirsk helped Syndar find her footing on the ladder. The pair exchanged another glance as Craster blew out the lantern, the night swallowing them.

⚬⚬⚬

Nollo led them to the warped peeling doors of the barn, wincing as the rusted hinges moaned when opened. Inside, the musty smell of hay, horses, and lantern oil greeted them. Poorly lit, they could hear the whinny of the caravan horses. Nollo crept forward, taking them around the back of one of the wagons, to a shroud-covered cage.

Nollo turned back to face them and said, "Remember, one coin each for a look, two if you want to touch it."

McDodd shook his fist as he spoke. "I'll give you two of something else if you don't hurry up."

Nollo ignored the threat, puffing out his chest in preparation for his performance. "In all the realms there is no monster so fearsome, no danger so . . . so . . . dangerous, no beast so horrible that they cause fear by their very name!"

Nollo gestured grandly as Syndar whispered to Kirsk, "Can a dragon be fearsome and horrible at the same time?"

Kirsk smirked as Nollo's voice rose. "Cast away your eyes gentle folk, for you dare not see what I am about to show . . ."

But McDodd had had enough. He pushed the smaller boy out of the way, and grabbed the shroud and yanked it off, revealing a battered steel cage. The bars were warped from repeated blows, and the top of the cage was punctured from dozens of rents and tears. The cage was more fascinating than the mottled brown creature curled up inside it. Dull scales adorned the torso, and a long thick tail curled tight to the sleeping body.

"Gods, the stink!" McDodd said as he wrinkled his nose in disgust. "That's the ugliest lizard I ever saw."

Nollo unsuccessfully tried pushing the burly McDodd back.

"It's a dragon you axe-head, and you're the one that stinks."

Syndar crept close, studying the creature as it stirred at the noise. One reptilian eye popped open, surveying the group. The beast opened its tooth-filled snout, a leathery tongue sliding out in a lazy yawn.

Nollo said, "See? No lizard has that many teeth. Them's dragon teeth. Stick your finger in and see for yourself. Just make sure you have enough fingers left to count your coins."

Kirsk smiled at Nollo's bluster, and looked to Syndar.

She shrugged, looked back to the cage, and said, "I've only read about them in my mother's book, I've never seen one. I expected it to be . . . to be . . ."

McDodd finished her thought. "Bigger, right? A dragon is as big as this barn, not smaller than my dog."

As if in answer, the creature let out a cry that sounded more like a squawk than a roar. Its tail flipped back and forth for a moment, rattling the cage, and it sent an expectant look Nollo's way. Disappearing behind another wagon, Nollo returned, struggling to carry a bucket stinking of day old fish. Grabbing one of the slimy offerings, he hoisted it toward the cage.

McDodd stole it from his hand. "Good thing this isn't really a dragon, you'd be too weak to even care for it."

As McDodd slid the fish through the bars of the cage, the creature grew more animated. Syndar and Kirsk looked at each other as a thin membrane momentarily unfolded from the side of the body before disappearing against the scales once more.

McDodd wasn't finished having his fun, and as the creature opened its mouth to take the fish, he snatched it back, laughing.

Nollo, furious, made a grab for the fish. "Don't tease it. Give it back!"

Kirsk started to complain, but McDodd drowned him out. "Ha! A dragon would'a ripped the fish right from my hands. They move so fast yer dead before you even see them. This is just a lazy, fat lizard."

McDodd held Nollo away with one hand, slowly swinging the fish in his other.

"McDodd, stop," Syndar said, but her warning fell on deaf ears.

"I'm helping it hunt, see?" the bully said. "It's moving its neck now."

McDodd swatted at the snout, landing a blow that caught the creature on the end of its nose. It croaked as it pulled back, a surprisingly dexterous claw pawing its face. It shuddered before sliding its neck back as McDodd leaned closer to the cage, laughing as the creature struggled to escape the smell. Kirsk had just decided it was time for that fight between him and McDodd, when the beast sneezed, sudden and violent.

A burst of flame shot from its mouth, promptly igniting McDodd's hair.

McDodd stood straight up, his hair smoking, then screamed as though he had seen the dead walk.

"Put it out! Put it out! Put it out!" he shouted as he ran in circles, swatting at his head.

Craster stood dumbfounded. Syndar burst into hysterical laughter, as Nollo ran to the cage to check on the wyrmling. Kirsk could only stare as his lips curled into a horrified smile.

"It's burning! It's burning! It's burning!" McDodd screamed.

He continued his frantic running, still smacking the top of his head.

Kirsk overcame his amused shock, yelling at Craster to grab a bucket that sat on the floor of the barn beside a trough. The two boys scooped their buckets into the water as McDodd screamed that he'd kill them all, running toward Kirsk and Craster. In one fluid motion, he bent over at the waist to expose the top of his head, just as Kirsk threw the water where McDodd's head used to be. Craster stumbled into McDodd at the same moment, drenching the bully from the waist down. Kirsk's water splattered uselessly on the floor behind the bully.

McDodd shrieked, his head smoldering. The captive dragon grew excited at the boy's terror, struggling against the confines of the cage.

Syndar steadied herself as she caught her breath, then noted the ends of her hair standing straight out from her head. She reached a hand to them even as Nollo felt the hair on the back of his neck rise. Kirsk and Craster were too busy swatting at McDodd to notice, and McDodd was too busy swatting back in pain and anger.

Nollo jumped back from the cage as the wyrmling's excitement turned to violent rebellion. It began ramming its head against the top if the cage as hard as it ever had.

A low hum sounded inside the barn, and Syndar tried to speak, her voice lost as the buzzing intensified. Her hair stood up even more, as did the boys', then the buzzing stopped.

Their world exploded in a shower of wood and debris.

The entire rear wall of the barn burst inward, the cries of the baby dragon lost as a massive shadow stepped into view. They all saw the horn-tipped snout at the end of a scaled neck that opened to reveal a row of horrifying fangs. The bellow started low and guttural, rising to a roar of unbridled fury. Blue scales glistened in the fragments of light from the moon that shone through the missing wall and roof.

McDodd sat up, many feet from where he had been standing, unaware that the blast of wind had finally extinguished his head. His favorite weapon, a quick tongue and blustering threats, were useless to him.

For a moment there was silence, then the rending sound of metal signaled the wyrmling had burst free from its cage.

That sound was followed by another roar from the blue dragon, causing them all to clutch their ears. One heavy claw from the blue ripped open the wagon, revealing a ruined cage and an unconscious Nollo lying amidst the debris. The blue had no appetite for the human boy, and snapped its head at the sound of clawed feet that scurried across the floor.

McDodd sobbed uncontrollably, his arms covering his head as Syndar rose to her knees, unsteady and bleeding from a gash to her scalp. Kirsk staggered to his feet. His heart nearly stopped when he saw the blue cross the barn, Syndar right in its path.

Without knowing how close to death he was, Kirsk summoned unknown strength and bolted across the path of the blue. Tackling Syndar, they tumbled to a stop as the dragon thudded past them on heavy, clawed feet. It walked right over McDodd, the heavy tail nearly sweeping him away.

Syndar shook uncontrollably, and Kirsk fought to keep

his legs from giving out. The horses in the barn made a sound Kirsk never wanted to hear again, driving themselves through the wooden doors of their stalls in their fear.

As the mounts bolted for the double doors leading outside, everyone felt their breath stolen from their chests. The air started to hum again, and Kirsk couldn't hear his own breathing. The air itself seemed drawn toward the blue, then snapped back hard in angry rage. A blazing white light exploded into the double doors, burning a hole and carrying on into the night. It caught one of the horses in its wake, and the animal shrieked horribly, spasming as it smoked and burned in the throes of death.

The noise around Kirsk sounded distant as he held his head. A brown, leathery shape slid across the floor under the wagon nearest to the jagged hole in the barn. The wyrmling looked at Kirsk and Syndar and squawked.

Kirsk found his voice, even as the blue whipped its tail, obliterating the wooden stalls. "Syndar, you have to run, we have to get it out of here!"

She sobbed, but moved when Kirsk moved. The boy grabbed at the wyrmling who croaked even louder. Its cry alerted the blue, which roared again, spinning back in their direction.

Kirsk yelled as loudly as he could, thrusting the struggling creature into Syndar's arms. "Whatever happens, don't let go! Run for the mill! Run as hard as you can!"

Syndar shrieked as Kirsk pushed her through the ruined wall, crying out as the wyrmling dug its' talons into her skin. Kirsk closed his eyes and prayed. With speed generated by fear, he ran out the opening in plain view of the blue. The nightmarish beast was as long as a wagon train, and far faster. Bellowing in protest, it followed Kirsk outside.

"Run!" Kirsk shouted to Syndar. "Run hard! Don't look back!"

Syndar's light feet carried her quickly, but the wyrmling was heavy, her arms already bleeding from the sharp talons.

"Kirsk!" she wailed. "Kirsk! It hurts!"

But she ran on, the wood mill looming through the trees ahead. Branches and brambles tore at her dress, and tears stung her eyes, making it difficult to see.

Kirsk ran into the thickest of the trees outside the barn, weaving left then right, desperately seeking protection. His breath left him, the air starting to crackle and hum. In a last desperate gamble, Kirsk dived forward. The entire forest in front of him was illuminated by a brilliant white light, then there was a roar and a snapping sound, and he was in darkness.

———— ❦ ————

Syndar struggled with the squawking wyrmling as as she made her way to the heavy door of the mill. Slamming her slender body into the door, she forced it open. Leaning with their combined weight, she managed to close it again.

Her hair stood up on end. With a cry she dropped to her knees as a bolt of lightning burned through the door, passing within feet of her. Slamming into a large steel saw, it splintered into a cascade of arcing lights. As the momentary brilliance of light vanished, Syndar raced for the stairs to the catwalks above. A roar from outside nearly deafened her, and she gritted her teeth, forcing her legs to move.

She ran across wooden walkways straddling piles of fresh cut trees. The smell of wood and sap mingled with burnt hair and blood. The building shook as a terrible blow shattered the door. A second lash of the blue's tail forced a larger opening. The gnarled horn of the blue's snout slipped inside the mill, slowly panning its head side to side.

The wyrmling squawked again, causing the blue to snap its scaled head in their direction. Tears stained her cheeks as Syndar ran, hoping to find another set of stairs down out of the mill. Winding her way through coarse bags of wood chips, a dark form appeared in an opening and she shrieked as Kirsk caught her in his arms.

"Syndar! It's me! It's me." Pulling himself the rest of the way inside the opening using chains that hung down to the ground below, Kirsk swatted away the thrashing tail of the wyrmling. "We can scare it off, but you have to listen. You have to stand exactly where I say, and not run no matter what. I promise you won't be hurt."

Syndar shook her head, then opened her eyes when she realized the wyrmling wasn't struggling. It looked at her with obvious intelligence.

Kirsk was covered in mud, leaves, and smelled of burnt skin, but she met his deep blue gaze with her own green eyes, looking for strength.

Her quiet reply was determined. "I trust you, Kirsk."

Creeping back along the catwalks, Syndar moved opposite where the blue stood thrashing its tail, unable to fly over the tall stacks of logs.

Lowering himself quietly to a table laden with saws and axes, Kirsk grabbed an axe. He crept away as the blue left long claw marks in the logs, attempting to climb them.

Syndar breathed deeply, standing very still as the wyrmling perched on her shoulders, its long tail wrapped around her waist. Her lips moved in silent repetition, reciting an incantation practiced over and over. Her voice rose as she did, and the blue snuffed loudly, turning on all fours at the familiar sound of spellcasting.

The dragon took several steps forward, seeking to blast the half-elf right off the catwalk, when multi-colored globes of light started dancing harmlessly in front of the blue's eyes. Snapping its head back in expectation of a biting spell, the blue roared in defiance as the futile dancing lights winked in the air.

It was then that Kirsk stood where he needed to be, lifting

the heavy axe and bringing it down on the tail of the blue with all his strength. The handle snapped in two as the blade cracked a scale, biting into the tough flesh underneath.

Howling in unexpected pain, the blue looked back to find Kirsk kneeling over the broken axe. Its thick tail cut the air as it swung down hard. Dirt shot upward from the blow as a bludgeoned Kirsk flew across the mill, as did the wooden pylon behind him that held the log pile secure. There was a sudden shift in the weight of the logs, and the momentum began, like the torrent of a waterfall, impossible to stop.

The blue roared again, its tail pinned by the first falling log, as the massive pile avalanched out of control. In reaction to its tail being caught, the blue turned, its strength ripping the tail free, along with dozens of scales, only to bring its horned snout into line with the next bouncing log. It took the heavy tree right in the face, knocking it backward.

Struggling to avoid the next missile, it unfurled its wings in a natural escape pattern. Touching the floor as they swept out, they were promptly trampled by the rolling, spinning logs. Clawed feet sought purchase on the churning debris and were swept under, sending the blue crashing to the floor.

Losing all sense of direction, the dragon fought to stand upright on the shifting mass of spinning wood. With a defiant roar it freed its massive wings and thrust upward with all its remaining strength, heaving itself through the roof of the mill. As shingles and support beams rained down, a solitary shriek signaled its flight into the night sky.

Syndar rushed down to Kirsk's prone body. Silent tears streamed down her cheeks, and she was almost afraid to touch him. Moonlight revealed the blood trickling from his mouth, his lips twitching, struggling to draw air. Gathering Kirsk against her she listened for his next breath. More tears ran down her cheeks when she was rewarded with a rattling exhale.

But her joy was short-lived. A shadow obscured the moonlight, and she heard the sound of heavy wings returning. Eyes widening in horror, she looked up to see the roof buckle as a massive dragon settled onto the ruined structure, the remaining beams supporting the roof snapping and cracking in protest.

The monster shifted, allowing moonlight to creep back into the barn, as a scaled neck slithered into view, dropping down into the jagged opening. The dragon's head slid back into a massive hardened plate. Through her terror Syndar noted scales glinting in soft brassy tones, not blue. The wyrmling squawked loudly, scurrying toward the brass dragon.

Spying the wyrmling, the brass roared in what could only have been relief. When the dragon reached down with a huge talon, the excited baby crawled up the scaled limb.

Syndar clutched Kirsk tightly, waiting to die. The dragon's snout lowered farther into the opening, studying the youth amidst the ruins of the mill. Syndar felt her matted and tangled blond hair waft with each smoky breath from the brass, and she dared to look death in the face.

The dragon watched her for a long moment before withdrawing its head. Reaching with a clawed talon, it tore loose a gleaming scale from its underside that tumbled down, slicing into the hardened earth as it landed upright. A storm of dust swirled as the dragon launched itself into the air upon mighty wings. Threatening to collapse once more, the roof held, just.

Shaking, unable to cry, Syndar stroked Kirsk's brow. She stared at the dragon scale as the dust settled. In the stark calmness of that moment she noted its shape was deformed somehow, two leathery straps clinging to the inside of the scale. A scale that looked less and less the skin of an animal, and more and more like a magnificent shield.

Beccard Rellock ran toward the barn, ignoring the shouts and cries as most of the men in the lumber camp sprinted toward the wood mill. Followed by his wagon team, they each ran in a different direction after the horses that survived the vicious attack of the blue dragon. Beccard ran through the trees, praying aloud that he would not find what he most feared. He stopped short as a pair of gloved hands grabbed him in mid-stride, spinning him around to face two shadows emerging from the trees. One was a bearded human in dull chain mail with a pair of swords on his belt and an axe strapped to his back. The other was a slender but no less dangerous looking elf. Supple leather adorned his lithe form, and a longbow, arrow notched but not drawn, was ready in his hands.

Beccard's fear intensified, and he took a step backward, even as he realized he couldn't outrun the two strangers, for they were not part of the lumber camp.

The human ranger spoke first. "You made a mistake Rellock, a big mistake."

The elf spoke in a quiet voice, and even through the elegant words of the Elvish language, Beccard could sense the anger directed at him.

The bearded human nodded, never taking his eyes off Beccard, and said, "You know who we are Rellock, and you know what we do."

Beccard nodded, swallowing, realizing he might not actually die, but that his danger was still very real.

"Please, my son might be in there . . . I have to find him," Beccard pleaded as he pointed to the ruined barn.

The elf spoke again, and the ranger translated: "That wasn't a two-headed cat you bought, it was a life. A life just like yours, just like mine. You couldn't possibly believe you'd haul it all the way to Suzail or Waterdeep like some cheap animal that does tricks for food."

Beccard shook his head, frantically glancing in the direction of the barn, looking for any sign of movement. It was the lack of it that terrified him.

He turned back to the pair before him and said, "I know. That's why I came here. It's quiet, remote. I didn't think anyone would find me here. I needed time to decide where to go. I had seen—" he gestured to the elf—"his kind following, but once we reached the camp here, they disappeared. I didn't know who else to tell."

The elf made one final comment, looking to the sky then back to Beccard.

The bearded ranger said, "Someone did find you. Someone big, blue, and angry. Brass is the natural enemy of the blue. You're fortunate the mother came along when she did. Scared the blue off before he tore this encampment to pieces. If there are any dead here tonight, Rellock, their blood is on your hands."

Beccard nodded once more, his intent to run to the barn obvious. The ranger grabbed him once more.

"If you ever want to earn one of these the right way, you stop making selfish decisions, and start making selfless ones."

The ranger unfolded his tunic collar underneath his chain mail. For a moment he flashed a pin carved in the likeness of a crescent moon and a harp, each inlaid with a sparkling dust.

The pin was gone as quickly as it appeared, and the two Harpers did likewise. Beccard barely saw them disappear into the darkness before he scrambled back toward the barn.

Beccard lifted away splintered boards to find the body of his son. Scooping the young boy into his arms, he gasped when Nollo squinted one eye at him.

"By the gods, Nollo!"

Nollo murmured in reply, then stiffened.

Beccard whispered, "It's safe son. The big one flew away. It flew away."

Beccard was surprised when Nollo jumped to his feet, disregarding his cuts and bruises, looking around the barn.

"Pap, the baby . . ."

Beccard hugged his son close, realizing what the entire journey had almost cost him.

"Gone, boy. It took it and flew away."

Hugging his father at first, Nollo pushed away suddenly and said, "Don't be mad, Pappy. I remembered!"

The young boy limped over to McDodd who was being helped to his feet by other men. Nimbly snatching the bully's purse, Nollo returned. Upending the purse he counted three copper coins.

"One for him," Nollo said as he pointed to Craster lying in a wagon, "and two for him!" He pointed to McDodd.

Beccard was too disoriented to ask questions, but Nollo smiled as he explained, "One each for a look, and one extra for him."

Nollo pointed back to McDodd.

Beccard asked the obvious: "Why one extra, Nollo?"

"Because, Pap! He's wyrm-touched!"

THE BOOK DRAGON

JIM PITRAT

Mid Hammer, the Year of Wild Magic (1372 DR)

The Red Wizard Nusair Darkul peered into the crystal globe before him. The visage of his master, Nevron, the Zulkir of Conjuration, stared back. The zulkir's ironlike face held a sneer that was old, angry, and as powerful from far away as it was in person. Nusair gulped down the knot in his throat that always seemed to accompany his late night meetings with the powerful conjurer. The zulkir had little use for the Guild of Foreign Trade, where he had assigned Nusair. In Nusair's opinion, it was an office designed for little more than to spy on Samas Kul, the guild's ambitious master. Nevron usually showed his contempt with short-tempered tirades at Nusair. But that night, the zulkir paid close attention to what Nusair had to say.

Nevron's angry voice boomed out from the

globe, "What news have you of this discovery?"

"*The Scalamagdrion* lies closer to us than you might think, Master—merely across the Alamber, in Mulhorand," Nusair responded, keeping his tone as respectful as possible to head off any potential rant by the zulkir.

He had tracked the powerful book from its discovery in Myth Drannor, two hundred years past, all the way to where it had come to rest: in a collector's home, deep in the capital of Thay's long-time enemy, Mulhorand. Nusair's contacts within the enclaves had located and tracked the artifact. In some small way he regretted letting the zulkir in on the discovery. But the opportunity to ingratiate himself to Nevron was too great a thing to resist. His recovery of *The Scalamagdrion* could mean the difference between wasting away as a mid-level bureaucrat in the guild for the rest of his life, and earning the favor of Nevron, one of the seven most powerful Red Wizards in Thay.

"Samas Kul?" the zulkir asked, no doubt wondering if Nusair had shared his secret with the hated guildmaster.

"He knows nothing," Nusair reassured his true master. If Samas Kul knew to whom Nusair truly answered, he wasn't sure if even Nevron could protect him.

"It would be foolish to waste such powerful summoning magic on that accursed guild. I, of course, could think of numerous alternative uses," Nevron said. His face twisted into that maniacal sneer once again.

"Of course, Lord Nevron," Nusair agreed. No doubt those alternative uses had something to do with the zulkir's rivals and their allies, Nusair thought—perhaps even Samas Kul himself. The tome and its magic would make a terrible weapon, indeed. Who needs an assassin, if a dragon will do the work instead? "I'll not disappoint you, Master!" Nusair added.

"Surely you won't," Nevron said in a threatening tone. His eyes smoldered as he watched his servant through the glass.

"The consequences for you would be most unpleasant. Are we clear?"

Shaking, Nuisair leaned over the orb. "Crystal clear, Master" he said.

It was popular knowledge that Nevron had summoned monstrosities from the underworld that he could command at will. Nusair wanted no part of an angry pit fiend.

With that thought, the powerful zulkir faded from view, his sneer still pasted across his face, and burned into Nusair's mind.

After the disturbing meeting with the master conjurer, Nusair hurried to his library. Despite Nevron's demands, Nusair would not be able to recover *The Scalamagdrion* on his own. Samas Kul watched him like a hawk, and expected to see him in Bezantur, minding his duties at the guild. Instead, Nusair would send his lead apprentice, Saura Umakra. The Rashemi wizard was ruthless. More importantly, she was someone he could control. And that was critical for what Nusair had in mind.

Finally, after all the years of licking Samas Kul's boots, Nusair could almost breathe the fresh air offered only by power!

Saura Umakra waited impatiently, staring through tall, arched windows at the Alamber Sea, all but black in the muted moonlight, thrashing at the rocks below. Winter's winds raced across the water, carrying with them what little natural moisture would come to Thay's arid coastal plain. Meager rains would soon fall to wash red slides of mud into Umberlee's emerald locker. The land was ever changing, she thought. Nothing stays the same, she assured herself. Nothing.

The wind whistled as it squeezed through tiny cracks in the windows of Darkul Tower. Behind her, the warmth of a raging fire heated her back while the coldness emanating through the window reddened her cheeks. The land was roasting hot in the summer and seemed equally frigid when winter's kiss was upon the barren plain. Saura pulled her cloak tighter, attempting to stave off the chill.

Nusair's library was easily the largest room in the tower and furnished in a comfortable, if dark, manner. Tapestries the color of a crimson drake, stretched down from the high ceiling, covering most of the walls in an attempt to imprison the warmth and deny the cold a foothold. Where there was no tapestry, shelf upon shelf of leather bound books lined the walls, like red bricks bound in gold. A rug of the same color as the tapestries languished on the stone floor. Comfortable chairs, upholstered in soft leather, were placed near the stone hearth and a heavy, wooden table, carved in intricate designs of twisting dragons sat like a draconic sarcophagus in the center of the room. Upon the table were several old books, half-rolled scrolls, and candles. The tiny flames flickered and wavered in drafts that slipped through the room's windows, their light lost in the blaze of the fireplace.

The large door that marked the room's only entrance swung open, drawing Saura's attention from the scene outside. In the doorway stood the master of the tower. On his face, Nusair wore a toothy smile.

Saura looked upon her mentor with thinly disguised scorn. Nusair was a handsome man to be sure. He was tall and thin, like many Mulan men, but he was strong, unlike so many purveyors of the Art who become soft with a lifetime of study. His shaved head, heavily adorned with twisting tattoos of magical script, glinted in the firelight. He wore red robes of the finest Shou Lung silk that ended just before the floor, giving the tiniest hint of soft black shoes beneath. He carried himself, Saura reckoned, with all the arrogance of an elf king, but possessed none of the substance.

For too long, Saura had stood in his shadow and shared

his bed, waiting for him to reward her with robes of red. To Saura's way of thinking, the Red Wizard's contempt for her Rashemi heritage was all that stood between her and the blasted robes. Unfortunately for her however, she would have to do his bidding to get the robes she coveted. So, she had swallowed her pride for five long years. Saura didn't know how much longer she could bare it. But retribution would come swiftly, when finally it came.

"I have awaited your arrival, as you commanded," she said and knelt before her master.

"You have," he agreed before waving her to stand up. "And you'll not be sorry for it."

"As you say, Master." She forced a smile.

Nusair stepped forward and touched her face softly, running his manicured fingers down across her cheek. The dragon's claw tattoo that encircled her left eye suddenly flared with an angry twitch, as it always did when he touched her. She sneered inwardly and swallowed the rising bile brought on by his touch.

"I have finally succeeded where all others have failed," he said.

He turned from her and faced the fire, letting his hand fall away to his side. Nusair was not a man of normal desires, even for a Red Wizard. Saura knew the man's obsessions better than anyone else. She was painfully familiar with his odd preferences beneath the silken sheets in his boudoir, his taste for bitter duergar ale, and his obsession for all things Draconic. The wizard's compulsive lust for ancient artifacts and his well-financed expeditions to recover them were common knowledge among Red Wizards, and often the center of jokes among them as well.

"What great thing have you uncovered?" she asked, only half believing.

When he turned once again to stare into her eyes, any doubt Saura had about the validity of this particular fool's errand was suddenly erased by the look of victory firmly planted on his tattooed face.

"You seek the robes," he said, ignoring her question.

"Of course," she answered, trying to keep her voice steady.

"I have but one final task to ask of you," he said in hushed tones, as though someone might hear his secret, even there, deep within his own house. He reached out again and touched her cheek, tracing his hand, nails teasing at her flesh, over the intricate tattoo that wound down her sensitive throat to plunge into her neckline. When his hand reached her throat, he dug his sharpened nails into her flesh. "I am sure that it will be easier to stomach than some tasks I have asked of you."

Saura couldn't doubt that. Her years of service in the wizard's bed were a steep price to pay for this apprenticeship.

"What could it be then?" she purred, teasing, trying to ignore the growing pain in her throat.

"If you are able to pull this one off, my dear, I shall grant you your greatest desire." He let the promise hang in the air for a bloated moment then added, "But Samas Kul must know nothing."

Nusair's hand lingered for another moment at the small of Saura's throat and he stepped past her to stare out the great, arching windows. Saura breathed a sigh of relief as he released her neck. Or was it the relief promised by what he had just offered? She would finally get the red robes that she had craved for so long—but was withholding information from the dangerous guildmaster a wise thing to do?

Saura thought about it for a moment then nodded and asked, "What must I do?" For the robes, and an end to her infernal apprenticeship, she would do most anything.

"I have found *The Scalamagdrion*," he said.

Saura gasped, unable to suppress her surprise. Nusair had sought the ancient tome ever since she had known him. She had begun to believe the thing was only a fairy tale, a myth.

The book was an artifact right out of Toril's dark past. Some said it was crafted in Imaskar, long before the destruction of the ancient nation. Others thought it originated in fallen Netheril. No one knew for sure. The book was said to hold the secret to summoning strange, magic-resistant dragons from a secret place beyond reach in any other way. In the hands of the right conjurer, the book meant power . . . and gold.

Her master smiled at her like an ancient red wyrm about to devour its prey. "I have tracked the book from where it was raided from a crypt in Myth Drannor to where it now rests, in the City of Shadows," he said, referring to the Mulhorandi capital. "From Skuld, you will recover my treasure."

One last time, Saura looked up at the door that marked her destination. To the west, the twin towers of Horus-Re poked into the sky from behind the rounded turrets of the Palace of the Pharaoh like two massive fangs. She had spent two days trying to locate the obscure shop deep within the market district of Skuld and she was growing impatient with her search. Nearly invisible in the quickly approaching darkness and rising fog, she waited for the opportunity to seize her prize.

When darkness was near complete, and the moon hung mostly hidden behind bloated rain clouds, Saura stepped from her hiding place in a narrow alleyway opposite the building. She pulled her hood lower over her eyes and skulked to the protective cover of the stone pillars to which the door was hinged.

Saura was out long after the city's curfew. With the army away in Unther, no one was allowed to prowl the streets, save the city watch and people on the pharaoh's business, neither of which she qualified for. Mulhorrand didn't take too kindly to Red Wizards stepping foot within its borders. In the event she was caught, she would be imprisoned for sure. Likely she'd never be heard from again. She pushed that fear to the back of her mind and reached out to the locked door.

Saura whispered an incantation into the night and the lock slid open, the door swinging mysteriously inward. Carefully, she stepped into the shop. Once inside, she ensured all the shades were drawn and blinds were closed on the two street facing windows. Then, crumbling a piece of phosphorescent moss to invoke the Art, she cast a simple light spell on the serrated blade of her curved dirk. The room was cast in an eerie yellow light, revealing thousands of ancient tomes, manuals, scrolls, and books stacked in a haphazard fashion around a room nearly twenty paces square. A small wooden table, empty except for a well-worn ledger, stood in the center of the cluttered room. Just opposite the door, another opening leading out of the room was covered with a hanging tapestry. She figured that the passageway led to the proprietor's living quarters, and she turned away from it, ignoring the possibility that her prize might lie in that direction. She'd deal with the proprietor later. It wouldn't do to go leaving potential witnesses about.

Saura whispered the arcane words and traced the intricate designs of a spell that would illuminate all items within the shop that possessed magic. Nearly one-in-four books showed some sort of magical aura, surprising her. Deciding to search for the strongest aura of magic, she stepped into the mass of tomes and began to sort through those items she identified with her spell, looking for the book whose aura told of ancient power, and matched Nusair's cryptic description: black dragon's hide, edged in beaten copper.

Soon after starting, Saura stopped her search when a voice called out from behind the hanging tapestry, startling her from the task at hand.

"Who's there?" The voice was shaky and unsure.

For a moment, Saura considered avoiding confrontation,

but the promise of her Red Robes drove her onward. She slid her dagger into its sheath, effectively plunging the room into blackness.

As quickly as it disappeared, light once again streamed into the room. The glow was faint, though, and coming from behind the tapestry that hid the room's exit. Saura quickly hid behind a large stack of leather bound books. From there, she watched as an old man carrying a low-burning candle in one hand and waving a wand before him in the other, stepped tentatively into the room. From her two days of surveillance, she knew the man as Mephnit Nandem, the owner of the establishment.

Mephnit was dark of skin and hair. He would have been tall, if he hadn't been bent over with age. He looked afraid. He wasn't much of a threat, as far as Saura could tell. That thought brought a tentative smile across the wizard's face. The old man was no warrior, nor was he a wizard to be feared.

Saura stood and said, "I am a collector . . . of fine books and ancient writings."

"More likely a thief," the old man said, startled. He backed away, waving the wand before him. "Why do you come here, breaking and entering and wielding magic in my home?"

Ignoring the man's question, Saura stated the obvious: "I'm looking for a book, old man. It's an ancient tome, if truth be told, with a black and copper cover."

Mephnit's eyes darted to her left and returned nervously to settle on Saura.

"Come back in the morning," said the old man. "I don't do business in the witching hours."

"There's a reason I'm here now," Saura hissed. She threw back her hood revealing the tell-tale tattoos of a Thayan spellcaster.

The man stepped backward once more. "I have wards up. The watch will come. You should go, wizard. Your kind is not wanted in Skuld," he continued to clutch the magical device in sweating hands. "If you're caught, you'll be killed."

Saura's patience wore thin with the old man. She doubted the old sage knew much of the Art at all—certainly not enough to ward the place against any sort of magic that Saura could wield. But she had no idea if he had somehow sent out warning to the watch. Time was slipping away. She decided to play on his greed, and took a bag from the folds of her cloak, emptying its contents on the small table. Ten beautiful rubies spilled out and rolled about the tabletop. The man's eyes widened in exasperation.

"My offer is high," she said with a smiled.

Mephnit hesitated for just a second. He was obviously interested in the offer. But Saura was disappointed at his response. "I am sure it is not high enough," he coughed out. "If I am caught dealing with Thayans, I too will be put to the sword."

"I grow tired of this talk." She put on her cruelest look, and shot out her hand to snatch at his shoulder, pulling him closer so that his face was only inches from hers. "That is the price," she rasped at him. "The next offer will be much higher!" she finished the last comment by raising her eyebrow and sneering wickedly. It was no threat, only a promise.

The frightened man's eyes darted once again to the corner, then back to hers. "H-how can I trust the word of a . . . of a Thayan wizard?" he asked, stuttering.

"You cannot!" she shrieked in final frustration.

Like a striking cobra, her hand lashed out and knocked the wand from his shaking hand. She could see the fear in his eyes as he backed toward the exit. Saura briefly considered murdering the man with a magic missile or some other spell that would be clean and sterile. Then she reconsidered. Sometimes, Saura preferred cold steel. As gracefully as any hunting cat, Saura drew her knife and went to work.

Three days after murdering the shopkeeper and making off with the tome, Saura stood in front of Nusair, holding a bag that contained the great artifact. The walls of the library surrounded them once again, and Saura bent a knee to her benefactor.

"I have returned, Master," she said.

The trip back to Bezantur was not nearly as long as the trip to Skuld. Nusair had equipped Saura with a stone imbued with a spell of recall, which allowed her to teleport back to her home base whenever she wanted. Of course, all that was predicated on the safe retrieval of *The Scalamagdrion*.

"Have you brought it?" He asked.

He should have known better. Saura would never have come back without the artifact. Failing on such a mission would have cost her her life, or worse, her position at Darkul Tower.

Still, she humored him. "Yes, Master, I have brought your prize."

Saura stood and dropped the bag on the room's great table, partially spilling the ancient tome onto the well-worn surface. Her master's eyes lit up and she could not suppress the feeling of victory that spread through her.

"Now for your part of the bargain," she said.

Nusair walked to the book, turning his back to the beautiful apprentice. He pressed his hand against the bag that held it.

"Yes . . . about that . . ." he started.

Saura's feeling of triumph fell through the floor.

───◦◦◦───

That night, Nusair slipped from between the silken sheets in his bed. He let his lips brush lightly against Saura's ear one last time. She knew how to please him better than anyone.

He briefly considered taking her with him to the library, letting her share in his victory. But that would be foolish. Why should he give her any more power than she already had? There were certain pleasures worth holding on to, no matter what the cost. Besides, he'd be damned if he would be one of the few Red Wizards to officially induct a Rashemi into his red circle. He'd be a laughing stock, and any chances of serving Master Nevron more closely would be dashed as surely as if he had hidden *The Scalamagdrion* with the intent of taking it for himself. That decided, as quietly as he could, Nusair threw on his red robes, and snuck from his sleeping room toward his library, leaving her dozing peacefully in his bed.

The Red Wizard opened the door to his library and looked upon the darkened chamber. On the table rested *The Scalamagdrion*, shrouded in darkness, its cover glowing with a faint red light. He thought about starting a fire to heat the cold room, but his own impatience wouldn't let him. He whispered a quick incantation and tiny flames leaped from his fingers to light the candles that graced the table and walls, casting out just enough light to read by.

Copper bindings wrapped about the ancient tome like the crushing arms of a monstrous drake. It seemed to Nusair that the forms of dragons, terrible to behold, writhed and undulated on the cover, each one seeming to snap at unseen victims, their talonlike claws and razor teeth glinting magically in the candlelight. Yet, strangely the cover bore no such markings.

For a moment, Nusair hesitated. But the promise of the book was too much. He had come too far to fear some petty illusion. Inside the bindings waited riches and power beyond even his imagination. The book would be his defining discovery. Once he unlocked its secret and gave the book to Nevron, he might well be catapulted to the highest levels of Thayan power circles . . . perhaps even to command a tharch or become a trusted lieutenant to the Zulkir of Conjuration himself.

Intent on unlocking his hard won discovery, Nusair swallowed the momentary pang of fear that had worked its way into his throat. He reached out with shaking hands to touch, however tentatively, the artifact. The book's age and power pulsed under his fingers, and he drew back.

The tome had been crafted long before even the coming of Mulhorand to Toril, in the dark and mysterious palaces and winding spires of Imaskar or perhaps Netheril, where brown deserts and wastes were all that remained—reminders of power gone awry. But that was long ago, and the roots of the long dead regimes were buried with the kings and pharaohs of old. The ambitious Red Wizard had better things to do than worry about long dead civilizations.

He reached out once again and gripped the cover in his trembling hands then allowed his fingers to crawl across the strange cover to the latch holding it closed. There, he flipped open the leather tongue securing it. Suddenly, he found his breath coming in short gasps of air. What had he to fear? Only words written on pages awaited him, he chided himself. But still, all his instincts told him to leave the book closed. Let sleeping dragons lie, the old saying went.

"Bah!" Nusair exclaimed aloud to the empty room. He was a Red Wizard, and ridiculous wives' tales and irrational fears would not cow him. He took a deep breath then slowly, deliberately, opened the tome. He leaned forward to peer downward upon the thing that he had labored so long to recover. A loud, deep groan, like a dying man's final pained breath, escaped the pages of *The Scalamagdrion* as the front cover struck the worn oak table.

Without more than that single groan as a warning, a monstrous reptilian creature leaped from the pages of the tome, its body growing to crush the table, sending splinters of oak flying in all directions. The dragon was twice as tall as

Nusair, with massive muscled arms and stunted wings. Its tail stretched another body length behind and was tipped in a bladelike plate. The dragon's gray-silver scales glinted like platinum in the firelight. Its jaws opened and revealed razor teeth that sparkled like diamonds.

"Loreat Levethix," the beast hissed, its voice scratching across its tongue and its breath hot on Nusair's face.

Nusair gasped. His heart accelerated, threatening to burst from his chest. He recognized the dragon's words at once—*Die Wizard.*

Then the room was plunged into silence.

Nusair fell back before the beast, scrambling to put distance between himself and its grinning jaws. The Scalamagdrion stared down at him with terrifying malevolence and advanced, watching Nusair's every move.

Nusair reached into his mind for the spells that he had prepared. Grasping on one that would roast the creature in a hellish fire, the Red Wizard muttered the words that would call the Weave to him. Nothing happened, his voice lost in the magic silence cast out by the dragon. Cursing to himself, Nusair rushed for the door.

He never made it.

The dragon launched itself between the Red Wizard and the door, coming down on the wooden floor with a loud *crunch* that shook the entire tower. The beast swung its massive claws at Nusair, but the wizard was too quick. He dodged to the left then dived to the ground. The beast's dagger-claws whistled as they passed within inches of Nusair's head. The Red Wizard rolled onto his back and tried to stand. Just then the second claw raked across his chest.

Both flesh and magic robes alike gave way before the terrible attack. Nusair bellowed a silent scream at the top of his lungs, as blood sprayed the floor behind him and ribs cracked like so many twigs under foot.

Gasping for air, he looked upward at his assailant, pain

thundering in his temples. The Scalamagdrion arched its back up and away, preparing to strike again, but with its jaws. It glared down on him. It seemed to relish the look of horror on Nusair's face, as its razor-sharp teeth gleamed in the remaining candlelight. Nusair shuddered in fear and prepared himself for the inevitable.

Just then, the Red Wizard remembered the magic ring that he always wore as a last resort. He didn't need to speak to activate the device—only a simple flick of the wrist. And so he did, desperate for anything to work against his murderer. Four blue globes of shining light launched from the ring and shot, like arrows, the short distance to the dragon's armored breast. The balls impacted on the creature in bright explosions of white light.

But Nusair's elation at the attack's success disappeared as the dragon's glimmering scales absorbed the globes of magical energy. Then, as quickly as the missiles hit the dragon, they reappeared, emerging from its very flesh and launched right back at Nusair. The Red Wizard barely had time to let loose yet another cry of terror that disappeared into the magical silence, before the first of the ball lighting bolts tore into him. The explosions wracked his body. He convulsed as the power of the charges surged through him, leaving him broken, burned, and writhing in pain.

Terribly wounded but still alive, Nusair rolled over and crawled desperately for the door, his bloody fingers digging holes into the fine wood floor, and leaving a bloody streak of glistening crimson behind. But before he could cover the last few feet to the door, the dragon leaped upon him, landing square on his back with sharp talons that punched clean through his torso to splinter the floor beneath.

At that moment, Nusair expired.

The dragon let the ring of silence fall. It flipped Nusair's lifeless body over and looked into the dead wizard's eyes. Then, with a final roar, the Scalamagdrion snatched the wizard up, and leaped once again upon the book to disappear into its pages. All that remained of the once powerful Red Wizard was a torn and destroyed red robe and a bloody trail that told of his demise.

A few moments passed before Saura emerged from a darkened corner, naked and holding her serrated dirk. She walked into the room and to the wizard's robe. She shivered then smiled smugly. Saura crouched over the object of her greatest desire and considered the implications of her betrayal for the shortest of seconds. Then she pulled the tattered and burned remains of Nusair's robe over her sleek shoulders and walked to the closed book.

"You have underestimated my powers, Nusair. I learned the secret of *The Scalamagdrion* long before I ever returned," she said, speaking to the tome. She added, "Samas Kul cares little about my parentage, and he will be most pleased with your gift."

Saura strode from the room carrying the ancient artifact and cloaked in her coveted robes, however tattered.

FREEDOM'S PROMISE

ED GENTRY

Kythorn, the Year of Wild Magic (1372 DR)

The ancient blue wyrm rolled lazily onto his stomach, fully rousing himself from his long slumber. He shifted, and coins and gems embedded in his azure hide fell from his body and clanked in the pool of treasure upon which he rested. His enormous orbs peered around the cave as he took note of every precious item that sprawled around him. The titanic beast magically dismissed the remaining wards around his lair with a sigh, allowing the visitor entrance to this innermost portion of the cavern.

"Well met, Gerinvioch," said the unfortunate intruder as he finally came into view, brushing sand and dust from his violet cloak.

Dampened by sweat, short, graying hair was matted so tightly against the human's steeply sloped forehead that it almost seemed as if his face simply continued on into his hair, flesh becoming strands of gray. The emblems embroidered on the sleeves of the man's robes announced him as a citizen of Estagund.

"You are Gerinvioch, are you not?" the man said as he continued to primp his robe.

A long moment passed as the dragon considered the human who stood before him, a wizard to judge from appearances. Gerinvioch blinked and let out a slow yawn.

"Dragon! You will hear me!"

The old wyrm sprang to his feet, lunging forward, coming to a stop with his single-horned snout mere inches from the stunned human's face. A smile widened on his reptilian lips as he slowly pulled his head back.

"I would ask you some questions, dragon," the wizard said as his body slowly gave up its rigid posture and went slack.

Laughter erupted from Gerinvioch's belly, resounding off the stone walls in a cacophony of mirth. "Would you give audience to an ant?" the wyrm responded. He continued, not allowing the human a chance to speak. "Seeking to procure some of my treasure for yourself? Where are your fellow thieves then, bug?"

"Treasure? Why would I want a pile of such worthless refuse as this?" the wizard replied, extending his arm to sweep across the cache of riches in the cavern. "What I seek, you could never own. What I seek requires real power to wield."

Gerinvioch stared silently at the man, the anticipation welling up in him.

"The item is somewhere here in the Dust Desert," the man began after clearing his throat. "You have made your home in these lands for many years, so I thought I might be able to use one relic," the wizard continued with a beaming grin, "to find another."

Gerinvioch returned the human's grin and replied, "Truly, you believe this item is valuable since you have come to face me, a *Great Blue*," the dragon said, emphasizing his heritage. "What is this object you seek, human?"

"It is called the Evise Jhontil. It was a *divinely* inspired gift from Set to his disciples," he responded sanctimoniously, obviously doubtful of the item's ecclesiastical origin.

Gerinvioch quickly cast his eyes downward.

"You've heard of it," the man stated more than asked. "Where is it? You must tell me!" he exclaimed, his bottom lip quivering.

"You do not want that item, wizard."

"Where is it?" the man replied, almost lunging forward.

"The finest clergy of Set and wizards in their employ could not control it," Gerinvioch asserted, pleased to see the man's anxious reaction.

"Where they failed, Kinase Bronihim will succeed, as he always does."

"Bronihim?" the wyrm said, his booming voice trailing off sharply. "Of Estagund . . ."

"Yes," the wizard replied as his head gave a slow turn.

"You are the one who defeated the Ancient Green, Ronatsinaderin?" the dragon said, hoping the man would take the bait.

"Yes, I dispatched the sniveling coward," Bronihim said, standing taller, his face flushing at the same time. "How did you hear of that?"

"All of my kind for hundreds of miles know of it," Gerinvioch replied, doing his best not to smile at the man's lie. The wyrm congratulated himself on the ruse. Ronatsinaderin's death—of old age Gerinvioch reminded himself—would serve an enjoyable purpose on this day. To be sure, the old green was no friend of Gerinvioch's, but no wyrm deserved to have his death attributed to some human peasant. "I battled Ronatsinaderin myself, once," Gerinvioch said, lifting one of his enormous wings to reveal a deep, pale scar of two long, jagged lines. If the human insisted upon lying, why shouldn't he?

"I see I fared better than you did," the wizard said, his arms wide, as he slowly spun around once in place.

"So it would seem," Gerinvioch replied.

"Where is the artifact? I did not come here to discuss the worthless carcass of that miserable beast," the man said, obviously anxious to steer the conversation back to his desired goal.

"Why do you seek it?" Gerinvioch asked, peering at the man closely. "For its power?"

"For the same reason you lust after treasure, I'd imagine. Because I want it, and it should be mine," the wizard said, sweat now forming on his face.

"Its power is too great, human. No one could control it forever," Gerinvioch said, closing his enormous eyes slowly and pulling in a long, haggard breath. "No one."

"I, unlike many," Bronihim said, casting a sideways glance toward the dragon, "am more than capable of mastering its secrets."

A soft growl began wafting from the dragon's throat, building to a grating rumble, though he wanted nothing more than to laugh. The human was perfect in his arrogance. The wizard's hands began the gestures of a spell. The dragon ceased his vocalization and took a slow step back. The man's gesticulations stopped.

Gerinvioch almost let slip his mirth, but chided himself and continued to slink away.

"You must tell me where to find it," the wizard said, his voice taking on a frantic velveteen quality as though he were coaxing a child.

Gerinvioch could enjoy his game for many hours, but reminded himself of the short attention span of humans. It was time to let the trap unfold.

"Leave this place and travel south, staying close to the mountain line. When you reach the tallest peak, turn east. After some distance, you will see an unusually large rock rising from the desert sands. It is near there," the dragon said, lowering his head slightly.

"Where from the rock?" the wizard shouted as he strode toward the creature.

"I left it near there long ago. I don't know exactly where," the dragon replied, recoiling from the man.

"If I find you have deceived me, wyrm. . . ." the wizard trailed off as he turned to leave.

"You will find your end lies within its magic, Gruanthe," Gerinvioch said, relishing that his genuine warning would only spur the idiotic human on further.

"Is that a derogatory term for humans in your language, wyrm?"

"My apologies. It is a name," Gerinvioch replied, hiding a smile. "You simply remind me of someone."

The wizard threw one last scowl over his shoulder as he departed.

After the man left, the great dragon lay back down on his bed of treasure, luxuriating in its cold embrace, and began to chuckle. Gruanthe would have liked this Bronihim, Gerinvioch thought. Then again, perhaps not. Shared goals often seemed desirable among humans, though the wyrm guessed that lust for power would be a rather divisive one to have in common. No matter, he thought. It always ended the same for those with the foolish desire to wield that kind of power and the single-mindedness not to recognize their folly. Gerinvioch had ensured that of two such fools now.

Kinase Bronihim floated several inches over the searing desert sands as he crested yet another dune. Finally, he spotted the stone he had been seeking. Standing three times taller than Bronihim, its ruddy form erupted out of the sand. After a quick inspection of the area, Bronihim continued east from the rock, figuring it as good a direction as any to begin his search. He cast a minor detection spell but could find no magic in the vicinity at all.

Bronihim looked up to the blazing sun and muttered curses at the blue wyrm under his breath. It had been many hours since he had left the dragon's lair, and he was beginning to think he had been deceived. He continued on, averting his eyes from the sun and blinking the spots from them. Suddenly he shifted his weight to the left and stumbled to the ground to avoid walking directly into the wall of a small hut. He stood, brushing himself off, and blinked in disbelief as he saw brightly colored thatched-roofed huts all around. Where there had been only the open desert a moment before stood a small town.

He turned to see a woman on the street run away, screaming as she went. Doors to many of the homes creaked open slightly as their wary inhabitants peered out. Emerging from a side street, a dark-skinned, muscular young man approached him and offered a smile.

"What is this place?" Bronihim asked, still craning his head around to take in the sight.

"Please come with me and I will take you to someone who can answer your questions," the man answered.

Bronihim followed the man to one of the huts closer to the center of town and entered to find a dim room. The air was full of incense and a plethora of furniture sat strewn about. A woman sat wide-eyed on a couch near the center of the room. She nodded to the young man who had escorted the wizard, and he took his leave. Her sharp, angular face held pleasant warmth but seemed almost harsh when viewed in context with her exceedingly lithe frame.

"I am Moriandro of Lliiress," she said.

"Kinase Bronihim of Chavyondat. What is this place? I know of no towns in Raurin."

"That you do not know it exists is not surprising," the woman said.

Bronihim considered her for a moment. Her eyes seemed to hold kindness and what he thought might be pity. Why this woman would pity him he could not imagine.

He said, "I came seeking—"

"The Evise Jhontil," Moriandro put in.

The wizard's face almost swallowed itself with an enormous grin. "You know where it is, then?"

"It is here, in the center of our town," she said, her shoulders slumping.

"Have you the authority to bargain for it?" Bronihim said.

The tall woman laughed, shaking her head. She motioned for him to have a seat.

Bronihim enjoyed bargaining, as did all his people. He doubted that the woman would be a challenge, but as he sat, he subtly began the gestures to a spell that would allow him to discern her honesty all the same.

"No! You must stop!" the woman shouted, lunging forward and grabbing his moving fingers with startling speed and force.

Bronihim sat in stunned silence for several moments as he watched Moriandro calm herself. He could not bring himself to mention what should have felt like an affront to him. Her touch was genuine and warm. She stopped him for reasons other than wanting to prevent him from gaining the upper hand in their dealings. Of that he felt certain.

"You are from Chavyondat, in Estagund," she said after several moments. "Do you know the name Aniolon Gruanthe?" she asked.

Bronihim's eyes widened at the mention of the same name the dragon had used.

"You do, don't you?"

Bronihim's brow furrowed and he found himself slowly sinking further into the chair opposite the lovely woman.

"The wyrm used—" he began.

"Gerinvioch," Moriandro said, interrupting Bronihim.

"You know . . ." Bronihim began but found that his throat was tightening.

"Yes, we know the name Gerinvioch here. We know it well. It does not surprise me that he taunted you with the name of Aniolon Gruanthe," Moriandro said, gritting her teeth.

"Who is this Gruanthe?" the wizard asked, his original goal unexpectedly seeming very far away.

"Let me tell you of him and those of our ancestors who followed him here to their end in the Year of Slaying Spells," she said.

"This town has been here for three-hundred and ninety-six years?" Bronihim said, the doubt clear in his voice.

"It has been that long, then?" the woman asked, her shoulders slumping. "A few generations ago people tired of keeping time, and without the records of those years we have found it fruitless to begin again."

"How could you not . . . ?"

"I promise, I will explain, but you must let me do so in my own way," she said.

Kinase Bronihim nodded, not knowing what he would say even if he were so inclined.

Moriandro paused, drew a long breath, and began her tale.

——◦∞◦——

Aniolon Gruanthe walked through the fledgling town he had so recently founded. He took in the sights of his people forging their new life in the wasteland. Workers dug foundations for homes, while mud for their walls was mixed with pigments of various sorts to make the new homes vibrantly colored. The short man ran his stubby fingers through his thinning black hair and smiled.

"Aniolon, are you sure this is the only way?" asked the redheaded woman behind him.

He turned to regard her, his eyes following the soft lines of her voluptuous curves hidden only by a few scraps of bright red silk that barely served to provide even minimal modesty.

Aniolon ran his fingers over her bared hip as he leaned into her and replied, "Lliira and Sharess have blessed our journey and our town. How can we be wrong?"

A tall, old man in robes similar to Aniolon's moved to stand next to the pair. "Aniolon, you do not devote yourself to either of those goddesses, so please spare me the divinely inspired oratory," he said, then sighed. "We are fools to do this. The rajah's cursed mercenaries are bound to find us, and the powers know it could be soon. We should face them."

"We must preserve our dream, my friend," Aniolon replied, acknowledging the old man's words though still staring into the eyes of the lovely young priestess of Sharess before him. "We cannot defeat the rajah's wizard mercenaries, the poor deluded souls that they are. They are interested only in what their cursed master tells them they are interested in and of course, in the coin he pays them. It is that persecution of a life of duty and obeisance to nobility that we have fled. You should know as well as I that they will never cease their hunt."

"The truth is that you have no idea what you're doing. You simply want to lead . . . to feel important," the old man countered. "Asking a wyrm for help? This is madness, Aniolon."

"I'm leading you to salvation," Aniolon replied, finally turning to look at the man.

"We can defeat these hired wizards," the old man insisted.

"The wyrm is one, the rajah's hirelings are many . . . too many," Aniolon said, stepping away from the woman.

"What could we possibly offer this dragon for its help?" the old man inquired.

"We will offer it treasure, or whatever else may interest it," Aniolon replied with a wave of his hand.

Aniolon turned and shouted to the working townspeople,

"We are off, friends! Pray to Lliira and Sharess that I will find our way to freedom!"

Those around the wizard shared a concerned glance at his exclusion of anyone other than himself in his declaration. A cheer rose from the crowd. Some of the people waved, others shouted phrases of well-wishing to the departing group, and still others simply took the opportunity to rest themselves.

Aniolon stared on as some of the people opted for more pleasurable endeavors during their break. He watched as a short man and a young woman many years his junior embraced, kissing deeply. Their hands explored one another, each slowly divesting the other's body of its minimal clothing. Many of the townsfolk stopped to watch the two lovers, some of them forming their own pairs or groups to pursue similar activities. Aniolon drank in the view before him and grinned. A scene like the one unfolding before him would have been akin to heresy in Estagund, he knew.

He had found these people and they had showed him a different way of living. In turn, he had promised to lead them to a place where they could practice their religions and lifestyles as they saw fit, free from Estagund's so-called noble rulers. All it had cost them was to include him in their ways. Aniolon had to admit to enjoying the deference these people offered. That was pleasant, indeed, he thought. He had railed against the tyrannical rulers of Estagund in his speeches to them, inspiring them to ask him to lead them. Freedom was precious, after all.

One of the other men standing near him tapped him on the shoulder. Aniolon nodded, sighing softly as he turned away from the lustful vista before him to leave on his journey. Leadership was a harsh burden, he decided.

Aniolon and those he had selected to accompany him arrived at the beast's lair a few hours after they had departed. The magically granted flight had made the trip rather expeditious. With him were two warriors formerly of Estagund, two priests of Lliira, the priestess of Sharess, and the old wizard who had joined her in questioning Aniolon's plan.

The imp that Aniolon had summoned days before, a devious little creature by the name of Quiono, had told him the whereabouts of the dragon and had warned him that the lair would be magically defended. Aniolon had expected no less. He and the old wizard inspected the entrance to the cavern. Much to their surprise, they could find no evidence of any active magical traps or barriers.

They entered, finding a single, large tunnel with walls so perfectly smooth that they could not have been naturally formed. Aniolon wondered how the dragon had carved them so perfectly. Magic? Dwarf slaves? The young wizard would pity any such workers. Fealty to something in which one does not believe deteriorates one's very being. Aniolon strode onward, more resolved than ever. They followed the tunnel for a long while as it twisted erratically, leading them ever downward.

—— ❧ ——

Never in his hundreds of years of life, had a living human entered Gerinvioch's lair. True, a lich had once come in search of a stash of enchanted sapphires for some grand spell, but liches were hardly living. With the proper application of spells of controlling, however, they made excellent guardians for a lair such as this. Gerinvioch mentally dismissed the wards and measures of protection leading into his den, including the annoyingly incessant one that had alerted him to the presence of the intruders in the first place. Excellent indeed, but annoying nevertheless.

Motivation for their intrusion was obvious. The wyrm glanced around his home, the sparkle of the many treasures reflecting in his eyes from their piles. Humans and their greed. Gerinvioch shook his head and prepared himself for a bit of merriment.

Seven? Only seven of these visitors, Gerinvioch thought. It was insulting. He could smell their filth and knew they would be within view at the mouth of his cavern at any moment. The great blue wyrm set his front legs firmly and craned his thick neck. The scales covering his body verily hummed with power and a familiar smell emanating from his own body filled his nostrils. The invaders rounded the final corner and were, at last, in view. He doubted they could see him as well in the murkiness of his home.

He opened his mouth and released the lightning that could accompany his breath. The energy poured from his throat and pulsed past his lips. It was invigorating.

The humans were ill prepared for the assault, as expected. Only one was spared. The tiny man had somehow managed to leap away, finding shelter in the deep shadows behind a stalagmite.

Another of the creatures was on the ground, smoke rising from his robes, but quite alive, no doubt thanks to an enchantment of some sort. A red-haired woman writhed in the last few moments of silent agony against the wall of the cave, while two other corpses stared blankly at the ceiling of the cavern, their clothing melted to their skin. The remaining two humans were no more than heaps of indistinguishable charred flesh.

"Please! We have come to talk! We do not wish to hurt you!" the human who had avoided the blast cried from behind the rock.

Gerinvioch advanced toward him slowly, wearing an amused countenance.

"Help us," the man whimpered.

"Help?" the dragon replied, intrigued and bewildered at the same time. "Come out."

The man emerged, crawling on hands and knees. His face reminded Gerinvioch of a coin, it was so perfectly round. His robes and other accoutrements identified him as a wizard.

"Please. Help my town and . . ." the wizard sputtered and continued, "me. You must help my town."

The wyrm peered closely at the man. "You came to ask for help?"

"Yes. M-my name is Aniolon Gruanthe," he stuttered, rising to his feet. "We—we cannot stop them. You must help us."

"Who is it you cannot stop?" Gerinvioch asked, pacing around the shaking man. The human winced with each echoing impact of footsteps. This was quite easily the most unusual and amusing event Gerinvioch had experienced in many years.

"Estagund . . . hunters from Estagund. Sent by the rajah himself."

"You want me to fight them for you?"

The man nodded, his head looking as though it might fall off at any moment.

A long silence dwindled between them and the human finally continued, "We could offer you treasure. We could even mine the mountains for you."

"Why not simply flee?" the dragon asked, still pacing.

"No! They must not have it!" the man said, as his head shook violently.

Gerinvioch stopped his pacing and grinned. "What is it in this town that you covet so?"

"The town itself. There is nothing of value in it," the wizard replied. Much to his own surprise, the dragon believed the man. "Other than the treasure we would like to offer you, of course," the man said, pursing his lips and casting his eyes to the ground.

Well, half-truths were better than no truths, Gerinvioch thought.

"This town of yours is near here, I presume. Long have I been asleep else it would never have been built," the dragon said more to himself than to the man. "Why should I not simply go and destroy it myself?" he added, looking directly at the man.

"No!" Aniolon shouted, panting hard. "Please, do not do that. It is my dream."

"Oh? And what is it that insects dream of?"

"Freedom," the man said, his voice dropping to a whisper.

"Freedom? That is what you lust after so desperately?"

The human only nodded.

Gerinvioch almost laughed at the word. Freedom. What could that mean to a human? Perhaps there was a way to find out, the wyrm thought. It was hard to keep from smiling.

"You are the leader of this town?"

Aniolon renewed his nodding.

"You led your people here from Estagund? For freedom from what?"

"The tyrannical rule of a madman," the man said as if repeating by rote.

"And your own rule is different?"

"Mine is benevolent," Aniolon said. Then the man shook his head and quickly amended, "We rule ourselves, we choose what we want. No one gives us orders."

Gerinvioch smiled and gave a nod. These humans were quite bold. To lust after treasure would be offense enough, but power? What could slake the lust of these humans, he wondered.

"I see. Freedom is an admirable gift to provide your people," he said, deciding to grant the man his gift. Thirsts must be quenched, after all.

The man's eyes grew wide. "Yes. It is. I am pleased that you . . . Thank you," the man offered with a bow.

"I will help you, Gruanthe."

Aniolon almost stumbled backward with surprise. "You will? That . . . that's wonderful! Thank you." The man stared off into the gloom of the cavern, obviously lost in thought. "That's wonderful," he repeated softly as a smile danced across his lips.

"It is an exhilarating feeling to wield power over others,

is it not?" the dragon said, no longer hiding his grin.

"Yes," Aniolon said with a distant look in his eyes. "Yes, it most definitely is."

How wonderfully oblivious these creatures were, Gerinvioch thought as he shook his head and chuckled.

The little man seemed to awaken from a daydream. "You will fight them?"

"That will not be necessary. I will come to your town and grant it a protective spell."

Aniolon shrugged and nodded.

"The cost you pay for my assistance will be high. You will obtain an item for me that lies here in the desert. Also, you will leave these others for me," the dragon said motioning toward the man's smoldering companions.

The wizard grimaced but agreed.

Gerinvioch told him where to find the item, the Evise Jhontil, which would seal their pact and instructed him to make contact again once it had been obtained. After Aniolon departed, Gerinvioch inspected the first of his payments.

The other man who obviously fancied himself a wizard was still alive, though immobile. Gerinvioch sniffed at the man, letting the aroma of scorched human skin overwhelm him.

"Ple-please," the man stuttered.

"I have answered one man's pleas today. I think that quite generous of me," Gerinvioch replied.

"You are going to he-help him?" the human asked, swallowing back an eruption of blood.

Gerinvioch cocked his head. "You muster the strength to ask me one question and that one is your choice?"

The man assented.

"He wishes freedom from this Estagundian tyrant and his killers. I will grant him that," Gerinvioch answered, leaning in closer to the man.

The wizard's face contorted in obvious confusion. "Why?"

"Humans need to learn that desire is a dangerous pursuit.

My desert has been invaded by your kind more times than I can count. I roam the skies beyond the desert and see that your disease has taken a firm hold in most of the lands I find. I tire of your endless quests and searches, your discoveries and advancements, your invasions and intrusions. It is in your nature to 'outdo' yourselves, so you say. What you are doing is outpacing yourselves, you are overstepping yourselves more and more each day. I tire of it," the wyrm said, his cadence slowing. "He wants freedom from this ruler when all humans do is imprison the world around them in their lustful, greedy pursuits? So be it."

"But our town is sm—" the man started, cut short by a surge of pain—"is small. We are but a few humans."

The wyrm conceded the point. "True. However, everything starts somewhere."

The man started to respond, but ceased abruptly as Gerinvioch's gargantuan maw creaked slowly open and lowered itself toward him. The wizard screamed so loudly as to cause his voice to crack and fade away.

"I have answered your question, human. Now you will answer my hunger," Gerinvioch said before he sank his teeth in slowly, savoring the squirming delicacy.

Aniolon returned to his town and shared the news with his followers. The people had their trepidations and were sorrowful over the loss of those who had accompanied him. He, naturally, didn't give all of the details of the journey, but insisted that the dragon would protect their new home.

A party of twenty was dispatched from the town to the location of ruins described by the dragon. Among them had once been a temple to the evil god Set. Aniolon told them the artifact would be there.

Aniolon enjoyed the attention of his people while they

waited for the party's return. This is one of the rewards for being a good leader, he thought.

Upon their return, almost a tenday later, the intrepid searchers described the ordeal of their quest. The wards and defensive measures surrounding the artifact, mysteriously still in place nearly half a millennium after the temple was abandoned, had claimed the lives of almost a dozen of their ranks. Another four were killed when they had encountered a roaming efreeti on their return journey. The others had barely escaped. Aniolon listened to the tale, adding empathetic remarks at moments he deemed most effective, attempting to console them for the loss of their friends. He was, of course, certain to remember to congratulate them on a job well done. The wizard turned leader took the item to the dragon. Upon his return to town he once again assured his people that they would be safe.

The next morning the great beast arrived at the edge of the freshly formed town, keeping his distance from the nervous inhabitants.

"Thank you for coming. Your largesse honors us," Aniolon greeted the Great Blue loudly as he approached, so everyone within earshot could hear his easy tone.

Aniolon led the beast to the center of the town, smiling at his followers and giving them reassuring nods. Gerinvioch produced the artifact the townspeople had retrieved for him as if from thin air. Aniolon looked carefully and still could not begin to guess where the dragon had hidden it on his person or how it had been hidden in the first place. The wyrm placed the object on the ground at his feet and nodded to Aniolon.

"You are using the Evise Jhontil in your spell?" the wizard asked.

"It is essential to your protection," the dragon responded.

Aniolon regarded the dragon curiously and finally shrugged. The enormous creature reared onto his hind legs, exposing the gold-green scales of his belly. They were dull and void of life compared to the dazzling azure that adorned the rest of his body. Gerinvioch looked equally comfortable standing on two legs as he did on four, Aniolon noted.

The dragon began chanting in a language Aniolon did not recognize, occasionally gesturing with his large, three-fingered hands. Aniolon chuckled as he wondered if they were called fingers and hands when it came to dragons. The wizard turned to see his followers watching the great beast carefully. He smiled as he watched them, knowing soon they would be safe under the protection he had procured for them. They would be in his debt and provide him with a comfortable, free existence for the rest of his life.

The dragon ceased its incantation and turned to face the wizard. "It is done."

"What does it do?" Aniolon said doubtfully, looking at the still inert object on the ground.

"The barrier will make your home invisible and impenetrable. And if these men hunting you cannot see you . . ." the dragon began.

"They will pass by and continue their search elsewhere," Aniolon said, a large grin spreading across his face.

"But surely they will detect the magic of the barrier itself," said a man with graying hair named Umbeso, once one of Aniolon's rivals for positions of power in Estagund.

Like many of the arcanists in the town, Umbeso had desired a respite from the Estagundian worship of a class of warrior nobility. Most citizens held those warriors in high regard, but the hierarchy often led to political conflicts with the magic-using citizens of Estagund, who did much for the country but were not very highly regarded under the current regime.

Aniolon spun to face the man, red with anger, but before he could speak, Gerinvioch responded, "I have concealed the magical emanations that are usually a natural part of both spells and artifacts of this sort. However, I will need to place a finishing charm on it once I depart."

"But they will still be able to detect the people here in this place," Umbeso interrupted again.

"Enough, Umbeso," Aniolon said.

"His questions are reasonable, Gruanthe. I will answer them," Gerinvioch said. "I have concealed this area and all in it from detection of any sort."

"They could simply stumble into the town. If it is invisible, they may think they are simply proceeding through the desert," Umbeso put in.

Aniolon saw the townspeople looking between Umbeso and Gerinvioch and suddenly felt very unnecessary. It was a familiar feeling and not one he enjoyed.

"The barrier will not allow them passage," the wyrm replied, locking eyes with Umbeso.

"Yet if anyone from inside the town," Umbeso said waving his hand over the gathered crowd, "should leave the town, this barrier will allow them to enter once again?"

Aniolon broke in before the wyrm could respond. "Silence, Umbeso! We have an arrangement with Gerinvioch. It is settled," he said, glaring at the older man.

Gerinvioch looked at Umbeso and the man took a step back. "You are wise to surround yourself with capable advisors, Gruanthe," the blue said.

Aniolon turned to face his town's winged salvation once again. "Yes. Very well. Thank you for your assistance, Gerinvioch," he said, dismissing the dragon's comment. "I will contact you when we have your first payment," Aniolon said, hoping his informal tone did not distress the great wyrm, but knowing the comforting effect it would have on his followers.

Gerinvioch smiled, his eyes shifting from their locked position on Umbeso to rest on Aniolon. "Enjoy the freedom you covet so dearly," the dragon said. He then leaned in to Aniolon and spoke in as hushed a tone as a creature so enormous may. "Continue to enjoy the power, Gruanthe," he said, a grin slowly overtaking his mouth. "I certainly shall."

Gerinvioch spread his batlike wings and gave a mighty flap. Coming to a hover some forty feet off the ground he made a final magical gesture and bellowed a last arcane phrase. Aniolon raised an eyebrow and watched the great wyrm speed away.

Aniolon heard a wave of gasps erupt from the gathered citizens and turned to see the inert artifact on the ground begin to crackle to life. Orange lights surged inside it drawing pulsing, racing lights that shone through its dull exterior. It rose from the ground, levitating slowly, coming to a resting position nearly sixty feet off the ground and began to spin in place.

The sky momentarily flashed bright orange, like a burst of sunlight, and everything seemed as it had been, except for the dull whir of the spinning object hovering overhead.

Aniolon turned to look upon his people. "We are saved!"

Cheers rose tentatively from the crowd as everyone gathered closer to the object that would save them. Aniolon barked orders for the celebratory feast to be prepared and everyone scattered to do their part. It would be quite a celebration and they had much to be happy for. Indeed, there was much to celebrate, Aniolon thought. His people would throw a victory celebration in his name. Aniolon smiled. His people.

The next day, Aniolon awoke to shouts and screams. He left his home and jogged south. The hedonistic celebration had endured for many, many hours. Remnants of food and drink were strewn all about. People were passed out everywhere, some in piles of spent carnality. Aniolon found a crowd of frenzied people and pushed through the gasping throngs to find a young man screaming, being held upright by two other men. Streams of air poured from the young man's right hand as he held it before himself.

"I can't stop it!" the younger man being restrained cried, his voice cracking. "I can't stop the spell! I was using a simple wind gust to clean the refuse from the streets, and now I cannot stop it!"

Aniolon noticed a woman convulsing slightly as she let loose a small scream.

"I tried to dispel his magic and—" she stopped abruptly, convulsing again.

With the eyes of every person witnessing the spectacle turned on him, Aniolon could only stare at the convulsing woman. Her face seemed to be wrinkling in waves before him. It was as if a ripple was moving across her stern features.

"Someone stop this! What's causing it?" Aniolon heard someone shout. Questions echoed from all around the crowd.

Umbeso stepped through the crowd to stand directly in front of Aniolon. "The boy may simply be inexperienced. She, however," the man said, indicating the spasming woman behind him, "is not. There is something wrong here, Aniolon. Many of us cast spells as simple as these daily here. These particular spells are two very different kinds as well. It surely is not the magic itself."

The crowd was muttering amongst themselves but Aniolon could not hear. It could not be the magic, he knew. He stared into the eyes of his former competitor. The man was calm, his lips pursed as if waiting for an answer to a question he had asked.

"What is it?" Aniolon asked quietly. He wanted to scream at the man but could find no voice to do so. This was no time to play the role of teacher.

"Think, Aniolon! What has changed?" the man asked, looking impatient.

"Tell me!" Aniolon cried.

Before the man could respond, a shrill scream rose above the din of befuddlement in the crowd. Aniolon turned to see a nude woman running toward the crowd, her auburn tresses bouncing around her shoulders. The crowd parted to admit her to the center.

"Daron . . ." the woman panted the name of a well-respected priest among the villagers. "Daron's dying!"

"Speak, child," Umbeso said calmly.

"Daron was praying to Sharess for . . ." she paused, looking flushed. "Praying for a spell to . . . enhance our pleasure in our . . ." she paused again, "activities this morning."

Umbeso nodded for her to continue.

"In the middle of his reverie, he collapsed. He's not breathing!" she said.

Umbeso turned to Aniolon and asked, "Now divine magic as well?"

Without another word, Aniolon pushed through the crowd and dashed to the site of the Evise Jhontil floating in the town square. Aniolon did not want his guess to be correct, but it was the only thing that had changed. The artifact's octagonal shape pulsed more brightly and was spinning faster than before.

Aniolon stared on in silence, hypnotized by the moment and the racing orange light that so entranced him. He felt a hand on his shoulder.

"It must be the Jhontil. Do you agree?" Umbeso asked.

Aniolon nodded weakly. "What do we do?"

"You are our leader, Aniolon. You tell us," Umbeso said with a grin.

"Damn you to the Hells! Tell me!" Aniolon said as he spun to face the man. "This is not the time."

The man took a step back and stared hard at his leader. "You are right, of course. We need to discuss this with all those learned of the Weave."

A short while later, in his home, Aniolon met with the most skilled arcanists in the town.

"As we can all see, something, presumably the artifact, forces the caster of any spell to perpetuate the spell infinitely," said an old man named Sohj, who had instructed Aniolon some years before.

Murmurs wafted around the room. Aniolon hushed them, intent on hearing the man.

"Eventually any spell will consume the caster," Sohj continued, pointing to the dead young man who had attempted to cleanse the street and the still-convulsing older woman in the corner of the room. "There have been four others so far. The priest Daron, two young apprentices who attempted to combine their talents to dispel the effect, and Elder Grashtio. The old fool took it upon himself to rid of us the Evise Jhontil. Each attempt has only made the damned thing spin more quickly and glow more brightly."

"Then we must leave this place," Umbeso said.

"No!" Aniolon shouted.

"Gruanthe, we must leave. There are hundreds of us here and magic sustains us by providing food, water, even shelter. Without it, we will die and now the magic itself will kill us!" Umbeso replied.

Aniolon looked around the room. He saw assent in every pair of eyes. He simply nodded and listened for the next hour as plans were made to abandon the town. It was decided that scouts would be sent ahead to find another suitable location for the town, somewhere in the desert.

Not more than an hour after all was decided and the scouts sent, a dark-haired woman, one of the scouts, burst into the room and reported her news.

"There is a wall . . . an invisible wall," the woman said, her face twisted in confusion.

"A wall?" Umbeso asked.

"Yes. We were headed east, farther into the desert. We were no more than a mile outside of town and we hit a wall. It appears as if nothing is there, but you simply can no longer walk forward. One of my men has the knot on his head to prove it," she said.

"Then try east, south, or north!" Aniolon said, standing up so quickly that his chair tumbled to the floor.

"We have, sir," the woman said, shaking her head.

"We're trapped then," Sohj said quietly as the other gathered scholars fell silent. "The Evise Jhontil has us, it would seem. Its barrier holds us, yet if we attempt to disarm it, we will get trapped by its power," he said, motioning again to the dead boy in the corner.

"Wands!" Aniolon blurted out.

The others in attendance turned quizzical looks toward him.

"We have not tried a wand or other magical tool on the artifact," Aniolon said.

The gathered scholars talked amongst themselves. Aniolon watched nodding and shaking heads, theorems and postulations discussed with wild gestures, and Umbeso. His rival stood alone, discussing the option with no one.

"I will attempt it," Umbeso said over the raucous debaters.

A hush fell over the room.

Sohj hushed the chatter in the room. "Are you certain, Umbeso?"

Umbeso affirmed his intentions.

A few minutes later, the group of academics reconvened in the town's center, beneath the light of the Evise Jhontil. One of the men provided Umbeso with an enchanted trinket he had once picked up from a Calashite magic dealer many years before. It was a brooch of fine silver laid over a polished onyx stone. He said it contained very powerful dispelling magic. The man imparted the magical command word unto Umbeso and joined the rest of his fellows several feet away.

Many of the townspeople gathered to watch as well and Aniolon could hear whispers among them, wondering why he was not the one risking his life for their benefit. He was their leader, after all. Aniolon did his best to block out their voices, but found he could hear nothing else.

Umbeso looked into the orange light dancing around the Evise Jhontil and took a deep breath. He held the brooch aloft and spoke the command word. After a few moments, he turned to face the other scholars and shrugged.

"You feel nothing?" one of them asked.

"Nothing," Umbeso said.

As the others gathered in closer to congratulate Umbeso on his courage, the brooch began to vibrate in the man's hand. As quick as thought, he hurled the brooch away from the crowd. As it spun through the air, it released a flash of bright light and landed softly on the desert sand. An inspection of the item revealed that it was spent, unusable.

Other items were brought to him and Umbeso tried them all. They attempted to dispel, disrupt, destroy and even push by force, the Evise Jhontil. Each attempt only resulted in a defunct item and Umbeso's arm growing increasingly sore. The Evise Jhontil seemed undisturbed.

A dust-covered man interrupted to report that attempts to dig under the mysterious wall were yielding no results as of yet.

Sohj stood before the gathered people and said, "I am, of course, open to other ideas. Short of any, I see only one other option. I have not mentioned it because I have my doubts about its success."

No further ideas came from the crowd. Aniolon felt as though every last eye was a boulder upon him, crushing him slowly.

"Very well," Sohj said. "I will attempt to teleport out of the city. If successful, I will return and escort others out the same way."

Cries of protest whirled around, but the old teacher ceased them with a pat of his hands in the air and said, "I have made my decision."

Sohj cast a look to Aniolon and rolled his eyes when the younger man shrank away. He glanced to Umbeso and gave a smiling nod.

He spoke the words to his spell. It was a simple one that would take immediate effect. His form disappeared from sight. After a few heartbeats the crowd began to cheer. His form reappeared but did not move. The noise from the gathered people ceased immediately. The wizard vanished again. Confusion took hold of the crowd and the shouting began. Sohj returned yet again, his form still frozen, and just as quickly left again.

Umbeso hung his head as he quieted the people. "He is trapped. His spell may not reach its fruition, so he is neither here nor at his destination, but constantly moving between the two."

No one spoke. Aniolon quietly weaved his way through the crowd and returned to his hut. He sat in his home with his head in his hands and laughed. He thought of Gerinvioch and what the dragon had said to him: "Enjoy the power, Gruanthe. I certainly shall." The words raced through Aniolon's mind again and again. His dream was lost to him. His people would never again look upon him as anything but the source of their doom.

Later that evening Umbeso entered Aniolon's home to find the man staring, sobbing and heaving, into a large bowl of water.

Umbeso gasped at the sight. He knelt next to Aniolon, tears welling in his eyes.

"I had to know, Umbeso. I had to. He took everything . . ." Aniolon said, his eyes never leaving the bowl.

Umbeso nodded, blinking away more tears. "I know, Aniolon. What do you see in your scrying?"

"He's laughing at me," Aniolon answered through his sobs as his mind's eye showed him the great blue wyrm chuckling to himself as he lay down to sleep another long sleep.

"He died shortly after, the scrying sapping the last of his life," Moriandro said, finally lifting her eyes to meet Bronihim's once again.

Bronihim ran from the small hut in disbelief, his head shaking violently. He stared a moment at the Evise Jhontil hanging in the sky a short distance away and raced toward the large rock he had used as a landmark. He ran past a pair of the homes and finally spotted it off in the distance. Suddenly he found himself on the ground, a dull ache in his head. He had collided with something. He rolled onto his side and saw Moriandro running toward him just as the light of consciousness flittered away.

When he awoke the next day he found himself on a couch in Moriandro's home. She was bringing him fresh water. The light fabric of her dress swayed in the slight breeze.

"How do you get water?" Bronihim asked.

Seeming startled, Moriandro struggled to keep from spilling the bowl, setting it down on a table in the corner of the room.

She asked, "How are you feeling?"

"My head is sore."

"I would imagine so," she said with a soft smile.

"The water?" Bronihim asked again.

Moriandro sighed and sat down opposite him. "The Evise perpetuates any spell that is cast, Kinase."

"Yes, but . . ."

The woman raised an eyebrow and leaned in slightly.

"Oh, you mean . . ." Bronihim said, genuinely shocked.

"Yes, Kinase. Whenever the need arises, one of us volunteers to sacrifice his own life by casting a spell to provide the rest of us with food, water, or whatever else we might need. We gather and store everything that is produced." She let out a long breath, stood, and walked back to the bowl.

"Occasionally desert animals wander in and we have food for a while that does not require such a sacrifice."

Bronihim nodded and moved to stand next to the woman.

"Has anyone else ever joined you the way that I did?" he asked, moving even closer to her.

"You mean has anyone else just . . . stumbled in?" she said, turning to face him, obviously surprised by how close he stood.

Bronihim nodded and smiled.

"Small bands of people, no more than two or three at a time have joined us. Except once, an entire nomadic tribe, more than a hundred people in all, passing through Raurin, came about twenty years ago," she said, flushing slightly. "We have since adapted to one another's ways of life and now we are simply one with them, and they with us."

Bronihim spent many days meeting the other townspeople and getting tours of the facilities. Many of the innovations in use to avoid the need for magic were truly marvels, he thought.

The months passed and Bronihim settled into his life in Lliiress. After his new duties were completed each day, he sat beneath the Evise Jhontil, watching the orange lights course through it like blood pumping through veins. He felt compelled to understand the thing that had led him there. He had once sought the Evise for power. Now he sought freedom.

He felt that he'd come to understand Gerinvioch as well. The wyrm had seen in Aniolon Gruanthe the worst aspects of humanity, though Bronihim had to admit that, in his day, he had known many men more deserving of punishment than Gruanthe. Perhaps he himself had been one of those men. Gerinvioch had seen those things in him as well, Bronihim thought, and maybe the wyrm had been right. It was not so bad here. These people were now his people. His life held no important schedules or constraints. Other than leaving, he said, felt, and did whatever he pleased and was granted the space and social leeway to do so.

"Kinase, it is very late, you should get some sleep," Moriandro said from behind him as he sat in the center of town one evening months after arriving.

Bronihim took his eyes away from the spinning Evise and turned to face her. "Soon," he said with a smile.

She turned to leave but stopped. "There is no way out, Kinase. Is your life here so bad?"

He took her hand in his. "It improves every day," he said.

She flushed briefly and brushed his face with her hands. "Then why do you still sit here, staring at the accursed thing?"

"There is always a way, Moriandro," he replied as they set off.

He glanced behind him one last time for the evening, letting the light of the Evise Jhontil burn itself into his mind. He would dream of that light, he knew. He would dream of it just as he had every night for tendays.

"There's always a way," he whispered to himself.

POSSESSIONS

JAMES P. DAVIS

Flamerule, the Year of Wild Magic (1372 DR)

The streets of Zazesspur were silent in the deep hours between midnight and dawn. Count Kelmar Dargren and his men waited patiently, sweltering in the summer heat that dominated even in the sun's absence. Kelmar's eyes were focused only on his quarry, his every nerve on edge for even the slightest sign of movement.

His men, all in dark clothing, wearing hidden weapons and used to long nights, watched him warily. Kelmar's demeanor had been erratic of late, secretive and prone to irrational bouts of rage. All of them were loyal to the count due to his allegiance with the School of Stealth, Zazesspur's guild of assassins, but lately they had begun to wonder at their guild's faith in the man.

Kelmar saw their searching looks, felt their

untrusting eyes on him, and heard their whispers, but he didn't care. He knew as long as the gold of coin graced their palms, they'd perform their duties. If not, the assassins guild itself knew how to discipline its own. Any threat he could have made to them would pale in comparison to the methods of the School of Stealth.

Most of them wondered if a cleaner death might be gained by abandoning the hunt entirely.

The past tenday had seen a series of grisly murders in and around the Merchant District. The bodies were near unrecognizable as having once been humanoid, only their perfect faces remained unblemished by cut or bruise. Faces locked in expressions of unspeakable horror.

Seasoned soldiers of the civil war that changed the political geography of Tethyr, grew visibly ill viewing the bodies. They noted that the blood remained a deep red long after death. Sure sign of a prolonged murder, terrible moments or even hours of fear before finally ending. This was no assassin or ambush killer, no simple street thug or thief. Only a pure, cold-blooded murderer could perpetrate such acts.

The seasoned assassins, sitting on the still warm cobblestones of a darkened alley, looked into the count's eyes and knew he held some secret to the puzzle of random killings. They could see the familiar spark of death in the man's stare and most privately feared it.

Kelmar grew impatient. His hand gripped the basket hilt of his saber in quiet anger. His dark black hair was matted to his forehead and beads of sweat collected in his knotted brow. With swift, precise motions he signaled to the four assassins behind him, his mastery of their silent language apparent, telling them to spread out in groups of two. Each would take a street and patrol, taking care to avoid the civic guard, which had become more difficult as the guard's numbers had nearly doubled since the killings began.

The men nodded and quietly padded out, clinging to

shadows, hands on daggers and poisoned short swords. Watching them go, Kelmar let out a long held breath, pain lanced through his head, spreading into his neck. The pain had been frequent lately, strong enough to bring him to his knees at times, and with the pain came the visions.

He tried not to think of the nightmares that plagued him when the pain was strongest, the images of blood, dead faces screaming their silent torment. Warmth flooded his chest as the sound of rushing blood thrummed in his ears. Reaching into his tunic he pulled out the amulet he'd found when this had all begun. Its large ruby heart glowed, beating in tune with some unknown rhythm. He closed his fist around its warmth, looking all around for some glimpse of the killer he knew prowled the streets at that very moment.

He couldn't help but recall the first of those nightmarish images. A vision of his own death.

He shuddered at the thought.

Borial was glad to be free of the count for a few hours. Kelmar's obsession with this killer business was strange and a little disturbing to him. Borial's companion seemed not to care much, Faerdral had ever been light of brains and even lighter of insightful speculation. They'd stalked the length of Ivory street on the western end of the Merchant District, shadowing another pair on the parallel Temple street, and had stopped on the rooftop of an abandoned warehouse to survey the area from above before continuing.

"Faer?" He whispered.

"Yeah Bor?"

"What do you think this is all about?" Borial was being optimistic in expecting any real answer from his less than intellectual partner, but felt a need to make the attempt.

"All about? I just figured we'd have a better viewpoint from up here is all." Faerdral continued scanning the lengths of street available to his well-adjusted eyes. Many of his brothers in the guild suspected him of having some elf blood due to his excellent night vision.

"No not that, I mean, why does this new count seem so keen on stopping this killer? He's no stranger to blood as I've heard tell, even put his own brother, Count Lukan, in the ground himself, so the rumor goes."

Faerdral squinted his eyes as he thought the question over. Despite what his fellow assassins thought, he wasn't as dim as they envisioned him, he just took his time. After mulling the question over he finally replied, startling Borial, who'd begun to focus on the view as well: "I suppose its just good business."

"Business?"

"Yeah, the count's got a lot of coin in some of the businesses in this area and still has to pay taxes and tribute to the duke and the Council of Lords. Blood in the streets doesn't exactly bring in the coin. Hard to make a single gulder if everyone's too afraid to come and spend it."

Borial had to admit it made sense, he'd seen more than one nobleman pitch a fit if profits suffered even the slightest.

"Not to mention the count's less than honest operations on the side. I don't know about you, but I counted at least three patrols of civic guard we dodged getting here. Keeping things under the table is getting a lot more dicey these days."

Borial stared down at the street, nodding his agreement. Still, though, that look in Kelmar's eyes seemed darker, more circumspect than a nobleman merely tightening his purse strings.

A strange sound brought them both to full attention, their conversation forgotten as they listened, trying to pinpoint the noise. Again, a muffled voice just to the east of them. Swift as cats they descended the building's side, moving in the direction of the disturbance to the night's silence.

Creeping to the edge of a shadowed alleyway, Faerdral motioned for a stop, both could hear labored breathing from within the alley. Peering around the corner, his hand ready to draw the daggers at his waist, Faerdral looked into the shadows.

Only a sleeping beggar greeted his piercing eyes, wrapped in a tattered old cloak and bundled against the wall. Disappointed, Faerdral slumped against the stone building and relaxed his guard. Borial rolled his eyes in irritation, but continued to scan the street hoping to spot anything that could be reported later to the count. Faerdral straightened himself and began to walk across the alley's mouth to the next building, Borial fell in step beside him.

Just then, as Borial looked north down the intersecting street, something warm and wet landed on the right side of his face and down his neck. Pure instinct caused his left hand to draw his throwing dagger from its sheath as he turned. Only Faerdral stood there, his eyes wide and his mouth gasping quietly. Two curious looking bone blades had sprouted from his chest and seemed to raise him off the ground, his toes barely twitching above the cobblestones as his life bled from him.

As Faerdral's dagger fell from his hand, it was only then that Borial noticed it made no sound when it landed, as it should have clattered like a hundred swords in the still night air. Unaccustomed shock flooded Borial's veins, an inexplicable fear paralyzing his body, allowing only his eyes to move.

He saw a thick-scaled limb of some sort trailing away from Faerdral's back, covered in spines and sharp, boney barbs. It ended at the figure of the now quite awake beggar in the alley, twisting out from beneath his tattered robes like the sinuous tail of a serpent. The beggar was lying on his belly, raising himself on gray-skinned arms. Only two glowing eyes the color of late sunset and a smiling mouth of needle-sharp teeth were visible beneath the hood of his dirty robe.

Every muscle in Borial's body screamed to move, but pulsing waves of power were pouring from the beggar's violently trembling body. Uncontrollable fear weighed Borial down, he fell to his knees, his own dagger silently clattering to the street as his hands went limp.

Watching the form of the beggar grow larger, his neck lengthening, the robes filling with small veins and stretching out on still growing bones, Borial realized he'd never once prayed to any god save Tymora, the Lady of Luck, in all his life.

He saw the body of Faerdral shake like a rag doll and fall as the incredibly long tail whipped its twin blades from his back.

Borial stared into the much larger glowing eyes, rimmed in small barbs and sharp horns, fangs like ivory swords shined in the moonlight as the beast's wings folded to its sides.

He never once prayed again. His last sight being the harsh red-orange glow of late sunset over a field of teeth.

Kelmar dressed himself the next day, angry, the past night's complete failure still fresh on his mind. Not only did the assassins fail to even spot the beast called Grim, two of them got themselves killed, increasing the level of alarm in the city. This game was drawing too much attention for his taste.

His head still ached from using the amulet. He knew somehow that it was either linked to Grim or its magic assisted in locating the beast's kind. He wasn't sure if the pain and nightmare of activating it were worth the insanity of hunting the creature.

He strapped on his sword belt and the elegant silver-handled saber that had earned him quite a reputation in days gone by.

For many a year he'd merely been the good for nothing youngest son of the Dargren family. A nobody in the shadow of his late brother Count Lukan. His family's piousness and loyalty to the throne sickened him and he'd taken to drinking and dueling. His skill with the blade had drawn the attention of the School of Stealth, who saw in him a chance to gain another contact among the nobles. Kelmar had seen in them a useful and profitable ally.

He walked down the stairs to the common room of the Whispering Maiden. One of the newer inns built in the Garden District as part of the reconstruction period after the war. He enjoyed the luxury of the place and its discreetness. He had his own manor a few miles outside the city, his family's estate, but he preferred it here in the city. It proved easier in keeping an eye on things.

The common room was mostly empty now, but the smiling barkeep graciously had a small breakfast prepared for the count, despite it being already late in the afternoon. Kelmar sneered at the quail's eggs and bacon on his plate, the pain in his head having affected his stomach as well. He drank lustily of the spiced ale the inn had become famous for, then ordered another. He'd tempered his drinking since his younger days, but never lost the taste for it.

The nervous barmaid brought his second ale, wary of catching his eye, well accustomed to his moods and tempers. Kelmar paid her no mind, his thoughts far away from the inn, staring into the frothy surface of the ale. He tempted the veil of memory between him and his recent past once again, trying to peer into those secrets being kept even from himself.

The pain returned with a roar of fury through his head, he screamed, his fists clenching, knocking over the ale he'd ordered. The barmaid flinched, the barkeep shooing her away to the kitchens with a worried glance at the count. Kelmar breathed deeply, his eyes tightly shut, focusing on the present, no more of the past.

As the pain receded, the images came again. The amulet was warm and glowing beneath his black silk shirt, he gripped it through the cloth as he experienced another grotesquery of bloody images, terror filled eyes, and the taste of blood in his mouth. He almost grew ill at the last, but held his composure as the images too began to fade away.

It is time to explore other options, he thought.

He knew he'd been foolish to use the School of Stealth in all of this. Without telling them the nature of their target they were too ill-prepared for the beast, but Kelmar was determined to keep Grim's identity to himself, until he knew more about the circumstances that had brought the creature to Zazesspur. He had other suspicions as well, feelings that stirred in his heart and chilled his blood, but those he could not even admit to himself just yet. He had to know more.

He left the inn and made his way to the Carpet District on foot, enjoying the stares of the common folk as he walked amongst them. He never denied the rumors that he'd killed his brother Lukan, but neither did he address them.

Let them think what they will, he thought, rumor and fear can be powerful allies.

He kept close to the northeastern curve of the streets, avoiding the glare of early sunset and the aching twinge it brought to his sensitive eyes. The Carpet District had once been an area of ill-reputation before the war, currently under reconstruction and new laws it endeavored like all of Zazesspur to restore a more favorable opinion to itself. Kelmar shook his head at fond memories long past as he surveyed the newly restored shops and productive citizens slowly beginning to return to their homes in the fading light. He nodded to a small patrol of civic guardsmen, noting their lighter numbers during the day and dreading their annoyingly greater presence in the evening.

At last he came to a small stone building, at one time having had two stories, but a fire had seen to the upper half long ago. The lower half remained in liveable condition, though he loathed entering it at all.

Opening its slightly charred wooden door without knocking, he peered into the darkness seeking a familiar form usually huddled there. The scents of jasmine and sandalwood greeted him mixed with other smells best left unknown. A voice called out from behind him as he shut the door and bolted the latch.

"I could have killed you, little nephew." The voice was a dry whisper that carried throughout the room like the echo of a waterfall.

Kelmar smiled as he turned to the speaker and said, "You knew I was coming, dear aunt, else you would not have left the door unlocked."

"Hmph," was all the reply he received besides some shifting noises and quiet mutterings about the arrogance of youth.

The count lifted a lantern from the small table by the door and carried it over to the stone fireplace where his aunt usually sat in a well worn cushioned chair. She'd refused his offer of a new chair when he'd taken over the family's finances and he did not push the issue. The offer had been reflexive and he didn't really care all that much for her comfort.

"Pyrasa," she said in the spidery and flowing language of magic, bringing the lantern flaring to life though there had been no oil in it for ages.

Kelmar looked at his aunt, his mother's twin sister, his expression unmoving and emotionless despite her hideousness. She'd grown bald long ago and one eye had been blinded by a falling cinder during the fire that had taken the upper floor of the house. She wouldn't stand for the touch of a healer, so it remained an empty socket surrounded by scar tissue.

She looked him over as well, noting the scar he proudly wore himself, a thin line on his left cheek, a reminder of an old duel and the pain of an inexperienced sword arm. It was his first and last scar. He still wore his coal black hair just past his shoulders. It contrasted sharply with his pale skin. An aftereffect of the nocturnal lifestyle he preferred.

In the silence of her gaze Kelmar began to feel his skin crawl, tiny tendrils of pain twisting through his veins. She was reading him, sifting through his being for the answers she knew she sought. He watched her reactions, reading her as well, waiting for her to find the pain, the nightmares.

Her single eye narrowed as it fell on the spot where the amulet rested beneath his shirt. He could feel it warming next to his skin, growing hotter as her magic neared it. His head began to throb again, the ache pulsing in time with the waves of heat growing from the amulet. He forced himself to remain still, fighting the sensation, clenching his eyes shut.

She gasped then as her magic brushed the edges of the amulet. Her body stiffened and she screamed—a strangled, scratchy sound that electrified the air as it escaped her, followed by a convulsing coughing fit. He heard her as she felt the amulet's power, an unbidden smile coming to his thin lips. He could not explain the feeling, but an acute joy overtook him as she suffered the amulet's touch with her mind. The sudden emotion was confusing and painful to him as well, bringing his headache to the edge of that dark place where the visions hid, the nightmares and omens that tasted of blood and fear.

Her quiet spell was broken. She sat hunched over. Her breath wheezing past wrinkled lips stained with small droplets of blood. The spell had cost her somewhat, using more power than she'd anticipated. She looked up at him, awaiting the answer to the questions she had regarding that same dark place, a place she dared not go.

His own pain subsiding, Kelmar opened his eyes and nonchalantly answered her, "His name is Xexillidaulgrymm, I call him Grim. A fang dragon. I feel his hunger, see through his eyes at times, and taste what he tastes, but all at the cost of the pain. I have no memory of encountering this monster before, I simply know things without knowing them." He stopped then, looking at her as she listened.

"There's more to it than that isn't there?" her quick, whispered query lashed at him. "What do you feel? What do you know?" Never once did her eyes leave the soft glow of the amulet, now visible through his shirt.

Kelmar shuddered at his own thoughts, anger welling up in him, his lip curled in quiet rage, and he said, "I think he's taken my soul."

"Possible, but souls are not easily taken. Especially by fang dragons, more known for their appropriate names than their skill with the more sophisticated sorceries involving souls." Her words seemed softer to him, causing the count to suspect she was withholding something, "I wish my sister was still alive, she was the soul-sorceress, more the necromancer than I."

She looked at him sideways, from the corner of her eye, "You will hunt the beast again tonight?"

His determined look had answered her question almost before she'd asked it.

Slowly, on creaking joints, she rose from her chair. She shuffled over to an antique cabinet, filled with bottles and pouches, the source of the room's vague odor. From it she pulled five slivers of string, interwoven with an odorless black herb. Returning to the chair, she handed them to him carefully.

"Tie these charms round the hilts of five swords using a cross knot. When the dragon is joined in battle, slip the knots and release their magic, they will protect you and your men and cause grievous harm to the wyrm."

Kelmar eyed the strings warily, remembering the faces of the dead assassins who'd met the beast.

She added, "Mind that bauble round your neck as well. I don't know where you came by it, but it seems to want to bring you and this Grim together. It will find the dragon for you, though you may well wish it hadn't."

The count stood and nodded to his aunt, still suspecting her for holding back, but he assumed she had her reasons. Without a word he turned and walked out of the uncomfortable stone dwelling, into the darkness of the early evening. Curiously, he heard the bolt latched quickly behind him.

———— ❧ ————

In the shadows of an abandoned shop in the Merchant District, Grim sat in the constricting form of the beggar, staring out at the street through broken windows. The visions had come to him again when he awoke there.

He'd seen the old crone in her little stone hovel, using her human sorceries and muttering little human words. He'd felt the mind of the count seeking him out, using the power of the mysterious amulet. The pain of the search was excruciating, though it thrilled Grim to feel it. His blood burned and his very soul writhed in agony, all the while he grew stronger, more powerful. More deadly.

The smell of fear from outside and the sound of beating hearts informed him that the count had been successful. He'd sent his men to prepare an ambush for him. Four assassins tried to hide amongst the shadows of the surrounding buildings. Clearly, Kelmar hadn't told them yet of Grim's true nature. Thin, ash gray lips pulled back in a smile, revealing an impossible number of sharp teeth.

Fine, he thought, I'll give them their ambush.

He stood then and walked to the door, affecting the limp he'd perfected while in the guise of the old beggar. He made a slow progress to the center of the street and stopped, standing in the moonlight of Selûne, waiting for his hunters to attack. He did not smell or sense the presence of the count, cursing Kelmar silently for his cowardice.

The quick snap of crossbows firing amused Grim as he felt the bolts hit his chest and shoulders. The poison they carried had a strong, pungent odor, potent, but useless against him. He shrugged the bolts away. They had only barely pierced the surface of his tough skin.

Taunting them, he used his natural ability to mimic sounds, reproducing the song of a young girl he'd hunted five nights ago. The child's voice floated through the dark streets, the lilting tunes of her rhyme chilling the air of the summer night. The assassins shivered involuntarily and gripped their swords tighter, preparing to release the knotted charms given to them by the count.

As they touched the magic strings, Grim's song stopped, his humor fading in the presence of their magic. Rage replaced it and he stood straighter, more focused. He would not suffer the arrogance of insects who sought death.

They came then on silent feet, from four directions, surrounding Grim. Faster than the eye, Grim rushed the assassin to his left, releasing his hold on the beggar's form. His body rippled as the bonds of magic faded, his bladed tail appearing whiplike from beneath his torn robes, which mended and began expanding into wings.

He twisted his footing and fell to all fours, his long neck turning to face the other three assassins while the fourth was cut in half by his deadly tail. Grim could see the magic glowing on their blades, but sudden fear slowed their steps as the dragon showed himself fully.

He was a horror to behold, every scale of his forty foot long form seemed dedicated to cutting or piercing, barbs and bony horns crowned his fang-filled mouth. His wings were short and unaccustomed to long flight, but were perfect for quick pouncing and leaping. He crouched like a large hunting cat as he approached them, his eyes glowing in anger at their audacity.

The man to Grim's left lunged at him, his faith in the magic blade giving him courage. Grim's tail blades knocked the sword from the assassin's right hand, severing the fingers neatly at the knuckle. Barely had shock begun to register before the tail whipped the man again, disemboweling him.

With Grim's attention diverted momentarily, the assassin to his right slid in silently, swinging his ensorceled blade and scoring a wicked gash in the dragon's right shoulder near his wing joint. Grim roared as the pain of the magic wounded him and reflexively clawed at the offender, talons buried deep into the assassin's unarmored chest sent him flying to crash in a bloody heap against a nearby wall.

All sense fled Grim as the pain in his shoulder became a dull throb. He roared again, releasing the dragonfear he'd kept within. The fear washed over the final assassin in waves, battering against his willpower in rhythm to Grim's massive heartbeat.

The man turned to run, dropping his sword behind him. Grim pounced then, painfully beating his wings in a single thrust, to land on the man's back. His weight had easily crushed the life from the doomed assassin, but in his blood-lust Grim tore the man's body to pieces anyway, crushing the bones and soft flesh in his powerful claws.

Then he stopped, hearing noises approaching from behind him, footsteps walking purposefully toward the grisly scene. Finally, Grim thought, the count arrives to see my work firsthand.

Appearing from a street to the north, a single guardsman stopped as the moonlight revealed the splashes of blood and crumpled bodies. His stomach twisted, seeing the violence of the scene. Looking up to his left he froze as he saw Grim approaching him.

Grim cursed himself for the noise he'd created in his killing. He'd attracted the attention of the civic guard. This one would soon be followed by many more.

Leaping forward before the man could scream or run for help, he clamped his jaws around the guardsman's chest, sinking his fangs through the thin chain shirt and drawing blood.

The man gasped and gurgled, one of his lungs punctured by Grim's bite, as the dragon carried him quickly away to hide in a darkened alley farther down the street.

The bite of the fang dragon, like all of his kind, was draining, stealing a victim's life, leaching one's spirit away in a vice grip of death.

The guard's struggles grew weaker as his life-force fed Grim's injuries, partially closing the wound in his shoulder. Despite the healing he received, pain flared through Grim's chest, causing him to squeeze the man's body even tighter as he collapsed to the ground, hidden in shadow. The pain was like before, but different somehow, coming from within as confusing images flooded his mind.

The amulet, the prize of his hoard that he'd left so long ago near Myth Drannor, floated across his vision. He'd forgotten it had once been his, a powerful artifact he had treasured for centuries. Ancient memories came rushing back to him, particularly the wizard who'd tried to steal his soul, using the amulet to augment his necromancy.

He remembered defeating the wizard, but after that his memories were broken and sketchy. Enemy after enemy had come searching for him, all with the amulet in hand, causing him pain and nightmares. Finally as the pain of memory grew to extremes within his mind, he saw the young face of the civic guard he just killed, stained red and framed in the amulet's glow.

The tortured face grew closer and new memories slammed into his mind with the force of ancient magic. Memories of growing up on a farm outside of Zazesspur, the smell of the fields at harvest, the desire to wield a sword, to help people, to become more than a mere farmer. The energy of the man's life, coursing in the dragon's veins, became a fire in his mind.

Grim passed out as the intensity of the barrage became too painful, his struggling mind too weak to resist such magic.

His skin grew tighter as his consciousness faded, scales disappeared and fangs receded.

The silence of the evening resumed its vigil, blanketing the remains of those that had disturbed it.

Three patrols of civic guard soon arrived from different directions. Their commander, one Captain Begg, began to oversee the investigation and removal of bodies. One of his officers approached him to report.

"Sir, our men have returned from Count Kelmar's estate, from which he'd been absent for a tenday according to the servants. They found no sign of him at the Whispering Maiden either. Should we continue searching for him?"

Captain Begg shook his head slowly, "Don't bother, some hunters found the count's body yesterday, hidden in the woods near where his brother had been killed."

Confused, the officer replied, "But sir, I *saw* the count just yesterd—"

"I know. And I don't know." The captain shook his head. It had been a trying tenday. He looked up, noticing one of his men standing just outside the murder scene staring aimlessly. "Thaedras? Where have you been? And what happened to you?"

Thaedras turned his head, looked at the bleeding gash in his right shoulder. He could feel a strange warmth against his chest, could feel a necklace of some sort beneath his tunic.

A flicker of pain pulsed behind his eyes as he tried to remember, to answer the captain's question. He clenched his eyes shut as the pain grew, a single vision passing through his mind as the ache slowly faded. A vision of his own death.

He shuddered at the thought.

QUEEN OF THE MOUNTAIN

JALEIGH JOHNSON

When the great wyrm Amrennathed, in peace and solitude, gave her last breath to the mountain, the village of Orunn died.

She knew it would be her last by the way the stone shifted, a final, protesting grate against scale and ribs that had shrunk to hold barely the breath of three men. Centuries had reshaped the mountain, sculpted it around her sinuous body, until bare stalactites plunged deep into her back, wormed thorny roots into her spine. There was no room left for life that was not stone.

Amrennathed couldn't see the changes in the mountain. Her far-staring eyes, bored out by stone into painful, dust-choked blindness long ago, gave her no hint as to the passage of time.

The dragon did not care to see her death

approaching, nor had she acknowledged the loss of her eyes. She had not cared to look at anything outside her mountain for a very long time.

Do you hear me?

Her body was dying, but Amrennathed's mind was alive and working as furiously as it ever had against a foe. Time was her enemy now—only so much of it left to communicate her wishes, to pass on her legacy. Her thoughts were a fever raw and unfamiliar to the sedate mountain, and some of her words and desires may have been lost in the contest of wills.

Mountains, by nature and custom, are not easily stirred to speak, even to a dragon.

I have been patient. The dragon's mind-voice rumbled, banked against stone like settling embers. *I have waited for you to slay my body, in your unhurried, meticulous way, a gift I would give to no living being. It is time for you to take the rest.*

And from the mountain, in its unhurried way, came answer.

Aged as you are, we measure the centuries a pace apart. I will claim you, in time. We will become dust together a thousand years hence, as Faerûn is reshaped, remade again and again.

Too long! Impatience flared—rock and slab felt the blow of the dragon's desperation. *There must be certainty. I must know that what is in my mind and breast will not be left to scavenge.*

If you leave nothing behind, will it be that Amrennathed herself never was?

This time, Amrennathed wasn't certain if it was the mountain speaking or her own traitorous thoughts.

It does not matter, the dragon insisted.

By the measure of your kind, will you have failed?

I am the measure of myself! Pride had not left Amrennathed's mind, though the mountain had laid waste to her body.

Arrow-bright, an image flashed before the stone. Unused to the hard color, light, and sound, the mountain shuddered at the sudden barrage of all three.

A Zhentarim spy crouched on his knees, head thrown back in agony as a purple-hued claw caressed his spine, shredding black robes and peeling a fine layer of flesh.

Radiances pulsed and fed from the man's slack mouth into the claw. Amrennathed's mind-voice was soft, at first coaxing, then demanding, as the man shrieked and sobbed and gave the last vestiges of the spells he'd gathered in his long life to the dragon.

The image dissolved in screams, and another memory swelled in its wake.

In a filthy Skullport loft, Iamras Sonmaire crouched before an altar of metal and bone, a bloodied dagger point thrust into the crooked planks next to his knees.

Runes glowed from the altar and the spine of the thick tome perched upon it. Their magic flooded the shuttered room with a sickly green light. Iamras trembled, wiped sweat from his forehead with his sleeve even as he fought to keep his other arm steady over the book. Blood flowed from a clumsy gash in his wrist into the runes, and the book hungrily drank.

Amrennathed felt amusement stir at this memory. She'd left him knowledge of the book's location and power but stripped the memory of how much was required for its opening from his mind. He would bleed out well before he re-learned what she had stolen from him.

I have raped the secrets of folk across Faerûn entire, made hoard of them in place of coin-mountains, she whispered to the stone, as if all Faerûn was indeed bent to listen. *I have knowledge stored that kingdoms would bleed for and may still, if it is not allowed to pass with me. My body, my mind joined to yours, will be safe.*

Safe from a fate you fear, from ghosts of the minds you've stolen.

Again, Amrennathed wondered if she was hearing her own voice echoing in rebuke. Either way, her once clever and manipulative mind was too weary to deny or circle the truth.

Yes. Safe. They will look for my bones and find empty stone. No one will beg secrets from a mountain. I will bury them in the deepest crevices where the lowliest creatures walk. Let them know the secrets of Faerûn's evils and her beauties, where great powers hide and sleep. Wisest of all, they will give no thought or care to my legacy. That is my wish.

None of us can know all that we leave behind.

But the mountain sensed the great wyrm fading. Its words became a sigh as it yielded at last, opening to Amrennathed's oldest, most closely kept magic.

Stone within stone within buried stone shifted and sighed in turn, bent, melted, and burned, reshaping ages of the world in one small space, for the beast that had slumbered within the mountain's breast for untold centuries.

Outside in the clear air, hundreds of feet above the joining, a pair of sharp-shinned hawks nested on a crooked slab of rock where the sun was kind. Beneath twig and talon, the mountain shuddered, heavy with the scent of burning rock and dragon death.

The female of the pair shrieked a cry and took flight, terrified as the unnatural scent wormed its way into the nest. Her talons came down in a rush of wings and scattering feathers onto her own eggs, crushing the shells.

Clouds of feathers separated and drifted down on the wind, far and down. They came to rest in a pool of soapy water at the bare feet of a woman who was singing softly to herself.

The old woman sang and scraped clothes over a wooden washboard in the same back and forth motion she'd used since her fingers had been straight and smooth with youth. She plucked stray feathers from the suds, added more soap and scraped harder, until her knuckle grated on wood, and came up raw from the water.

She didn't notice when the moss-covered rock behind her changed.

The green carpet joining stone to the nearby trees ran dark, purpling like a new bruise. It covered the tree in thick veins, blotting out the hot sun streaming behind.

Cast in sudden shadow, the old woman turned on her knees to look as the first wave of magic slammed her.

She overturned the bucket in her fall to the ground. At first, she thought it might be that her heart had finally failed her, a death, living alone on the mountainside, she had always assumed would be hers. She'd accepted, even welcomed that fate. It was not a bad way to die, not an undignified way. In the end, the pain would have been brief.

Gods' laughter, this was none of those things, the old woman thought, gasping for air and clutching her chest reflexively, though in reality it was her head that felt as if it would burst from the pressure.

Images careened through her mind: a mountain that spoke—her mountain—to a dragon that looked like it was made of purple stone.

"Am-Amrennathed." Dry lips formed the word, and a wave of fresh agony rippled over her. The name crowded more images into the old woman's mind, of wizards being drained to husks even as she was being filled up—up and over with . . . what? To her, it was only pain. She was drowning in it.

The old woman shuddered up to her knees and crawled blindly to the side of the mountain, grabbing at roots and stone to drag her body up the slippery rock.

"Please, lady," she sobbed out, as if the dragon might hear her, "I don't w-want this—"

Roots snapped, and she was falling again, but her ankle remained tangled with skirts and mountain. There was a second, harder crack, and the world went blessedly dark.

She returned to consciousness slowly, to the sound of a voice—her own voice, pleading with the empty air as the dark trees and mountain loomed over her prone body.

"Lady, be merciful. I don't know . . . what to do with this."

She dug the heels of her hands into her eyes until stars swam. The memories were still spinning themselves out inside her head. If she concentrated hard enough, she could separate and see them.

In one, there was another dragon in a very different mountain, tossing in a fevered dream of madness and death. In another, a man was on his knees before a glowing altar, screaming in agony as his life's blood spilled onto the stones. And more, so many more. . . .

Whimpering, the old woman curled into a ball. Her quivering lips picked up her work song again. She sang, low and unintelligible at first, then louder, faster until she was screaming to drown out the memories flitting across her thoughts as if they'd always been there.

Beneath the shuddering pain and the drumming of her heart, she didn't notice when the mountain began to shake.

And as Amrennathed's clever mind finally slowed, joined and shaped to the grace of the mountain, the stone began to tremble.

The entire exchange had taken no more time than the dragon's last, faltering breath, but outside the trembling mountain, seasons passed, the land was reformed . . . and the village of Orunn died.

25 Flamerule, the Year of Wild Magic (1372 DR)

"Set it on fire and burn her out then!" The wizard pressed furiously trembling hands to his face and cursed as they came away ribboned with blood.

Bahrn did not immediately reply. He stood at the edge of

a high cliff and gazed down on the ruins of a house that had suffered that precise fate.

From any perspective, the village of Orunn had already seen enough abuse by fire. To put torch to one more of the sagging dwellings in the midst of the devastation caused by looting and abandonment seemed as arbitrarily cruel as a child squashing five ants because the first four weren't sport enough. Still, he could sympathize with Arlon's mood. Diadree had always had a temper.

Intact, her home perched less than ten yards from the ledge where he stood. Bahrn's dizzying view straight down ended at a lake called the Fox Ear, a sapphire triangle closing off the horseshoe of tiny houses and surrounding farms. Years ago, several men from the village had insisted on erecting a thick plank fence along the treacherous cliff edge for Diadree's safety.

He recalled vividly the old woman's wrath at the perceived insult.

"More likely they're afraid I'll push one of their little bratlings off the edge into the lake. A fence won't cure that temptation!"

Bahrn wasn't surprised to see the fence dismantled, a few stray planks sticking slantwise up out of the ground.

"You're, ah, wizardly cousin did not appear happy to see you," he said as Arlon continued to curse.

Actually, Diadree had come up behind Arlon as they searched for her and leaped, screeching, atop his back. Before he could wrench her off, she'd set both hands at his cheeks and raked from eye line to bony chin. She'd then barricaded herself inside her home and refused to come out.

Arlon wiped a spot of blood from the cleft of his chin and glared at the mercenary. "You could subdue her," he suggested. "For her own safety, of course."

"Of course." Bahrn cocked an ear, listening as Diadree continued her tirade behind the door. Eventually, it leveled off to wordless squalling punctuated by the thud of what sounded like furniture disintegrating as it hit the wall. "I could overpower her," he acknowledged. "I could also pin her to the ground with my morningstar—" he ignored the distinctly hopeful look Arlon shot him—"but she stands less chance of being harmed if we allow her to wear herself out first." He paused as another crash and shriek rang out. "Considering her current state, it shouldn't take long."

Arlon eyed the trembling walls skeptically but didn't argue. He settled down on the ground to wait, scrubbing at bloodshot, tired eyes and the beginnings of dark stubble at his cheeks.

"What kept you awake?" Bahrn asked, recalling the young man's restlessness the previous night as they drew closer to Orunn.

"Nothing—startled by a dream."

Bahrn turned his attention from Diadrec's door and found Arlon looking at him, as if quietly daring the mercenary to find humor in that. He had portrait eyes—slow to move and barely noticeable when they did. Yet he still managed to draw in and absorb the space and people around him so completely, Bahrn wondered if the wizard had ever been denied anything in his short life and if those who had dared the defiance were still alive.

"What kind?" asked Bahrn.

"I dreamt the earth was shaking."

"You weren't dreaming," Bahrn said. "The tremors are the reason the village stands empty today. Orunn was abandoned this time five years ago." He pointed down to a bare patch on the opposite side of the lake where crops had once been sown. A jagged crack cut across the barren soil into the foundation of a nearby house. "Almost overnight, the land became too unstable for farming or living."

"What caused them?"

Bahrn shrugged, the armor plates at his shoulders creaking.

"Caprice of the Gods? Magic? You, wizard, would be better qualified to speculate than I."

Arlon snorted. "You're capable of many things, Bahrn—claiming ignorance is not one of them. Qualification was the reason I hired you. You know the roads south of Ironfang Deep, when I wasn't aware there were mercenaries, especially educated ones—" he swiped a vague finger at the double painted dots creasing Bahrn's forehead—"who traveled extensively through this area."

"I grew up here," Bahrn said and smiled blandly as Arlon's face tensed, "Since we're discussing qualifications. . . ." Then he added, "Yes, I knew Diadree had no family . . . and that she is no wizard."

There it was, spoken aloud, the lie that had followed them all the way from the dwarven city, where Arlon had paid him to act as guide to Orunn to find Diadree. Bahrn had been surprised a foreigner had even known of the tiny village's existence.

Comprehension dawned on the wizard's face. "The burnt home you were staring at over the cliff."

"Mine."

"I do not understand you. Why did you agree to lead me here, then?"

"I never thought we would find her," Bahrn admitted. "But, if we did, to ensure nothing happened to her."

"You think I intend her harm?"

"Few have ever borne her love." Himself included, Bahrn thought. "What do you intend now we've found her?"

"Foremost, I intend to staunch this bleeding," Arlon's eyes slid away from Bahrn's, and the easy manner he'd adopted during their journey to Orunn was back as he busied his hands tending to the cuts. "And I will question her—in your presence, of course. What can you tell me about her?"

"There's little to tell. When I was young, Diadree rarely left her home here on the mountain." Though insignificant amongst the Mountains of the Alaoreum and greater Turmish, the broad peak easily held both the village and the Fox Ear in its shadow. As far as Bahrn knew, Diadree had lived on the mountain all her life. "She is harmless."

Arlon dabbed at the bloody marks on his cheeks. "Forgive me if I doubt you."

"She was angry."

"She is out of her mind," Arlon said. "She's been living alone in a dead village for a very long time, and it's cost her her sanity."

Silence followed the pronouncement. Bahrn's eyes darted to Diadree's house. It had ceased shaking.

He positioned himself to block the front door just as it burst outward, Diadree following in a rush. Bahrn snagged her round the waist as she flew by and lifted her gently off her feet.

Gods, she has a bird's bones, he thought. How long had she gone without a proper meal?

The rest of her, if possible, looked worse, like a garden grown wild from seasons of neglect. Her long gray hair hung in the same thick braid he remembered, but it had not seen soap or brush in all that time. Greasy mouse-tails of it escaped all over, hanging down in her eyes and trailing over loose cords of flesh in her neck. She wore a patched apron on top of filthy skirts, all of which gave off a jaw-clenchingly unpleasant smell.

Diadree flailed arms and legs, but Bahrn simply gathered her in against his armored chest.

"Well met again, Diadree. It's been a long time," he said.

Bones cracked as the old woman swiveled her head around and up until they were practically chin-to-chin. To his surprise, recognition flashed in her milky blue eyes.

"Bahrn? Norint's son, Bahrn?"

"You remember me?"

She grunted. "Bahrn the bully—the fat one with crooked

teeth who used to slobber and stare in my windows with his bully friends." Her eyes narrowed. "I broke a broomstick over your head for it."

"Did she? *Practically* harmless, Bahrn, I agree."

At the sound of Arlon's voice, Diadree resumed her violent midair kicking. Bahrn allowed her to slip down to the ground, but as soon as her feet were planted, he dug in, and forced her to stand in place.

"We're not going to hurt you, Diadree," the wizard soothed in a voice that prickled the skin at Bahrn's neck.

"In that case, you can turn around and follow the cracks back the way you came," Diadree snapped. "Watch you don't trip and fall into one."

She tried to back away as he approached, and she stumbled.

Bahrn steadied her and noticed a dark brown stain soaked into the hem of her torn skirts.

"You're hurt," he said.

"It's nothing—old." Diadree shrank back as Arlon bent and gingerly probed the bone. "Healed now, as best it can be. I don't feel it on level grass, but walking up and down the mountain puts me in the Nine Hells of hurt."

"It's a miracle you've survived on your own for so long," Bahrn said.

"Why? Because of the orcs and other uglies scattering through here to pick the houses clean?" She laughed scornfully. "They don't come up here. No one does. No one needs to."

"We've come to take you out of here. You're not well, Diadree," Arlon said, straightening.

Diadree smiled unpleasantly. "You mean I'm crazy. Yes, I heard you. It's true I am many things." She paused, her hand straying to her cheek to scratch at the grime darkening her face. "Crazy might be one of them," she conceded, as if she'd never given fair consideration to the possibility. Her eyes snapped to Arlon's face. "You are many things as well, some of which may even be true." She wrinkled her nose. "You smell of magic even if you don't flaunt the power." She jerked her head at the wizard's pale, bare forehead. "And I'm sure you're highly intelligent, for someone who reeks so thoroughly of magic, but you're looking for the wrong woman—"

"But the *right* mountain," Arlon interrupted. "I'm looking for Amrennathed's home."

Diadree went rigid under Bahrn's hands and said, "Amrennathed is even less your affair than I am."

"Who is Amrennathed?" Bahrn wanted to know.

"A dragon. In local legend you know her as the Queen of the Mountain," Arlon explained. "I came here searching for her."

"For a children's story?" scoffed Bahrn. "You've wasted your steps. The mountain has no queen but Diadree, and she's not a dragon, except in speech." The old woman's shoulders quivered with what might have been laughter. Bahrn couldn't be sure. "Your queen was used to scare children into good behavior."

"Never worked," Diadree muttered.

"Amrennathed is a dragon of amethyst, older and stronger than this mountain," Arlon persisted. "By all accounts, she came here a great wyrm and rarely left the lair she made for herself." His voice rose with excitement. "Don't you see? When you were a boy, she was practically beneath your feet, and you never knew."

Bahrn was unconvinced. "What does that have to do with Diadree?"

"Nothing," Diadree interjected, but the wizard was smiling at her.

Arlon turned, murmured something Bahrn didn't hear, and stepped close to the cliff wall. The grass and dirt shifted, as if a swift, momentary breeze had passed over them, and Arlon lifted his arm into the air. He clutched a dirty scrap of cloth between two fingers.

Diadree made a small, constricted noise of fury in her throat. Bahrn recognized the piece of the old woman's bloodstained skirt. The breeze plucked the fabric out of his grasp and bore it on the air for several seconds before allowing it to float gently to the ground. The rush of air streaked away from the cliff and blew toward the back of Diadree's home, ruffling flowers and bushy plants from her garden in its wake.

"This way," Arlon said, following the breath of magic.

A rocky outcropping rose up behind the small dwelling. The trail they had been following ended there, cut off by a steep climb up the rocks.

"A blood scent spell," the wizard explained when Bahrn came up behind him. He pointed to the rock wall.

Puzzled, Bahrn walked farther around the outcropping.

Roots of small trees and brush sticking out from the cliff formed an ascending carpet of rough stepping places and handholds. Halfway up the roots were torn, and there was a dark stain dribbling down the rocks.

"You tried to climb this?" Bahrn asked, turning to Diadree. "This is where you broke your ankle."

"She must have been looking for something terribly important," Arlon remarked. "I wonder what it could be, Diadree." His tone was conversational, but his eyes were fixed on the mountain, as if with enough force of will he could draw in and open the rock.

Murmuring under his breath again, he levitated up vertically along the cliff wall, steadying himself against the wind by grasping at outthrust rock.

"Follow him!" Diadree shrieked. She grabbed Bahrn's arm as the wizard disappeared from sight over the outcropping. "She won't like it if he finds where she slept!"

"Who won't?" Bahrn asked, his patience rapidly thinning. "Arlon's dragon? She's dead, Diadree, if ever she existed at all. Either way, she's not going to care who visits her grave."

"He's looking to pick through whatever she might have left behind. That's what they do, don't you see?"

"If that's all he intends, he's welcome to . . ." He trailed off as Diadree's face went livid.

"Stupid, insolent child," she spat. "Why did you come back here—bringing a sniveling, arrogant, cult mage in tow!" She shoved at him. He half-expected her to reach for the nearest broomstick as she had almost two decades before.

Bahrn raised his hands. "He hired me to bring him—for you. I didn't know what he was. Why does it matter what he takes?"

"Doesn't it matter to you? Of course, seeing your own home picked to bones by the vultures didn't seem to slow you, so why should I be surprised?" Diadree snorted with disgust and swiped at him again.

Deftly, he plucked both her fists out of the air and forced them away from his face. "A pile of sticks, to my memory. I only came back to see if you were well."

And if Arlon was a cultist, as Diadree claimed, he'd brought her much more trouble than he could have saved her by staying away.

Diadree's grip slackened, but her eyes remained raw. "I don't understand you."

Bahrn sighed and stooped, offering his broad back to the old woman. "Neither do I, at the close of most days. I'll carry you, but only as far as the roots go up."

Diadree closed her eyes briefly. "Thank you." She wrapped her thin arms around his neck and said, "I was wrong. The years *have* changed you a little. You're much less a fool than you used to be, even if you are traveling with the Cult of the Dragon."

"How do you know he's a cultist?" Bahrn asked as he began to climb. "He's not mad, not like—" he stopped and clenched his jaw.

"Like me." Diadree cackled. "You turn the same open mind

toward the world you did as a child, Bahrn. You'll want to be careful of that in the future. You've seen his look. Amrennathed knew ones like him would get around to coming after her eventually. She was prepared, don't you doubt it."

Bahrn did doubt and refused to ask how an imaginary dragon might have prepared against the fanatical cult or how Diadree would know about it, but he felt compelled to make some argument.

"I am not the same boy you chased with a broomstick, Diadree," he said.

"That's true. You didn't have this when you were a child." She thumped his armor beneath her knuckles.

"I didn't have it *because* I was a child. I left Orunn when I was thirteen."

The old woman shook her head impatiently. "I mean your father didn't pass it on to you. Norint was a farmer."

"Yes. I turned mercenary after he died."

Bahrn glanced back as he felt her hand rest on his shoulder. Her fingers absently traced two of the spiral designs on his shoulder plate, carved into the metal like a second set of eyes. Inlaid with lapis lazuli, the swirling patterns appeared in mottled blue-white pairs all across his armor, contrasting sharply with his darkly tanned face and black mustache. Frankly, he enjoyed the superstitious notion of having extra eyes to guard him, though the patterns resembled no human or elf orbs he'd ever seen.

Watching Diadree stare into them was uncannily like watching a child gazing at her reflection in a mirror.

"Why did you stay, when everyone else had left the village?" he asked quietly.

She looked up, and smiled. "Because I'm old. Bratlings and cult mages have driven me mad, and I'm too feeble to move on, no matter how hard the earth shakes my bones."

"The tremors could have killed you," Bahrn pointed out.

"Yes, but they were not her fault." Diadree sighed. "Be

grateful at least one dragon managed to pass out of this world with so little fuss, boy."

"You believe Amrennathed's death caused the tremors?"

"Why not? The power of a dragon dying—one so old and tightly linked to the earth—is bound to be felt, no matter how gentle she tried to be."

"You wish to protect her memory." Bahrn shook his head. "Yet she destroyed Orunn—not in fact, but as a result of her death."

"It was her time, and she chose to go as her dignity—greater than an army of greed-driven cultists—demanded. I can only hope to be offered that same grace someday." Diadree tensed. "Careful now, the mountain's about to have another fit."

"What—?" Bahrn cursed as the rock beneath his fingertips shifted, and began to tremble. Metal armor rattled against stone, jarring both of them, but Diadree seemed at peace with it.

Hooking an arm around the thickest root he could reach, Bahrn pulled the old woman in close until the shaking slowed and finally subsided.

"How did you know?" he asked when the rock was firm beneath them again.

Diadree didn't answer. When he craned his head around to look at her she was gazing back down at her house. From the high vantage, Bahrn saw that a section of the roof had collapsed in on itself.

"Diadree," he pressed, and she blinked and turned away from the sight.

"Keep climbing," she said. "We're almost there."

Bahrn followed her eyes to a ledge snugged against the cliff several feet above them. At its back hung a tunnel.

Diadree slid off onto the ledge when they reached the top. There was enough room for both of them to stand comfortably outside the tunnel. Squinting into the darkness, Bahrn thought he caught the glimmer of tiny lights.

"Arlon!" he called out, but the lights didn't move. He slipped a torch from the pack on his shoulder and spent a moment lighting it. When he raised the flaming end inside the passage, Diadree was already several steps ahead of him, examining the tunnel walls. He caught a flash of colored light against the flame and blinked, thinking he'd imagined the sight.

"What is that?" he asked, then answered the question himself: "Amethyst."

He flattened his free hand against the stone. In the shadows, deeply embedded, the formations were a mural of sparkling purple and white, swirling designs not unlike his armor.

"Watch your step," Diadree cautioned as gravel and something firmer crunched under Bahrn's boot.

He stepped back quickly and shone the torchlight over a dirt-caked bone that had been snapped nearly in half under his weight. He noticed a skull lying nearby.

"Human," he said. The entire back portion of the skull was caved in. "Others have come here?"

"Several others," Arlon's voice echoed out of the darkness ahead of them. They heard the wizard's footsteps as he trotted into the torchlight. "There are other sets of remains in the larger cavern," he said, then shot the mercenary a look of triumph. "And two eyes," he added, motioning for them to follow him back down the tunnel.

The ground sloped downward for several feet, emptying into a dome-ceilinged chamber. Directly ahead of them loomed two identical, man-sized oval alcoves buried a handspan into the wall.

The cavern was full of the sparkling amethyst. Crusts of it speared out from the wall and druzes carpeted the ground around his boots like a crystal maze in miniature.

Arlon moved his palm over the largest of the spears. Light haloed up from the crystal, illuminating the entire chamber in painful, lavender light.

Bahrn could pick out other glittering objects strewn about

the floor—gems of varying colors and sizes amongst gold and silver coins.

"She was here," Arlon said. "These are remnants of her hoard. Tell me where she is!" he demanded, whirling on Diadree.

"Arlon." Bahrn casually pivoted between the pair, ignoring the dark look the wizard threw him. "You truly believe she's hiding Amrennathed in one of her pockets?"

"For a brief time, I thought she *was* the dragon." He spoke to Bahrn in that same easy manner, but the wizard's eyes followed Diadree's every step around the cavern with the glittering fascination of a man who does not realize he is being observed.

Bahrn was observing though, and Arlon's eyes told him more than enough. The mercenary's hand slid to his waist, where the handle of his morningstar waited.

"The others who returned from the mountain never found this cave," Arlon went on. "They claimed the only living soul on the mountain was one crazy old woman . . . a woman who refused to leave Amrennathed. They didn't know she was speaking of the dragon, the Queen of the Mountain. Only a very few know her by name."

Diadree paused and glared back at him, her hand raised at the ridge of one of the stone eyes.

Bahrn thought of Diadree's reflection in his armor. He shook the memory off. "That's absurd. She isn't a dragon, she—"

"I know that!" Arlon said. "But she knew the dragon's true name. She tried to get up here herself. Why?" The wizard scraped up a handful of coins, jewels, and dirt from the floor and hurled it at the wall inches from the old woman. "Not for this! You're not a looter, not an orc, are you, Diadree? However much you smell like one. Where is she? Where are the dragon's bones?" he shouted.

Silence reigned in the cavern. A single coin from the

wizard's tantrum rolled to a stop at the toe of Bahrn's boot. The mercenary glanced down at it and caught movement out of the corner of his eye.

For a moment, Bahrn thought the left eye of the cavern had blinked, but it was only Diadree, shifting restlessly beneath the low-hanging stalactites suspended above the hollow in thick-set lashes. He opened his mouth to call her back to his side.

And one of the rocky spears broke away from the wall.

Not a stalactite, Bahrn realized—at the same time his voice shouted to the old woman to move—and it wasn't falling.

It was crawling down the wall.

Detaching from a cluster of stone, the thing shuffled down into the circle of purple light cast by the enspelled amethyst. Bahrn could make out an anvil-shaped head that swiped, pendulumlike, from side to side, and four stony feet dragging awkwardly across the ground.

Its body swung toward Diadree as she stumbled away.

Bahrn drew his morningstar and ran forward to push her aside, but Diadree's ankle had already given out beneath her.

She slid to the ground as the creature charged by, raking her side with its stony belly. Diadree cried out as she was dragged forward, bare flesh caught on protruding shards of rock and crystal.

Bahrn swung the morningstar underhand at the creature's other side, taking both front feet out from under its body in a cloud of dust and shattering rock. The creature skittered wildly across the floor like a puppy on slick cobbles, allowing the old woman to fall free.

Bahrn wheeled around for another strike but checked the swing as Arlon's hands began cutting rapid patterns in the air. The coins and jewels and chunks of stone he'd hurled earlier rose up from the floor and shot toward the creature like a dozen tiny sling bullets. More pieces of the creature's stone body fell away as the pellets impacted. Stung, the beast swung its attention immediately to the wizard.

"Watch her." Arlon raised his hands again. "I don't want her dead yet," he snapped at the mercenary.

Diadree lay curled into a fetal ball against the cavern wall. Her shirt was shredded—stone and bits of sharp crystal were embedded in her side.

"She's protecting herself," Diadree moaned as Bahrn tried to tend the cuts in the dim light.

"Arlon will kill it," Bahrn soothed, adding silently, and perhaps he'll move on to us. "It appears your dragon left a few pets behind to guard her lair."

"No," Diadree said. "They're like children, only not, not really. She's left pieces of herself behind."

"That thing isn't alive, Diadree," Bahrn assured her. "It's made of mountain rock, and gold and gems. I pulled some out of your wound." He pointed to the bloodstained pieces of wealth on the floor beside him.

The old woman lifted her head from her hands and reached for him, her fingers finding and clutching an exposed bit of tunic. Her eyes, dulled by pain, focused on him, pleading.

"Could you take the rest?" she begged.

Bahrn's heart wrenched. "They're all gone, lady, I promise you."

"No, they're not. Amrennathed's not. The pieces are still there." She tapped her temple hard with a dirty nail. "It's not her fault I got some of them. I'm stubborn—I loved the mountain as much as she did. I wouldn't leave."

"What are you saying?" Bahrn gripped her shoulders as she began to tremble. "Where did Amrennathed go?"

"The mountain. She was old and didn't want to leave or be scavenged after her death. Would you, if you had lived half so long, want your bones looted for trophies? I didn't blame her. I watched it happen to Orunn. So she joined her body with the mountain. It upset the balance of . . . everything—shook the earth, these caverns. Everyone left the village except me. The mountain and I . . . somehow the pieces got mixed, and now I've got some of her in me and . . . and I just wanted to stay in my home, to be safe." Tears welled in her eyes. "Or maybe that's her voice, her wishes. I don't know anymore. But it doesn't matter if he kills it," she moaned. "There're still too many pieces."

"Gods, Diadree," Bahrn said, feeling helpless. He rubbed his hands over her shoulders as she cried, trying to calm her.

His hands stilled abruptly as her words sank in.

Too many pieces.

Bahrn squinted at the walls of the cavern, letting his eyes become absorbed by the rocky fixtures and shadows. He remembered as a child lying on his back on the Fox Ear's shore, hunting for cloud shapes in the sky. As he looked, his eyes picked up more of the vaguely serpentine shapes sprouting out of the rock at various points around the cavern. They remained still and silent.

Behind them, Arlon dropped to his stomach as the stone wyrmling twisted, slamming its hindquarters into a rocky shelf jutting out from the far wall. It fell hard to the floor and shattered.

The wizard stood and said, "The amethyst dragons are powerful psions. I should have realized—wyrms animated from stone. Amrennathed allowed her body to waste away into the mountain, and her mental essence followed intact. But your proximity to her and the mountain—somehow a bit of that essence seeped into you."

He strode toward them, his expression frozen on Diadree in triumph as he began to mouth the words of another spell.

Bahrn wasn't about to wait to find out what magic it might be—at best, a spell to kill or contain them both, anything to keep Diadree's mind intact.

His hand moved to his weapon, but he hesitated. The

wizard was too far away. If Arlon ducked, if he missed his target, he and Diadree were dead.

He scanned the wall, following the spines of serpentine, stone bodies, as if he could will them to move, to leap down upon the wizard.

Arlon raised his hands.

Bahrn smiled grimly and hurled his morningstar into the space between them.

Arlon's eyes bulged. His left hand trembled violently, but he continued to weave the gestures of his spell even as his right palm spasmed weakly, pinned between the cavern wall and the head of Bahrn's morningstar. Blood streamed down the rock into the dust, but he kept speaking, spitting the words of his spell with flecks of saliva.

He didn't see the rock shifting behind him, stirred awake by the impact of the morningstar on stone.

Two more serpentine bodies uncurled. They caught Arlon's movement as he completed the gestures of his spell.

"Stay behind me," Bahrn commanded as Diadree tried to raise herself up to a sitting position.

They watched as a tiny wisp of flame hovered into being above Arlon's unruined palm, flowing and expanding into a blue-orange sphere of fire.

"Get ready to run," he hissed, knowing that Diadree would never be able to get out of the way of the flowing missile.

The sphere burst in the air where it was forming as a third anvil-shaped head swung out from the wall next to Arlon's raised hand. It struck the glowing sphere and the wizard in the same movement.

The magic dissolved as the anvil drove Arlon's body into the uneven cavern wall as the morningstar had buried his hand. His head snapped back against the stone, and he slid, limp, to the floor.

Bahrn held himself rigid. He pressed Diadree behind him as the wyrmlings came down from the wall. They stalked the cavern with their sightless eyes, heads drifting from side to side as if they could scent the air like bloodhounds on a track.

Finally, finding nothing moving, they slowed and collapsed to the cavern floor in a pile of rock. After a moment, they became indistinguishable from the other stone formations.

"Is he dead?" Diadree asked, looking from behind Bahrn's back at Arlon's still form.

Bahrn nodded. "Are you ready to go home, Diadree?" he whispered, hardly daring to breathe for fear the stone dragons would awaken again. "Amrennathed is sleeping again."

"Not yet," Diadree answered. "I have to stay."

Somehow, he wasn't surprised. He doubted she was in any condition to make the jostling trek back down the mountain. Her eyes were glazed, staring at something far away, and the hollows of her cheeks seemed deeper sunk into her face. It struck Bahrn that despite all of these things she looked much the same as she always had, back to the time of his childhood. She had been old then and was old now. He could never recall a time when she was young. He wondered why he was just realizing that.

"For how long?" he asked.

"Long enough to get the pieces out," she said. "Don't ask me how much time it will take. I've no idea."

"I mean how long have you lived here, Diadree—on the mountain?" He hesitated. "You knew Amrennathed, didn't you? You spoke to her."

"You're implying, I suppose, that she, I, and the mountain are of like age?" She offered a raspy chuckle. "No, boy. I'm not as old as the mountain—not quite. Amrennathed told me her name and exchanged words with me because we understood each other—two old women wanting a good place to live and die in peace. The mountain suited us." Her eyes turned heavy, dark. "Wouldn't you prefer that, human man, or would you be skewered on the point of spear and sword?"

"I am not a dragon, lady." Bahrn spoke gently, but for the first time since he was a boy staring in a window, he felt unsure and a little afraid of the old woman. He swallowed, forcing the feelings away and a smile to his lips. "Neither are you, Diadree, despite all accounts."

"This is no way to die either." Her eyelids fluttered—the darkness passed from her face, and a bit of the old humor returned. "Don't listen to me. If I stay here long enough, she will take them—the rest of the pieces. I hope."

Bahrn didn't know what to say.

"I'll mend your roof for you before I go," he found himself offering. "When you decide to go home."

"That's kind of you. You've not turned out too badly at all. I'm shocked almost to the point of exhaustion." She laid her head against the mountain and slept, a satisfied half-smile curving her lips.

THE STRENGTH
OF THE JESTER

Murray J. D. Leeder

Mirtul, the Year of Rogue Dragons (1373 DR)

There was news from far and wide in the Jovial Juggler Inn that day. News of dragons. It was hearsay, mostly, but it had enough of a ring of truth to put everyone present on edge. Vague reports out of the north of a new Flight of the Dragons, like the one over the Moonsea and Dales seventeen years before, only wider-ranging and more deadly. A bulbous merchant from Hillsfar recalled the dragon slain over the city that time, so great that its corpse blocked the harbor for a month.

From a vacant table Khalt sat silent and listened. Most occupants of the tavern glanced at the elf occasionally but none dared approach him or question him. Wiry and leonine, with a tawny countenance and a huge dagger at his belt, he looked able and willing to fight at a moment's notice. The tattoo across his cheek told them that he was feral and dangerous, a reputation his people did little to discourage among outsiders. The fact that the tattoo was a dragon, its silver tail dangling down his chin and onto his neck, probably drew some interest, but Khalt didn't care to explain himself. Beregost was a merchant town, serving those traversing the Trade Way between Baldur's Gate and Amn, and certainly saw a great many types better not questioned.

Khalt kept his focus on a shadowy corner of the taproom and the two figures meeting there. If the others knew who they were or what they were talking about, they would have cause to be much more than concerned.

A traveler from Turmish told a story he had heard in Erlkazar a tenday before. It concerned a dragon that supposedly emerged from its lair in the mountains near Saradash and laid siege to the city, destroying much of it before finally being slain by the town guard and two local wizards. The Turmishan saved the most shocking part for last: "It was a brass dragon."

A gnome roared in laughter, perched atop a tall stool. "If a metallic dragon did all that, Saradash must have done something to deserve it."

"Don't be so sure," the burly barkeep replied. "They say these Flights have been going on for centuries, and I always wondered why only the evil ones should be affected."

Khalt's eyes narrowed. One of the two figures in the shadowy corner, the one clad in purple with a wild shock of white hair, was a man Khalt trusted more than any being on Faerûn. But Trinculo's face, rarely seen without a wide grin, looked grimmer than Khalt had ever seen it. The other man, whom Trinculo called Chalintash, had a ruddy complexion and hair the color of rust. Khalt didn't trust him in the slightest.

The two of them roared in laughter a moment but soon returned to solemnity. Khalt wondered what could be so funny.

"Listen to yourselves," the gnome protested. "Your minds drift comfortably to the worst case scenario."

"He's right," piped in a black-haired trader from Waterdeep. "If something new is going on with the dragons, the right people must already know about it and are now taking actions to protect us all."

"Spoken just like a Waterdhavian," the Hillsfarian scowled. "Put your faith in your lords and your Blackstaff. Tell me, what actions did they take the last time this happened? What will they do to defend Hillsfar?"

"From what I've heard of Hillsfar," the gnome said, "it's a shame that dragon didn't raze it to the ground."

"Hold it now, little friend," said the barkeep. "The Lathand'rites run Beregost and they don't look kindly on that sort of talk. So either you—"

The gnome leaped off his stool in Khalt's direction. "Don't you know?" he proclaimed. "If you walked into his city, you'd be tossed in jail and fed to monsters in an arena!"

Khalt didn't say a word in response and kept his gaze trained on the pair across the room, but lowered his hand to the hilt of his dagger.

The two across the room, lost in conversation, took no notice of the disturbance.

"If you don't stop harassing my customers," said the barkeep, his voice barely raised, "you'll be spending the night in a cell instead of in your nice, warm bed."

The gnome walked upstairs, huffing, and the various merchants returned to their conversation, switching suddenly to topics far away from dragons. But the tension stayed and Khalt's hand remained on his dagger.

Fools, Khalt thought. The world is blazing and they gossip over it. Pettiness turns them against each other. Truly the Rage will bring out the worst in all folks, dragons and otherwise.

Khalt watched Chalintash turn and look directly at him.

He extended a finger and pointed. And Khalt saw the anger sleeping in his eyes.

With a cool breeze and a rustle of leaves, the dragon swept among the branches like a flash of lightning, its slender body weaving in and out of the majestic trees with seemingly impossible speed and grace. Its long, thin tail slashed its way through the passing branches but disturbed nary a tree, while what sunlight flowed through the thick boughs caught the dragon's polished wings and sent silver light filtering all across the shadowed settlement below. Each of the Trunalor stopped and beheld the spectacle playing out in the high trees, even those who had seen it a thousand times before. It was a marvelous vision, to be sure, but it had far greater significance to those elves. It meant that Trinculo had returned.

Each time, they suspected that he would not come back. Few voiced it, except perhaps in those periods when he had vanished and wandered Faerûn for years on end. Mercury dragons were creatures ruled by whims, who catered to the moment's impulse and the instant's pleasure. Some called it freedom, others irresponsibility, but mercury dragons could rarely be tied down. The bonds of friendship and honor that held Trinculo to the Trunalor, the wild elves of Amtar, were tight indeed.

Khalt Laathine never doubted that his friend would always return. The dragon tattoo on Khalt's cheek was a constant mark of their connection. He knew Trinculo better than anyone, and even as the mirror-scaled dragon touched down amid the green shadows, he could tell something was wrong. As the children of the tribe came to greet him, his smiles were forced, his laughter mirthless.

Khalt finished setting a new snare on the perimeter of the camp and walked over to join them.

"Child of Avachel," said Ferla, the tribe's leader and shaman. Under centuries of his leadership, the Trunalor had survived near-constant hostilities from their many enemies, including gnolls and other evils spilling out of the Gate of Iron Fangs to the southwest and the degenerate drow-spawned men of Dambrath, who had hunted the Trunalor for sport for centuries. "We welcome you back to the heart of the forest. What news do you bring of the outside?"

Trinculo's vast silver bulk seemed to melt around him as his form shrank and contracted into the appearance he usually took with the Trunalor, of a white-haired yet youthful wild elf dressed in outlandish green and purple robes. The form was much more accommodating within the tight nest of trees, and he enjoyed interacting with the elves on their own level. Trinculo was so full of energy he could barely withstand a moment of stillness. He wore on the nerves of many Trunalor but he was so relentlessly upbeat and good-natured as to win over even the most hard-hearted.

"Much news, Treeclimber," said Trinculo. His clownish spirit was often put to use deflating Ferla's occasional stoicism, but now Trinculo seemed almost as serious as the shaman. He spoke slowly, for one thing, uncharacteristic for him—when excited he could speak so quickly that no one could understand his words. "I won't be able to stay long."

"So you have said many times," said Khalt, emerging behind Ferla. "Even those times when you ended up staying decades."

Trinculo let out a ring of liquid laughter that cheered the hearts of all who heard it. He stepped forward and embraced his friend. "It's true this time, Khalt," he said. "There's much I must tell you."

When Trinculo was properly greeted by all the folk of the tribe, Ferla, Khalt, and he retired to Ferla's shadowed glade, sacred to Rillifane Rallathil. Trinculo paced constantly and spoke in fast bursts. He told them that the wyvern their scouts had battled near the Landrise was not alone in its apparent madness. He saw much more evidence of the same phenomenon, and heard travelers discuss such on the road to Three Swords. Finally, he received a magical missive from an ally of his, a copper dragon.

"Some sort of sickness is enveloping dragonkind. Fits of insanity, afflicting dragons of all kinds. This isn't the first time this has happened, but this is different . . . I don't know how, exactly. I don't have many details. Chalintash was concerned for the security of the message."

"A sickness of dragons," Ferla repeated, as if to dispel the ramifications of such a thing.

"Are you in danger?" asked Khalt.

"I don't believe I am," Trinculo said, in his haste running the words together. Khalt doubted his answer. "I don't know if this will affect the Trunalor. You can deal with the wyverns easily, but there may be other dragons lairing in the forest that I don't know about. Try not to attract their attention. And if the blues in the Gnollwatch Mountains rouse, we can only hope they point their claws at Dambrath and not here."

"But you cannot stay to help us face these possible dangers?" said Ferla, a hint of accusation in his voice.

"No," Trinculo said, his eyes drifting downward. "I have my own mission. I'm going to meet Chalintash for more information. I'm afraid I can't keep to Avachel's pledge right now."

The silvery dragon Khalt bore on his face was not Trinculo, though Trinculo often liked to pretend that it was. It was the Jester. Some knew him as Aasterinian, but to Khalt he had no name but Avachel. Many centuries before, the vicious Arkaiun Empire, the barbarians who fell to the dark elves beneath their homeland, interbred with them and became the Dambraii, terrorized their neighbors without mercy. They enslaved the gentle folk of Luiren and even dared challenge Halruaa, and among their conquests they sought the Forest of Amtar, invading the trees with a force armed with flame and axe.

But Avachel, a great quicksilver wyrm who spent his time traveling far and wide, happened upon the war and joined the elves against the Arkaiun. Many Trunalor died in the defense of their homeland, but the Arkaiun were repelled and never returned to the Amtar with such numbers. Erevan Ilesere, the Seldarine's Unseen Trickster and the god of elf rogues and wanderers, took notice of Avachel's actions and took him as a companion. In time, Avachel became a god in his own right, revered by all the goodly woodland races, and a diligent protector of wild elves across Faerûn. When Trinculo pledged his undying loyalty to Avachel, his spirit was forever bound to the wild elves, and he spent much of his life living and fighting with them.

"I will not lie to you," Ferla said. "I would rather you stay. Our tribe values your counsel, your aid, and your spirit. I cannot hold you here, but I must ask, is there not danger to our tribe that you might defend us from better than any?"

Trinculo nodded solemnly. "Yes, Ferla, there's danger everywhere now. I don't want to leave, but I think I can best protect us all far away from here. Chalintash and his allies want me to go on a mission. He says that I might help put an end to the Rage."

"You cannot be dissuaded, I see," Ferla concluded. "I wish you luck and speed. May Avachel's strength never fail you."

"I hope you'll offer the same wish to me," Khalt said. "I shall accompany Trinculo in his task."

"Khalt, no!" Trinculo protested.

"You are needed here, Khalt," Ferla reminded him.

"Trinculo is in need," Khalt said. "He has helped us so many times, it's only right we do the same. I was weaned on the stories of the Unseen Trickster, Avachel, and all their adventures—would Erevan abandon Avachel in such a crisis?"

"Tell me, Khalt," asked Trinculo. "Just how would I be upholding Avachel's oath if I deprived the Trunalor of one of their best warriors in their time of need?"

"And tell me, Trinculo," shot back Khalt. "Just how do you except to get through this mission, whatever it is, without me?"

Trinculo fought it for a moment, but it was no good. He broke out into a stream of laughter that Khalt suspected could be heard in Dambrath. Khalt turned to Ferla with his index finger pointed squarely at his own cheek. "This tattoo is meant to remind us that the pledge goes both ways. We owe Trinculo much more than he owes to us."

Ferla sighed. "The impetuosity of youth. I leave it to you, Trinculo."

Trinculo shook his head. "I'll regret this later, I know. Saddle me up."

<hr />

"What were you laughing at?" asked Khalt. Trinculo's discussion with Chalintash had concluded and the two of them had retired to their room in the Jovial Juggler.

"Laughing?" asked Trinculo as he paced back and forth. Trinculo was always filled with restless energy, but now Khalt could see every vein of the human form he wore bulging and pulsing. "When?"

"At one point you and Chalintash both laughed. What was that over?"

"Oh," said Trinculo, stopping in place. "It was at the idea. It's absurd. The Talons of Justice are rounding up metallics who defy Lareth's plan. 'Justice and good above'—that's their code of honor. And 'Honor and respect to righteous innocence.' Where's the justice, where's the good in this? Chalintash told me that two silver Talons came by his lair and he had to fly halfway around Anauroch to escape them.

We're nothing but rogues and fools to His Resplendency, just because we don't want to stick our heads in the ground, go catatonic, and hope for the best! Now if that's not funny, I don't know what is!" He resumed pacing.

Khalt understood Chalintash's decision to meet with Trinculo in an inn called the Jovial Juggler as a deeply cynical one. Chalintash was a copper dragon, and alongside mercuries they were said to be the most lighthearted of all dragonkind, famous lovers of humor and jokes.

And when the strength of the jester fails. . . .

"Why did he point at me?" asked Khalt. "And you know what I'm speaking of."

"Yes, that." Trinculo looked down. "It wasn't about you in particular. It was about elves. Nobody's saying that elves are behind what's happening today. Not at all. In fact—"

"What are you telling me?" Khalt demanded.

Trinculo looked him in the eye. "Elves did it. The Rage. Elves designed it. Gods know how long ago . . . but it was your people, Khalt."

"Why?" asked Khalt. "Why would the elves do that?"

"To hold us back." The words seemed to give Trinculo pain even as he said them. "Dragons once ruled this world, and the elves wanted to take our place. So the high mages designed this curse of insanity. It made dragons reckless, fighting each other, leaving their lairs to get killed. It even made them devour their own eggs. Draconic numbers decreased, and so the elves could build their civilizations."

"But surely this was only evil dragons?"

"Maybe, but I doubt it," Trinculo said. "The curse affects all dragons today, good and evil. Some might say that was how it was inttended."

The color drained from Khalt's dusky features. "You didn't know about this curse before?"

"No. The Flights happened, but I don't know the cause. And Chalintash didn't know either, until he learned it from a kinsman of his who drew the evidence up from a human ruin under the Moonsea."

"But he blames me, nevertheless," said Khalt

"No," Trinculo protested. "He doesn't blame you. How could he? This happened millennia ago! And the mission he's given me . . . I need to tell you my mission. Would he give me this mission if he hated the elves?" Suddenly, an oddly genuine smile crossed Trinculo's face that seemed to erase all of what he had just said. "We're going to Evermeet."

"Evermeet?" asked Khalt. When he was young, a bronze-skinned sun elf came to the Forest of Amtar astride a white pegasus. The Trunalor politely refused his offer to abandon their ancient homeland, won time and time again with their people's blood, but his stories stuck with Khalt—could any place be as he'd described?

Trinculo nodded. "Elven high magic created the Rage, and so perhaps high magic has the solution to it as well. That's my part. We go to Evermeet and seek the aid of the high mages."

This is all happening so fast, thought Khalt. A tenday before he had barely set foot outside of the forest, and now he was on a far coast of Faerûn, planning to go across the ocean to a place that some of his people thought nothing more than a myth.

"Why you?" asked Khalt. "Why didn't another dragon just do it instead?"

"They thought my closeness to the elves made me ideal," said Trinculo. "The elves are surely aware of the Rage and likely to attack any dragon that came close. But perhaps they wouldn't fire at a mercury dragon, especially with an elf on his back. Good thing I brought you. And there's something else. It's often hard to find Evermeet, even from the air. It's hidden by very intricate illusions. But I know the way perfectly. Truth is, I was born there."

"You were born on Evermeet?" asked Khalt. "Why didn't you ever mention this before?"

Trinculo smiled. "You never asked."

A sound like a mighty crash of thunder came from outside, and screams filled the night. Khalt and Trinculo ran over to the window to see. It was a clear night with many stars shining down, but no moon. Still, the improved vision of both elves and dragons showed clearly the glossy golden-rust form of a dragon swooping its way over the rooftops of Beregost. Its copper wings beating, its great tail lashed and slapped the passing buildings, breaking apart the wood and stone structures where it struck.

In one claw the dragon clutched a uniformed human, a member of the town's guard, still squirming and struggling. The claw squeezed deeper around him until his writhing ceased, and the dragon let the inert guard fall to the street below.

"It's Chalintash!" Trinculo cried. "He's returned, and he's lost. Khalt, he's lost to the Rage."

Khalt rushed to fetch Trinculo's harness, stowed underneath Khalt's feather bed.

"There's no time for that," said Trinculo. "I have to get him away from the town. Join me in the ruins." And with that, Trinculo reared back and jumped through the window, sending a shower of glass down to the street. With arms outstretched, he shed his false form, wings sprouting, his clothes melting away as silvery scales grew up all around him. Khalt snatched up his bow, quiver, and some other equipment, then quit the room with lightning speed. He dashed down the stairs, through the empty taproom, and out of the inn. Above, Trinculo made a high-pitched squeal that assaulted all of the ears of Beregost and alerted Chalintash to his presence.

When Chalintash came about to face Trinculo, he instead saw four luminous mercury dragons swooping toward him from different directions. The polished scales of each caught every point of light from the night sky and reflected them like a mirror, sending shards of light all over Beregost's sleeping streets. Snorting in annoyance, the copper dragon spat a thick line of caustic acid at the closest image. When it struck, the phantasmal dragon vanished in haze and the acid raced off beyond the town, splashing down into an open field to the west.

The three remaining dragons, which Chalintash scrutinized to find the real one, all wove and twirled identically in the air. Chalintash alighted on the temple of Lathander that dominated Beregost, clutching a towering spire in his hind talons, foreclaws and teeth ready to attack. A sudden burst of speed brought all the dragons sailing toward him. He slashed and snapped as the mercuries narrowed in, but his teeth and claws met only empty air as the illusions vanished before him. Instead, claws closed around him, the real Trinculo grasping onto his legs. With a powerful upward thrust, Trinculo uprooted the copper dragon and spun him upside down as he hauled him up into the sky.

Chalintash was larger than Trinculo, so the grapple could not last. Struggling with his great bulk, Chalintash lashed his tail, digging his sharp claws into Trinculo's flesh, bending his long neck backward to try to get a clear bite with his sharp teeth.

"I'm sorry I have to do this," Trinculo told him, wondering if Chalintash could even understand. Adjusting his flight downward, Trinculo held on slightly longer, grimacing as Chalintash's claws dug deeper, then released.

The copper dragon fell like a stone. As he plummeted to the ground below, Chalintash rolled over in the air and extended his wings to their widest, trying to use them to slow or halt his fall. Trinculo hovered above him and put his own breath to good use. A brilliant gold beam of light burst from his maw, catching his opponent full on. The light shone like a beacon that lit up Beregost and all of the surrounding farmland. Chalintash buckled under the intense heat, but his wings he kept spread wide.

Khalt watched breathlessly as Chalintash careened through the air, but knew that Trinculo's plan hadn't worked. They'd done it together fighting wyverns in the Forest of Amtar, but a copper dragon was much larger and stronger than any wyvern. By the time Trinculo's breath was spent, Chalintash had recovered into a secure soar, and was in no danger of striking the ground. Still, part of Trinculo's plan had succeeded. The course of the battle would depend on Trinculo's superior speed and wits.

Khalt ran past the ruins of buildings brought down by Chalintash. Men and women tore through the rubble, desperately trying to find survivors. Just outside the town, Khalt saw a line of city guardsmen under the leadership of a yellow-robed cleric of Lathander. They were standing in a long line armed with longbows, flame arrows at the ready.

Khalt ran up to the cleric and startled him when he shouted, "Hold!"

The cleric whirled to face him. "Who are you?" he demanded.

"Don't do anything to enrage the copper dragon," Khalt advised.

"He looks mighty enraged already," the cleric protested. "We must protect our temple and town."

"He's distracted now," Khalt told him. "Launch your arrows and you run the risk of bringing his attention back to the town. Let my companion and I try to deal with him." He paused a moment before adding, "But if we should be lost, show no mercy."

With that, he bolted off into the dark fields, hopping fences and dashing past frightened livestock, making his way to the ruins. Occasionally he cast a look back to see the two draconic forms racing across the heavens, mere spots in the night sky.

Soon, Khalt reached the ruins south and east of Beregost. Once it had been Ulcaster's school of magic, but it was destroyed by Calishite rivals centuries before and now was little more than a number of stone walls and crumbling towers. The ground was slick with sheep droppings and surprised, luminous eyes stared at him from the darkness. All was quiet and still, and it seemed far away from the deadly dance still playing out far above.

In the ruins there were two reasonably tall pillars, twenty or so feet apart. Khalt ran up and inspected them carefully, running his hands over one of them until he found a deep groove cut into the side. Its original purpose was ornamental—it outlined a panel where the dim impression of a bearded wizard stood—but Khalt knew a more functional use for it.

He pulled open his bag of tricks and started to work.

The cloudless night sky sprawled before Trinculo, each star like a tiny candle lighting the roof of a vast cathedral. As he spun and flitted through the night, he lost all track of up and down, so that the sky might be the carpet of the world, and the ground the ceiling. How he loved this! To fly through the night, every star rippling off glossy scales—the freedom of it! But not tonight.

Trinculo made every twist and turn his slender body could manage, every unpredictable move to keep Chalintash away from him. He pushed ! ... to the limits of his endurance to keep from thinking ... the fate that befell his friend. Every now and again, Trinculo would catch just a glimpse of the copper dragon on his tail, but it scared him to look. The turquoise gleam in his eyes had faded away, degenerating into a dull reddish glow.

Chalintash's blithe and generous soul was gone replaced by the cold instinct of the reptilian brain. With all gentleness and warmth shorn from him, Chalintash knew nothing but fury and that gave him strength, but also made him reckless and thoughtless. That was Trinculo's advantage. Occasionally he would slow and almost let Chalintash catch him, and fly away in a new direction, and listen to Chalintash's growls of frustration.

Trinculo saw a white flare go off far below him and pointed his nose down toward it. But as he did, he passed closer to Chalintash, who belched his breath weapon—not the line of acid, but a white gas that rolled out of his throat and all across the sky in a noxious cloud. Trinculo swept through it, and gulped as he realized that Chalintash's breath had impaired his mobility. He travelled toward the ground just as fast, but not in a controlled dive but a random, dangerous free-fall, and with his enemy so close behind. As the ground got larger and larger, he didn't dare look back to see just how close the copper dragon was . . . he could almost feel claws grasping or teeth snapping at his flailing tail.

Like a silver comet in the night, his luminous, reflective form rocketed to the ground. Trinculo was plunging toward the darkened ruins of Ulcaster's school, frustrated by the tortuous lethargy that vexed his limbs and wings. If he could not react in time, he knew he would surely strike the ground. Though he could not see Khalt among the ruins, he knew the elf was there and what Khalt had planned. They had perfected this technique against wyverns in the Forest of Amtar. He located two central pillars that looked high enough and sturdy enough to stand in for the thick trees.

"Avachel, bless the fools!" Trinculo cried as he was set to plow into the ground.

Gritting his teeth, he tried to force his heavy body into action, pulling himself upward and directing himself forward. His bones were slow to respond and he felt unimaginable pressure as he struggled. His scaly belly raked against the grassy ground as he finally pulled free of his dive, sending frightened sheep scrambling. His torpid form sped through the pillars and when he allowed himself to turn his head back, he saw Chalintash do the same, just as he hoped.

An arrow hit Chalintash from above, penetrating the scale and embedding just at the point where his wings met his body, and just where he could not pluck it out with his teeth. He snapped back to find its source, only to see a gleaming white line tied to the arrow and leading back to one of the two pillars he'd just passed through. The tether pulled taut, and the arrow ripped a path through dragonflesh.

Chalintash let out a sharp squeal as sublime pain wracked his entire body. The shaft in his wing was an elven arrow of attraction, designed to penetrate the target and stay in place through practically anything, and the line was enchanted with considerable strength, wrapped firmly in place around the broken pillar. Chalintash broke off his pursuit of Trinculo and spun back to find who'd shot him. He saw the elf standing atop the pillars where the line led, another arrow at the ready.

Khalt fired, the arrow flying right toward Chalintash's face. The dragon just barely dodged it, and closed a claw around the thin line that tied it to the pillar. Chalintash yanked as hard as he could manage, but the pillar was secure and barely trembled. Khalt nimbly leaped off the top to the ground beneath and dashed off, unseen, somewhere into the ruins.

Chalintash took the line in his teeth but could not break it. He flew forward to the pillar, inspected it closely. The tether was down in a groove set into the side of the pillar. The dragon scratched at it with his claw but could not disturb it. Something crossed his face, as if he were trying to dredge up from the quagmire of his mind the best solution.

"Back here!" came a voice. "Have you forgotten me so quickly?"

Trinculo had perched farther away in the ruins. Chalintash spun around to face him, but even in his Rage-impaired state, he was too smart to plunge forward and let the line pull tight again. Instead, Chalintash snatched up a large piece of rubble in his talons, lifted it up into the air as high as he could, and tossed it at Trinculo.

Surprised, Trinculo tried to scramble for safety, but still affected by Chalintash's breath, he was too slow. The stone struck Trinculo in the face hard and crumbled with the impact. Trinculo opened his mouth wide, blood dribbling from his broken teeth, and spat his renewed breath weapon at the copper dragon. Once again, the beam of light flashed from Trinculo's mouth to illuminate Chalintash's brilliant russet color, bathing him in scorching heat. Chalintash made no effort to escape, but simply stared at Trinculo, as he was cooked alive.

* * *

Khalt crouched in the darkness at the foot of a ruined wall and watched, amazed, as Chalintash hovered in midair, beating his wings slowly as Trinculo's breath consumed him.

It must be the Rage at work, Khalt reasoned. *Is he not feeling the pain, or is he simply past responding to it?*

But soon Trinculo's breath was spent, and Chalintash's only response was to shake his great mass so that steam escaped from beneath his scales.

Then, Chalintash turned back and pointed his nose at the pillar to which he was tethered. He was clearly weak, breathing heavily and his wings drooping with each powerful beat, but he rallied all his might and plunged forward. In a flash, he struck the pillar head-on, ramming it with his great forehead. The crack of bone against hard stone was deafening and horrifying. The pillar trembled but still stood, so Chalintash pulled back and struck again, and again, harder each time.

Khalt drew an arrow from his quiver and shot it. Chalintash spun at the motion, but the arrow was not aimed at him. Its path was between him and Trinculo, and when it burst into a white flare that lit up the ruins brighter than midday, Trinculo spread his mirrorlike wings to catch the light, redouble it, and direct the reflection directly at Chalintash. The brilliant flash of light burned into the copper dragon's pupilless eyes and dazzled him.

Khalt drew into his quiver again and launched arrow after arrow directly at Chalintash, each of them sinking into the copper scales.

The howling dragon, burned, blinded, and wracked with points of pain throughout his body, located Khalt's direction and bounded after him, summoning the remainder of his power. Khalt was well beyond the range of the tether, but when it pulled tight Chalintash pushed forward, his shoulders straining till bones bulged through scales, until the pillar behind him snapped at last. With a mighty *crack* it collapsed, and the copper dragon was free. Khalt fled as Chalintash barreled toward him.

But before Chalintash could reach the elf, Trinculo flew in from the side, striking Chalintash full-on and knocking him against a broken wall that collapsed under the impact. The effect of Chalintash's gas was only just then wearing off, and Trinculo pummeled him with laborious blows of claw and jaw. Trinculo pinned the copper dragon to the ground, and held down his writhing, struggling body. A hard-planted claw on Chalintash's neck kept the snapping, drooling mouth at a safe distant. Chalintash's struggling began to slow.

"Elves . . ." muttered the copper dragon through clenched teeth. Khalt sidled up next to Trinculo, holding an arrow at the ready, trained at Chalintash's face.

"What about elves?" asked Trinculo, digging his claws deeper into Chalintash's scales. "What about them?"

Instead of responding, Chalintash darted his head quickly, breaking free of Trinculo's restraint. His massive, snapping jaws thrust directly at Khalt, who loosed his arrow. It drove directly into the dragon's eye, and Trinculo closed his teeth around Chalintash's exposed neck. Trinculo pulled away a mouthful of flesh and Chalintash collapsed, a twitching wreck lying across the ruins of Ulcaster's school.

Spitting the meat out, Trinculo spun around until his back was to the dragon's carcass. He slowly walked forward to the fallen pillar that had restrained Chalintash. Khalt walked next to him.

"A brute!" Trinculo shouted. "A brute—that's all the Rage made him. He could have turned this pillar to mud, Khalt! It shouldn't have held him at all. But he didn't know his own powers."

"And a good thing too," Khalt said. He regretted his words immediately, and he saw a certain barely perceptible twitch run all through Trinculo's silvery body.

The dragon's claws dug deeper into the ground and he tensed.

"We've got to go now," Trinculo said. "We don't have much time."

"Where are we going?"

"Where do you think?" asked Trinculo. "Evermeet."

❦

By the time the sun rose, Khalt and Trinculo were well over the Sea of Swords. And by the time it was beginning to set again, they had passed the Moonshae Isles, keeping high and fast so as not to draw attention from any angry humans, or worse still, other dragons. As the sunset spread orange and red light all across the Trackless Sea, Khalt, harnessed safely to the back of the speeding dragon, asked Trinculo about their destination.

"It calls me back," the mercury dragon told him, his scales shining crimson. "Evermeet's crystalline lakes and graceful trees . . . and the harmony. Yes, Khalt. Everything you've heard is true. If your people had taken the Retreat, you wouldn't have to contend with Dambrath, bandits, or gnolls. You could have lived and made your life in peace."

Trinculo had barely spoken since they left Beregost, and Khalt was pleased to hear him speak so fondly of his birthplace.

"No struggle?" said Khalt. "Where's the fun in that?"

"Why do you think I left?" asked Trinculo. "When I took the pledge of Avachel, it gave myself an excuse to leave, to travel Faerûn helping your people. But part of me always stayed on Evermeet. Even I need a little peace and quiet sometime.

"We'll land in Leuthilspar," he went on, "and seek audience at Moonstone Palace. I met the queen once at night, on the banks of the Lake of Dreams. For once in my life I couldn't find words. She'll help us. I know it."

A voice deep within Trinculo asked, Or will she?

"What will it be like when we arrive?" asked Khalt.

"They'll have a name for you," he said. "You're a windrider. All those warriors who ride dragons, eagles, and pegasi are windriders."

"I like the sound of that," said Khalt, feeling the breeze through his hair.

"The world's most beautiful cities, and the most temperate forests." Trinculo's tone became more distant. "Evermeet is paradise. To think, the elves only achieved it with this curse."

"How many millennia ago was this?" asked Khalt. "Probably no elf lives that remembers it."

"Still," Trinculo said, "it says something of the elf mind that would design it. To exalt themselves at the expense of all others."

"There is no excuse," agreed Khalt. His heart was beating faster. He needed to pacify Trinculo, and quickly. "I wish there was some way I could make up for the sins of my ancestors."

"Hopefully that's what the queen will do," said Trinculo. Khalt hoped that was the end, but then Trinculo started up again. "I just think it's funny," he said. "I'm a dragon, my life bounded by my pledge to some elves. Avachel is, or was, a dragon and a companion to an elf god. Does he know about it? The truth of the Rage, I mean. Or is Avachel kept in the dark as well?"

Khalt looked around him, knowing exactly what he'd see. There was no land in any direction.

"Trinculo, you're worrying me," he said, as he gripped the hilt of his dagger. He looked back at his bow and quiver, both lashed to Trinculo's side farther back along the dragon, just out of his reach.

"I'm really sorry, Khalt, really I am," the mercury dragon hissed. "But when you've just torn out the throat of one of your friends, we'll see how chipper you are."

"You had to do it. He would have killed us both, and destroyed Beregost."

"You must have enjoyed sinking that arrow into his eye," Trinculo said, "and tethering him to the rock like a dumb wyvern."

"I hated it," Khalt said. "I hated that I had to do it."

Trinculo laughed. It was not the joyous sound that Khalt had so often heard ringing through the trees of Amtar, nor the cheerless cynicism he'd gotten used to those past days. It was a terrifying, hollow sound, bubbling out from darkest corners of Trinculo's collapsing psyche.

"Don't do this." Tears were dripping down his cheeks, rolling down the tattoo of Avachel. "Do you want to be Chalintash? Stay with me . . . please, Trinculo. Don't leave me." And he drew the dagger from its sheath as quietly as he could.

"Are you going to stab me, Khalt?" Trinculo muttered through clenched teeth. "Sink it in the back of my neck? Or maybe if you slash my wings, you'd hurt me so badly I couldn't reach land. Is that what you're hoping to do, dear friend?"

His eyes full of tears, Khalt swung the dagger, snapping

the harness that held him in place. He dropped the dagger and hopped backward to reclaim his bow, scrambling for handholds. He pulled an arrow of attraction from the quiver and spun forward quickly, ready to launch it into the back of Trinculo's head. But Trinculo dived sharply, pointing almost directly down into the vast, red-tinted sea below.

Khalt never fired his arrow. By the time Trinculo straightened out his body and flew forward, the elf was left far behind. The harness and the rest of the supplies slipped off the dragon's body as well. Trinculo didn't turn back, didn't look, didn't even listen for the splash. But a minute later, he felt a sharp pain, as if that arrow had dug into his brain. His senses unclouded and there was clarity again. His fury left him, replaced by something else.

Replaced by shame.

"Khalt," he gulped.

He spun back and scanned the water for the elf, desperate for any sign of him. But the waves were rolling and fast, and he found not a trace of the wild elf.

"Avachel!" he shouted. "Avachel, aid me!"

But the god was silent.

"I've failed!" Trinculo cried. "I've broken the pledge. I've shamed Avachel."

He closed his eyes tight, trying to shut it all out, but the Rage was not a force from without but from within, bound to the very soul of dragonkind. It thrived in weakness, in anger, paranoia, and shame. All that was Trinculo melted away, lost like a single teardrop into the sea.

The mercury dragon flew toward the sunset. He would not look back before he reached Evermeet.

An excerpt from

THE PRIESTS

MAIDEN OF PAIN

KAMERON M. FRANKLIN

The knock on the door startled Ythnel. It was late. Her birthday party had lasted longer than expected, but some of the older sisters finally paired off with their male counterparts after most of the wine had been consumed, signaling the end of the public festivities. Ythnel had retreated to her room and prepared for bed. She wasn't expecting any visitors.

Pushing herself up from the kneeling position she had assumed, Ythnel walked the three steps to the door and opened it just enough to peek outside. When she saw who it was, she swung it open the rest of the way.

"Head Mistress, I thought you were with . . . I-I'm sorry, I was just beginning my evening prayers." Ythnel stammered, her face flushing.

"Follow me," Head Mistress Yenael said then turned and walked back down the hall.

Ythnel wavered for a moment, but realized there was no time to put on something over her linen shift and hurried after.

As they passed the closed doors of the other initiates' quarters, Ythnel's mind wandered with the possibilities of where they were going, and what would happen once they got there. She was pretty sure she hadn't done anything wrong, or at least nothing serious enough to warrant a late night visit from the head mistress herself.

Maybe it is a surprise birthday present, she thought. Or maybe she was being taken to the ceremony that would ordain her as a handmaiden. It would make her the youngest initiate the manor had ever raised to the position.

The pair made their way down a flight of steps at the end of the hall. Smoky torches sputtered in black iron sconces every few feet. Even though Ythnel had never been down there, she knew where they were going. Every initiate knew about the lowest level of the manor, and what went on in those rooms. Ythnel shivered, and not just from the cold stone under her bare feet. She heard the moans and cries before they even reached the bottom of the stairs.

A floor of packed dirt ran the length of the hallway, with iron-banded doors of thick, rough wood set every ten feet in damp, rock walls that glistened in the torchlight. Each door had a small, barred window, but Head Mistress Yenael kept them moving swiftly enough that Ythnel thankfully couldn't see inside any of the rooms to discern what was happening or who it was happening to.

The head mistress stopped at an open door at the far end of the hall and ushered Ythnel inside. Ythnel bit her lip and hesitated, trying to brace herself for what she might see. Yenael's face darkened. She grabbed Ythnel's arm and shoved her in.

The room was hardly any bigger than Ythnel's quarters. A torch sat in a sconce on the wall just to the right of the doorway. In the far corner stood a brazier of glowing coals with a poker shoved in amidst them, its tip bright orange. On the wall to Ythnel's left were several metal pegs bored into the stone. Whips of various kinds hung from them, coiled and waiting. Finally, Ythnel let her eyes stray to the center of the room. There, bent over a bench, his wrists and ankles bound by manacles anchored to the floor, was Oredas, one of the few male clerics serving at the manor. Oredas's back was exposed, muscles rippling under sweaty skin as he shifted position slightly. Head Mistress Yenael entered, closing the door behind her.

"I remember when I was brought down here for the first time, on my thirteenth birthday," the head mistress said. She considered the row of hanging whips for a moment before choosing one that ended in three tongues about six inches long. A single small, smooth, steel bead was fastened to the end of each tongue. "There comes a time in every woman's life when classroom lectures no longer suffice. You must turn theory into application. Loviatar demands service through action, not endless discussion." She dropped the coil to the floor and lazily twisted the foot-long handle, causing the whip to slither in the dirt.

"I don't understand, Head Mistress," Ythnel lied, afraid she understood all too well. It had been one thing to sit in class and discuss the need for pain and suffering, to study the best ways to inflict it. Ythnel agreed that pain purified the soul and shielding others from suffering only made them weak, unprepared for the tortures the world would subject them to. Yet, suddenly faced with hurting someone, she doubted she could do it—that she *should* do it.

"That's all right," Head Mistress Yenael reassured. "You have much yet to learn. Tonight is just your first step toward using what you have been taught." She smiled and moved behind Oredas. "I will show you how it is done. Then it will be your turn."

The head mistress brought her right forearm up, perpendicular to the floor, the whip handle held loosely in her fist. With a flick of her wrist, the three feet of plaited belly leaped back then snapped forward, connecting with Oredas's flesh. Ythnel jumped at the sharp crack. Oredas merely grunted.

"There are many kinds of whips, Ythnel, and it is important to learn the purpose for each and how to use them." The head mistress struck with the whip again, leaving another set of welts on Oredas's back. "It's just as important to know how much pain your subject can take."

When the whip hit again, it broke the skin, eliciting a moan from Oredas. Blood began to seep from the wound. Ythnel felt a flash of heat, accompanied by a wave of dizziness. She was sure her knees would buckle at any minute.

Head Mistress Yenael returned the whip to its peg and reached for another that hung from a loop at the end of its handle. The stock was braided with leather that divided into nine different tongues at the end. Each strip was punctured with bits of glass, metal, and bone.

"This is a scourge. It is the preferred instrument of suffering for all those who follow Loviatar. It also requires the most skill to use effectively. If you're careless, you can easily kill your subject."

Ythnel watched with horror as the head mistress slapped the scourge against Oredas's right side then raked it across his back. The glass, metal, and bone caught the flesh and tore chunks of it away, leaving jagged stripes of blood. Oredas could not hold back his cries. She repeated this from the other side then dragged the scourge down his back from shoulder to waist a few times.

"There are signs to watch for in your subject to make sure you don't go too far. The rise and fall of the ribs—" the head mistress pointed—"indicates that they are still breathing."

Ythnel looked at the limp form of Oredas and felt bile rise in her throat. Was that bone she saw peeking out as his sides expanded with each shallow, labored breath?

"Tensing of the muscles as the scourge hits means the subject is conscious."

Oredas jerked slightly as Head Mistress Yenael lashed him once more.

"When the subject reaches the threshold between life and death, it is time for Loviatar's Mercy. Not for the purpose of relief from pain and suffering, as some gods instruct their lackeys, but so they can endure more."

The head mistress chanted a request in the tongue of devils, her free hand moving over Oredas's torn back. As her voice grew stronger, a harsh red glow enveloped her hand. Where it passed, blood would flow back into wounds and flesh would mend. With each stripe that disappeared, the red glow deepened, until it was as black as the Abyss and Oredas's back was whole. Head Mistress Yenael ended the chant and the glow around her hand faded. She stood and faced Ythnel.

"Now, it is your turn," she said, thrusting the stock of the scourge at the young girl.

Ythnel stumbled backward until she pressed against the hard stone wall.

"No," Ythenel protested.

Her heart had climbed into her throat and she could feel knots forming in her stomach.

"What did you say?" the head mistress asked, eyes narrowed.

"I-I mean, shouldn't we wait? Brother Oredas probably needs more time to recover." Ythnel knew she was walking dangerous ground, but she had to find some way out.

"Brother Oredas is fine. You saw me heal him. Besides, he is serving his goddess. Nothing could make him happier. Right, Oredas?"

"Yes, Head Mistress." Oredas turned his head to peer up at the two of them. Ythnel could see the glint of fervor in his eyes. "Please do not be afraid for me, little one. I would suffer a thousand beatings for the name of Loviatar and the advance of her cause. Come, take your turn. I am honored to be your first subject."

"You see. Everything is all right. Now, take the scourge." Head Mistress Yenael's voice was stern, insistent.

"No. I can't." Ythnel could feel the tears welling up.

"If you do not beat Oredas, you will take his place," the head mistress said through bared teeth. "I had high hopes for you, Ythnel. Do not make me regret them."

Ythnel shook her head then succumbed to the sobs she had been holding back, sliding down the wall to curl into a ball on the floor. Rough hands grabbed her and she looked up to see Brother Oredas sneering at her. He ripped the shift from her body before pushing her down over the bench and clamping the manacles over her wrists and ankles.

Then sobs became screams.

June 2005
From Wizards of the Coast

An excerpt from

THE FIGHTERS

GHOSTWALKER

ERIK SCOTT DE BIE

Torlic spun back and around, bringing his rapier singing up to parry his opponent's blade. The guardsman barely touched the half-elf's sword before he flashed the rapier down and thrust under Torlic's guard. The nimble half-elf twisted his blade around, sending the thrust out harmlessly wide. The guardsman Narb, his opponent, slashed right to left, and Torlic picked off the attack with a neat, almost casual parry.

An attack high and then a thrust low met a similar fate, parried by flicks of Torlic's wrist. Narb lunged—a strike Torlic easily dodged—and faltered in his step. The half-elf slapped him twice with the flat of his blade, making a "tsk" sound in his throat. Torlic leaped out of the way, landing on the balls of his feet as Narb slashed high to low, and slapped Narb's backside with his blade. Torlic covered his yawning mouth with one dainty hand.

Angry, the larger man lunged at Torlic, but the half-elf leaped back, spinning and landing lightly on his toes. The dancing half-elf flicked his sword back and forth, tempting his opponent.

"Try harder, Narb," Torlic said. "I haven't broken a sweat yet."

The two were standing in Torlic's training room. It was a wide, open square, thirty feet on a side, with walls lined with weapons and practice dummies. Members of Quaervarr's Watch sometimes used the training arena for dueling and working on their sword skills. Most of them took instruction from the half-elf Torlic himself, whose sword's sharpness was only matched by his tongue. Criticism was his habit.

Narb, shaking his hairy mane, growled a negative. "Sorry, Captain," he said. He turned away and took a few steps. He definitely limped from where Torlic's blade had slapped his thigh. "Me bed's callin' me louder than your sword be callin'." He fingered the scar running down his face.

"Tired, are we?" Torlic asked. "Too warm? Do I need to add another scar for you?" He cut his light rapier through the air, then stretched his arms. "It's a little too warm, I agree."

He turned to open the window, letting in the cutting chill of the breeze. The guardsman was walking away when Torlic cleared his throat.

"Narb, have you forgotten that you work for me?" he asked.

At the door, the guardsman stopped. "No, but . . ."

"Then put up your guard," Torlic said. "I'm not done with you yet."

As he turned, Narb opened his mouth to protest, but then staggered away, gaping.

As though he had stepped out of the air itself, Walker stood between them, the black fringes of his cloak rustling in the breeze and spiky strands of his dark hair shifting around his face. His muddy blue eyes were fixed on Torlic.

"It looks like your replacement . . ." Torlic started, but his voice trailed off as the weight of the dark man's presence fell upon him. His knees felt weak and the rapier in his hand, heavy.

"Yes," Walker rasped. "Send him away."

Torlic seemed to gather his senses again. "Go," he said to Narb without taking his eyes from his new opponent.

"Should I . . . should I call Unddreth?" Narb stammered.

"Yes," Torlic said. He flicked his eyes toward the guardsman. "Someone has to cart away the corpse when we're done."

A hint of a smile stole across Walker's face but he said nothing.

Narb wasted no time running out the door, and the two listened to his rapid footfalls and the outer door slamming shut. Torlic tossed his rapier from hand to hand, cutting it through the air. The man in black did not move.

"So, Walker—if I may call you thus—how long would you guess we have?" Torlic asked. "Five minutes? Ten? It's a disorganized watch, and Unddreth is a heavy sleeper."

"How quickly do you want to die?" Walker replied.

"How about not at all?" Torlic asked with a smile. "It's more about how quickly *you* want—"

Walker smiled.

He stepped aside as Torlic's blade flashed past. Faster than the eye could follow, the half-elf had darted forward and thrust, thinking to end the battle right then. Walker swept a silvery long sword out of the folds of his cloak and knocked the rapier to the right, then parried to the left when Torlic tried to reverse his strike. Walker leaped away, his cloak swirling around him, and brought the blade left to right, low to high, throwing the rapier up wide when Torlic thrust the third time.

As the half-elf danced back, his offensive momentum spent, Walker continued his movement. He spun a complete circle and slashed at chest level left to right. Eyes popping wide, Torlic barely got the sword up in time to knock the blow high enough to keep it from taking his head from his shoulders. Walker's mithral blade screeched against the rapier and Torlic pulled the weapon away as quickly as he could. He leaped back and wove his blade through the air to distract and ward off his opponent.

The warrior in black did not hesitate. He charged in, seeming to ignore the whipping blade. Torlic snapped his legs and dived aside of the slashing long sword, turning a somersault across the floor and coming up with a main-gauche in his left hand, drawn from his belt.

Walker slashed in with the long sword, and Torlic hooked it on his rapier's basket hilt. He pulled back his left arm to jab, but Walker's fist was faster. The half-elf went tumbling backward, his face stinging, but kept a firm hold on his weapons.

That was fortunate for him, since Walker was right there, slashing his long sword down over his head. Torlic barely deflected it with both weapons. The black-clad warrior was deceptively frail—his slender build belied strength greater than even Unddreth's might. Torlic was on the defensive, constantly retreating, keeping his blades weaving to ward off Walker's blade.

"Is this all you can do?" Torlic sneered. "You call that *skill?*"

Growling, Walker slashed diagonally, and Torlic parried, but the warrior in black slid the sword down the rapier and main-gauche, locking the hilts on his own. He gazed into Torlic's eyes in fury. Torlic took that as a good sign.

"Difficulty, eh?" the half-elf mocked.

Walker did not reply, but he gritted his teeth.

Torlic peered harder at his opponent. Walker was younger than he had seemed at first.

"Impressive entrance, frightening dress, but no skill. You have no business fighting a real man, boy," Torlic said.

Walker smiled slightly, then threw Torlic tumbling back with a heave of his shoulders. The half-elf rolled, blades held wide, and went into a crouch. He came up slashing, but Walker had not followed.

The black-clad warrior was standing calmly in the center of the arena. The only difference from when he'd first appeared was that he held the mithral sword outside his black cloak. His eyes seemed to flash with sapphire sparks in the torchlight.

Torlic felt the weight of his presence once more, only it seemed sharper, more focused.

"That's a shatterspike blade, is it not?" the half-elf asked. He looked at the nicks it had left on his rapier. Walker didn't answer. "Interesting. Come dance with me, whoever you are," Torlic said, weaving his blade before him. "I wasn't careful before, and you caught me. It won't happen again. I'm through toying with you. Dance with me, boy. I'll be the last thing you ever see."

Even as Torlic spoke the words, he could feel the heat bleeding out of the room and Walker's stance becoming firmer. His confidence seemed to increase, almost as though Torlic had just thrown down his blade and admitted defeat. Above it all, though, Walker seemed to pulse with an icy resolution that set the ever-confident Torlic back on his heels.

A memory flashed through Walker's mind. A cruel voice, paired with Torlic's face.

Come dance with me boy. I'll be the last thing you ever see . . .

Walker smiled thinly at Torlic. "I remember you as well," he said.

His arm pulsed with remembered pain.

Cold strength flooded through him.

December 2005
From Wizards of the Coast

An excerpt from

The Fighters

SON OF THUNDER

Murray J.D. Leeder

Under the guidance of Rask Urgek, the Thunderbeast party traveled through the deepwood of the High Forest. The changing leaves of the trees shone like fire in yellows and oranges. Only occasionally did they catch a glimpse of their destination, the fog-shrouded Star Mounts, through the dense trees. On the whole, they made good time. The farther south they traveled the more level the ground became, as though it had been worked over by some ancient woodworker's plane.

Three days of travel passed virtually without incident. Late the third night, however, their rest was disturbed by a cacophony of high-pitched squeaks.

"Bats," said Rask. Traces of Selûne's light filtered down from the sky, illuminating the thick trunks of the overgrown trees and brief flashes of movement. Soon the whole forest seemed alive with them.

"Are they dangerous?" asked Thluna.

"The High Forest houses certain carnivorous bats," Rask said. "But they usually live far to the northeast, near Hellgate Dell and Stone Stand."

"The dangerous part of the High Forest," Thanar elaborated. "Only marginally more dangerous than the rest."

"There must be thousands of them," said Kellin Lyme,

watching the trees. The sounds of the swarm came closer and closer and the occasional bat darted overhead.

"They find their paths by sound, do they not?" Keirkrad asked Thanar. The druid nodded. "Then I know a simple enough way to keep them away." The shaman motioned with his ancient, lined hands and the chiropteran squeals ceased, and with them all sounds of the night.

What did you do? asked Vell, but the answer came as he opened his mouth and no sound came out.

Kellin smiled. *Clever,* she mouthed, and patted Keirkrad on the back.

The area was deathly quiet. As planned, any bat that flew into the area where the Thunderbeasts and their allies huddled quickly became disoriented and retraced its path. Though the area outside writhed thick with the bats, it was calm and silent inside the radius of Keirkrad's spell. But the bats did not move on, and the spell would not last until morning.

Then the silence turned deadly. Without warning, a jagged spear sailed down from the trees above. Crudely aimed, it nevertheless caught the unsuspecting Thunderbeast Grallah, embedding itself deep in his chest. He collapsed, blood bubbling from his mouth. Thluna and Hengin caught him and lowered him to the leaf-strewn ground. Grallah's lips moved without sound. The others scanned the sky revealed in shards of moonlight, in search of this new foe. Flashes of movement revealed larger, man-sized forms swooping between the trees.

Werebats, mouthed Rask.

The party knew if they stayed huddled in close quarters they would be easy targets, and they did not know if the lycanthropes would be inhibited by the silence spell the way the bats were. Vell looked down at his hands to confirm that they were still flesh. Then he called the scales and they came, the restless behemoth spirit within him eagerly rising to the surface. He grimaced at first as the lizard scales sprouted and crawled along every inch of his flesh, but it felt comfortable, even normal. Lanaal's teachings have had an effect, he observed. It was a mixed blessing. It was useful to be able to call on those powers so readily, but worrisome that it felt so natural to be wearing a behemoth's skin.

Every inch of his human form coated with brown scales, Vell walked outside of the protection of Keirkrad's spell and into the tumult outside. Dozens of bats set upon him, swarming so tightly that his whole body seemed to writhe with their presence, but their teeth could not penetrate his natural armor. He reached out and drew back handfuls of them, crushing them in his grip.

A figure swept down from the trees: a slender hybrid with thick bat wings and sharp white teeth jutting from a hideous rodent face, headed straight for Vell. Kellin jumped out of the silence and howled in its direction, conjuring a tremendous burst of sound from her throat into a low-pitched boom of fantastic intensity that echoed off into the trees. The sound blast struck the hybrid in midair and sent it careening against a tree, thick nails grasping at its enormous bat ears. Vell ran over to the fallen hybrid and delivered a bare-fisted blow to its head, crushing its skull. The hybrid crumpled, its leather-winged form collapsing into a twisted heap. All around, stunned bats plummeted from the sky like fat raindrops.

Unnoticed, a strange pellet fell down from the trees directly above them. It landed next to Keirkrad and erupted into a mesh of substance like thick spidersilk that wrapped its way around the ancient shaman, binding his hands and gagging his mouth. The more he struggled, the tighter it cocooned him.

As the warriors Ilskar and Draf ran over to hack at the netting, a second wave of bats assailed the party—not the normal-sized bats of the swarm outside the silence efffect but a variety as large as dogs, triangular in shape, and red of fur.

Night hunters. Like their smaller brethren, they seemed to loose their ability to navigate once they entered the silence but instead of turning back, they panicked and randomly slashed about with their spiny tails, drawing blood wherever they struck.

Thluna bashed one solidly with his Tree Ghost club, damaging its wings before crushing it underfoot. Ilskar and Draf found their blades had no effect on the thick webbing and turned to help fight the night hunter bats.

Amidst the confusion, a few werebats swooped down from the treetops and crept into the silence. They caught hold of the strange web that held Keirkrad and began to pull him aloft. Rask hit one of them solidly with his battle-axe but it bounced off the lycanthrope without leaving a mark.

Thanar clapped Thluna on the shoulder and pointed out the werebats working on Keirkrad. Thluna swung his club at one of the struggling werebats, catching it just above the knee. The werebat released its grip on Keirkrad and turned to face Thluna, hissing and snarling in silence. Thluna struck again with the enchanted club just as a red-tinged bullet of magic struck the other on the side of its head, crimson streamers reaching back to Kellin's fingers. It too released its grip on the webbing, flying off to shelter in the trees. Still bound, Keirkrad tumbled unceremoniously to the ground, rolling face down in the dirt.

Outside the silence, Vell found himself assailed by two more werebats. Their speed and flying enabled them to evade him and keep him occupied while increasing numbers of bats swarmed around him until he could hardly see. Thanar, deprived of his magic, slaughtered one of the night hunters with his sword before rushing outside the silence to join Kellin.

"They're not trying to kill us," he yelled over the clamor of bat shrieks. "They want Keirkrad."

Thluna killed a werebat with a blow from the Tree Ghosts'

club. The others slashed their way through the remaining night hunters.

Kellin, looking down at Keirkrad's bound form, asked, "Did they bind him because he's the most powerful of us?"

Thanar shook his head. "They probably thought he was the least powerful. We need to free him."

Kellin and Thanar rushed to Keirkard's side, spun him onto his back, and dragged him out of the silence. He was still conscious, and his ancient blue eyes darted about in fear, but before Kellin and Thanar could dispel the magical webbing, more werebats appeared above them. Kellin quickly conjured up a spell bolt and blasted through one of the rightmost werebat's thin wings. Thanar called down a powerful blast of wind that tossed the other werebats astray.

But still more werebats came, flying down and striking before retreating to the trees and calling forth more of their servant bats. Knowing they could not endure much more, it was all Kellin and Thanar could do to grip the webbing and haul Keirkrad back into the silence.

"It won't last," Kellin said just before the world went silent again.

With Kellin and Thanar's retreat, Vell was alone outside the silence. Having finally succeeded in catching one of the werebats, he squeezed its neck until its huge rodent eyes went blank. Then, ignoring the other werebats, he also pulled back into the silence. It was deceptively calm inside. The werebats swooped around the boundaries of the spell, testing its limits and baiting those within it, baring their sharp, white teeth and tempting the barbarians to let their rage get the better of them. The night outside writhed thick with bats and the occasional night hunter swept into the silence to be swiftly dealt with by the weapons inside. Inside the radius of Keirkrad's spell there was no longer an air of safety or comfort. The silence crashed and crescendoed in their ears.

Unable to communicate with each other inside the unnatural

silence, the party found it difficult to regroup and plan their next move. Kellin drew her father's enchanted sword from her belt and passed it to Rask, who laid his battle-axe on the ground. They fanned out around the incapacitated Keirkrad, ready for the inevitable. Before long, the walls of silence fell and the cacophony of the outside world assailed them full strength.

Immediately upon the fall of the silence, the werebats and their servants plunged in to fill up the space. Kellin unleashed her ear-piercing sonic spell again, deafening a host of mundane bats and hobbling a number of the werebats. Thanar launched a strong wind that filled outstretched wings and sent werebats flying backward to crash against trees. Vell snatched a werebat from midair and drew it into an embrace as a shambling mound might, crushing it with the full force of his strength against his scale-coated body. The warriors swung their weapons, but only Thluna with his club and Rask, armed with Kellin's sword, did any damage. The nuisance of the bat swarm filled the air, the disgusting mass of them teeming in such a way that none of the party could move without their limbs brushing against hairy bodies and leathery wings.

Theirs was a doomed effort. More werebats appeared above, swooped down, and wrapped their claws around the netting that bound Keirkrad. No one could so much as turn around before the shaman was lifted off into the trees and away. The other werebats withdrew and followed, vanishing swiftly until it was as though they had never been there, and the defeated Thunderbeast party continued hacking their way through the thick bat swarm until it dissipated with the first light of day.

January 2006
From Wizards of the Coast

An excerpt from

THE WIZARDS

BLOODWALK

JAMES P. DAVIS

Leather gave way as crimson hands and a bloodstained torso burst from the innards of the unfortunate recipient of Morgynn's journey through the bloodwalk. The man's broken and torn body slumped to the ground behind her like a useless second skin. She stood before the circle of the seven remaining Hunters, her wet lips already mouthing incantations through the froth of her fallen victim's life as her targets slowly recovered from their initial shock at her gruesome arrival.

Rhaeme blinked and reflexes took over. He and those three closest to him unslung their bows, dropping their swords point down into the dirt. Drawing arrows from low hanging quivers, they assumed the traditional stance of the Hunter bowman, relying on their thick *eshtahks* to protect their bow arms and exposed sides.

The three closest to Morgynn raised their curved swords and charged, but it was too late. The final words of her incantation were complete and her spell caught them full in the chest. A wave of power, like focused wind, slammed into them, knocking the swordsmen to their backs and tumbling Rhame and his archers backward before they could loose their shots.

Morgynn laughed, enjoying herself, and letting everything

within her take over, releasing herself to the magic and to her frantic pulse. Her dark eyes welled into black pools of blood that spilled down her cheeks and danced in symbols and runes as she cast another spell, waving her hands in the air between her and the fallen bowmen. She turned to the three swordsmen and winced as light spilled from a small stone one of them drew from a pouch at his side, illuminating the cleared ground and broken plants.

Shaken but undeterred, the remaining swordsmen charged again, attempting to get close enough to disrupt her casting. Morgynn frowned and brushed her left hand across her collarbone, setting the scars there on fire. They hissed as they burned away, channeling their held magic down her right arm. A scent of coppery ozone filled the air as reddened bolts arced from her fingertips and struck the two brave swordsmen.

They had no time to scream before their muscles convulsed and tensed, threatening to tear away from the hidden bones beneath. One man fell almost instantly, a young man she noted, with dusty brown hair and striking blue eyes, now clouded with blackened tissue. As the arc of energy still gripped him, she could taste him in her mouth, his fear and the gamey taste of his cooking flesh.

The other man's eyes were lost to her now, bursting within their sockets as the spell coursed through him, showering his face in blood and the pinkish fluids of the ruined orbs. He collapsed to the dirt as his muscles suddenly relaxed, but remained trembling as he whimpered and hoarsely tried to give voice to his pain through a raw and bleeding throat.

The thrumming sounds of released bowstrings, followed by hissing charges of energy drew her gaze back to the archers. Rhaeme and his companions had risen to one knee to steady their stance and aim, but their arrows stopped short of their marks, bouncing away from an invisible barrier that crackled and flashed with each strike.

Smiling at their futile attacks, she brushed her right hand across the scars on her neck as she heard the last of the swordsmen approach. He was unable to control the fearful groaning yell of his own voice. The magic responded instantly to her touch, scars disappearing in a sizzling line of thin smoke, tracing the runes inscribed in her flesh. Thrusting her left hand forward, an acrid, caustic scent accompanied the crawling spell as it sizzled across her skin harmlessly.

The Hunter's powerful stroke fell short as crimson arrows of acid pierced his *eshtahk* and buried themselves deep in his chest and side. A wet gasp escaped him and she could feel the flooding hole in his right lung, and the impact of each arrow as it found his insides and ate away at the tissue and muscle. His veins and arteries became inflamed, showing starkly against the skin of his neck and face. Her heart responded to his pounding pulse as her blood grew more familiar with her enemy's.

The bittersweet flavor of adrenaline danced ghostlike across her tongue and her eyes rolled back. She moaned as he staggered back and dropped his ineffectual sword, his heartbeat slowed, pulse by pulse, and she felt drawn into his death.

Gaping oblivion yawned in his mind and showed itself to her, that second between life and final rest: The twilight of existence where she'd been for the past decade, borne on the currents of blood from a death that would not have her. Buried once in a ground that would not keep her, she'd risen to a power bound only by her skin.

"Toys and playthings," she whispered, "They barely know they're alive."

Rage replaced her ecstasy as the man fell lifeless and she turned, furious, on the archers.

Rhaeme fired one last arrow in frustration, but once again it was reflected away just inches from the mage's breast. He rolled forward to grab his sword, abandoning his bow.

"Run! We can't win here!" he yelled to his fellow Hunters who gave no argument and turned to escape only to see, through the dim glow of the dropped light-stone, the edges of the closing path behind them. The tortured sounds of another spell being cast hummed behind them, scratching at their ears.

Laen turned back, and Rhaeme could see the fire of youth and anger in his eyes and tried to grab him, but the young man was faster. Running toward the casting wizard, he yelled a war cry common to the Hunters and grabbed his ready sword from where he'd left it.

"As Savras sees, so shall I see you fall!"

Morgynn finished the spell in a crescendo of sound, drowning out Laen's yell and opening her mouth wide beyond its natural limits. Her scream became an enshrouding buzz as red-eyed insects flew in a crimson and black mass from between her thinly drawn lips. Each finger-long locust was colored in bands of dark rose and onyx. Their emotionless eyes glowed, giving the swarm a hellish light of its own as it streamed forward to meet the charging Hunter.

Laen met the mass head on, swinging his blade once or twice valiantly, but the locusts were too many and quickly found the small openings in his armor and clothing, flying inside his hood and hungrily feasting on his scalp and the back of his neck.

Rhaeme's sense of helplessness angered him and thoughts of Elisandrya came unbidden to his mind. His remaining two companions sprinted forward to retrieve their own swords, determined to make their ends proud and honorable. Rhaeme felt the world slow around him as he realized that he was going to die. It came with a peace that put steel in his nerves and speed in his step.

Ahead of their grim charge, Laen's writhing body was lifting into the air, his boots scraping the ground for just a moment before the momentum of the swarm bore him down, stripping his flesh to the bone. The locusts' incessant buzz drowned the young Hunter's muffled and weakening screams.

Morgynn watched as the warriors advanced. She saw death in their eyes and hated them for their acceptance of its inevitability. Righteousness fueled their spirits and the sight of it sickened her. Whispering a drone of grating syllables she pulled the threads of the Weave to her will, determined to teach them the true nature of death and their far too casual choice born of courage.

At a single word, the lead Hunter's sword flashed and steamed as cold flames enveloped its length. He screamed as his hand froze and became fused to the blade's handle, his flesh burning and brittle. He tried to push on past the pain, to wield the weapon against the spell's mistress, but the sword cracked and split, shattering in an explosion of metal that left his arm a cauterized stump and his eyes, blind.

The second Hunter was closer, and Morgynn had no time to cast again. She spun away but his blade glanced across her left arm, opening a small wound that sent shudders through her body as her blood recoiled from the open skin. Growling another quick spell, she roared the words madly and swung her right arm around before the man could strike again.

Her fingers popped and grew, extending into long blackened claws as she raked them across the Hunter's face and chest. Like ephemeral knives of ice and shadow they melted through flesh and bone leaving gaping scars in his spirit and mind. The man's eyes rolled and his arms went limp, dropping his sword and feebly waving in a spastic effort to maintain control. He babbled nonsense as he fell to his knees, weakly pawing at his head, searching for some wound, some way to make sense of and hold on to reality.

Rhaeme was the last, just a few yards away, and she pitied him for a second as she whispered quietly to the dagger at her belt, freeing the clasp that held it in its sheath. She touched its jeweled pommel once and it flew at her command, slamming into the lone Hunter's gut with a force born of old Nar magic. It knocked the wind from him and laid him flat on his back, the carved figures on its handle squirming against one another and quietly mouthing.

Picking up his dropped sword, she stopped to watch his slow agony. He refused to scream and met her gaze, grasping at the dagger planted in his stomach but unable to pull it free. Her red-black eyes looked straight through his, not seeing him, and focused on the branching rivers of blood beneath his skin. The bleeding streams of her eyes changed shape on her cheeks, mimicking what she saw inside of him, matching his swift pulse in twin red image of upside-down trees, stripped of leaves and laid bare for winter.

"They barely know they're alive," she mumbled as the rage bled from her limbs, dispersed by her arcane tantrum, "Then they die."

Around the pair, the locusts moved from body to body, devouring the fallen and eliciting more howls from those not quite yet passed on. Long she stood, lost in thought as the swarm finished each man, leaving nothing but bones and bits of cartilage under loose fitting armor and clothing. Finally they gathered in a cloud around her legs and Rhaeme awaited the command that would send them feasting on his own body.

Morgynn hissed a sibilant word and the swarm faded into thin air, returning to whatever foul realm had spawned them.

"You serve the whores of Savras?" she said emotionlessly, drained and calm for the moment.

Rhaeme tried to spit, to show some defiance in the face of his killer, but it was all he could do to breathe and force back the burning vomit in his throat.

Twitching her fingers, the dagger responded, lifting up and carrying Rhaeme's weight with it. His stoicism failed and he gasped, gurgling as a wave of nausea and blood flowed from his innards and into his mouth. He felt he would tear free at any moment, disemboweled by the vile weapon, but it would not release him, however much he wished it would.

The blade pushed him against the trunk of a tree, pinning him to the wood. Morgynn followed closely with his sword held in her hands. With a powerful thrust she buried the blade just beneath his right shoulder and deep into the tree. Rhaeme's pain was almost beyond him and his vision narrowed as spots of darkness and streaking stars clouded his sight.

"You would die for peddlers of visions and prophecy? Does your life mean nothing to you?"

Morgynn twirled her fingers languidly and concentrated. Rhaeme's bowels lurched as the dagger worked itself free and returned to Morgynn's hand.

"Kill me witch! F-finish it!" he spat through clenched teeth.

She glared at him and lay a gentle hand on his impaled shoulder, caressing the bloodied flesh and calling to his pulse, feeling it roll and tumble in his distress. His blood pushed back, fighting weakly against the walls of muscle and skin that bound it within him. She called to it, exerting her control over its ebb and flow.

Rhaeme tensed as his body seemed to reject itself. Pressure pushed behind his eyes and his skull felt as though it would burst. Sharp needle-like spasms caused his limbs to twitch. Time slowed again and the end of his life loomed in his mind, more real this time and yet still unreal, unbelievable. He saw Eli again, still watching him on the low road to Littlewater as he rode away into the forest.

"Elisandrya. That is her name," Morgynn said as she experienced his agony and witnessed his thoughts. "You still love her. She seeks the Hoarite."

Unbidden primal panic stole over Rhaeme at her words and

Morgynn withdrew her fingers, ceasing her pull on his blood and satisfied that fear of death still hung with him on the tree. His head drooped and he managed a single sob.

Without a word, her hands melded into his chest painlessly, opening the doorway of the bloodwalk through his body. Rhaeme had already passed out. The warmth that her passing sent through him was gone almost immediately and did little for the cold that crept into his extremities.

Then he was alone.

November 2006
From Wizards of the Coast

J.L. Collins always wanted to be an artist like many of his friends. In a page of his sketchbook, he drew a character sketch and proceeded to use the next three pages writing a detailed back story, which read suspiciously like a short story. It was three pages long . . . double-sided, and he hasn't stopped writing since.

James P. Davis is a freelance writer and is rarely seen without a notepad and pen close by, just in case. He is currently at work completing his first novel, *Bloodwalk,* for the FORGOTTEN REALMS series The Wizards due out in the fall of 2006. He lives in Shreveport, Louisiana with his wife Megan and their polydactyl cat named Graz'zt.

Erik Scott de Bie blends action, adventure, and magic together with a touch of mystery to create his tale, "The Hunting Game." His first novel, *Ghostwalker*—a tale of dark heroism, love, betrayal, and vengeance—is due out April 2006. de Bie's degree in English literature comes from Willamette University of Salem, Oregon. He currently resides in the Northwest with his beautiful wife Shelley, five swords of different styles, and in the near future, a dog.

Kameron M. Franklin lives in the Pacific Northwest, with his wife, son, and their cat. His first novel, *Maiden of Pain,* will be released in July 2005. Visit his web site at www.kameronmf.com.

Ed Gentry started writing when he entered the *Maiden of Pain* open call and plans to continue doing so for many years to come. Another of Ed's short stories appears in *Goblin Tails,* *the Anthology* (2004) from Poison Clan Press. You can visit Ed's website at www.edgentry.com.

Jaleigh Johnson lives and writes in the Champaign area of Illinois. "Queen of the Mountain" is her first contribution to the FORGOTTEN REALMS, and she couldn't be more thrilled about it.

Rosemary Jones works for an opera company, where she meets enchanted swans and singing dragons on a regular basis. Her fiction can be found in the Phobos anthology *Hitting The Skids In Pixeltown*. Her nonfiction work includes a four-volume series on collecting children's books published by Schroeder.

Murray J.D. Leeder, a native of Calgary, is currently pursuing an M.A. in Film Studies at Carleton University in Ottawa. He made his professional debut with "The Fallen Lands" in *Realms of Shadow,* the characters from which will be revisited in the novel *Son of Thunder,* scheduled for January 2006, which he's finishing up in the time left over between papers, presentations, and TA duties.

Jim Pitrat and his wonderful wife Marie live in Southern California where they stumble through the maze of insanity that is parenting. For his meal ticket, Jim plies his trade as a CPA. When not crunching numbers or chasing his two children around the house he writes tales of dark sorcery and ferocious beasties.

Harley Stroh began submitting stories to Wizards of the Coast when it was still TSR. Sixteen years later, he sold one. Too excited to know when to stop, he went on to found Poison Clan Press. Their first anthology, *Goblin Tails,* was published in September, 2004.

Erin Tettensor took up writing when it became clear Fate had no plans afoot to make her the heroine in some grand adventure. Since then, she has spent an appalling amount of time daydreaming on paper. Her contribution to this anthology owes much to her cat Sinatra, who provided invaluable insight into the world of small, neurotic creatures who insist upon being the center of attention.

FORGOTTEN REALMS®

NEW YORK TIMES BESTSELLING SERIES

R.A. SALVATORE'S
WAR OF THE SPIDER QUEEN

The epic saga of the dark elves concludes!

EXTINCTION
Book IV

LISA SMEDMAN

For even a small group of drow, trust is the rarest commodity of all.
When the expedition prepares for a return to the Abyss, what little
trust there is crumbles under a rival goddess's hand.

ANNIHILATION
Book V

PHILIP ATHANS

Old alliances have been broken, and new bonds have been formed.
While some finally embark for the Abyss itself, other stay behind to
serve a new mistress—a goddess with plans of her own.

RESURRECTION
Book VI

PAUL S. KEMP

The Spider Queen has been asleep for a long time, leaving the
Underdark to suffer war and ruin. But if she finally returns, will
things get better...or worse?

www.wizards.com

ED GREENWOOD

THE CREATOR OF THE FORGOTTEN REALMS WORLD

BRINGS YOU THE STORY OF
SHANDRIL OF HIGHMOON

SHANDRIL'S SAGA

SPELLFIRE
Book I

Powerful enough to lay low a dragon or heal a wounded warrior, spellfire
is the most sought after power in all of Faerûn. And it is in the reluctant
hand of Shandril of Highmoon, a young, orphaned kitchen-lass.

CROWN OF FIRE
Book II

Shandril has grown to become one of the most powerful magic-users in
the land. The powerful Cult of the Dragon and the evil Zhentarim want
her spellfire, and they will kill whoever they must to possess it.

HAND OF FIRE
Book III

Shandril has spellfire, a weapon capable of destroying the world, and
now she's fleeing for her life across Faerûn, searching for somewhere to
hide. Her last desperate hope is to take refuge in the sheltered city of
Silverymoon. If she can make it.

www.wizards.com

NEW TALES FROM FORGOTTEN REALMS CREATOR
ED GREENWOOD

THE BEST OF THE REALMS
Book II

This new anthology of short stories by Ed Greenwood, creator of the
FORGOTTEN REALMS Campaign Setting, features many old and well-loved
classics as well as three brand new stories of high-spirited adventure.

CITY OF SPLENDORS
A Waterdeep Novel

ED GREENWOOD AND ELAINE CUNNINGHAM

In the streets of Waterdeep, conspiracies run like water through the
gutters, bubbling beneath the seeming calm of the city's life. As a band of
young, foppish lords discovers there is a dark side to the city they all love,
a sinister mage and his son seek to create perverted creatures to further
their twisted ends. And across it all sprawls the great city itself: brawling,
drinking, laughing, living life to the fullest. Even in the face of death.

SILVERFALL
Stories of the Seven Sisters

This paperback edition of *Silverfall: Stories of the Seven Sisters*, by the creator
of the FORGOTTEN REALMS Campaign Setting, features seven stories of
seven sisters illustrated by seven beautiful pages of interior art by John Foster.

ELMINSTER'S DAUGHTER
The Elminster Series

All her life, Narnra of Waterdeep has wondered who her father is. Now
she has discovered that it is no less a person than Elminster of Shadowdale,
mightiest mage in all Faerûn. And her anger is as boundless as his power.

www.wizards.com

THE ELVEN NATIONS TRILOGY GIFT SET

FIRSTBORN
Volume One

PAUL B. THOMPSON & TONYA C. COOK

In moments, the fate of two leaders is decided. Sithas, firstborn
son of the elf monarch Sithel, is destined to inherit the crown
and kingdom from his father. His twin brother Kith-Kanan,
born just a few heartbeats later, must make his own destiny.
Together—and apart—the princes will see their world torn
asunder for the sake of power, freedom, and love.

THE KINSLAYER WARS
Volume Two

DOUGLAS NILES

Timeless and elegant, the elven realm seems unchanging. But
when the dynamic human nation of Ergoth presses on the
frontiers of the Silvanesti realm, the elves must awaken—and
unite—to turn back the tide of human conquest. Prince Kith-
Kanan, returned from exile, holds the key to victory.

THE QUALINESTI
Volume Three

PAUL B. TOMPSON & TONYA C. COOK

Wars done, the weary nations of Krynn turn to rebuilding their
exhausted lands. In the mountains, a city devoted to peace, Pax
Tharkas, is carved from living stone by elf and dwarf hands. In
the new nation of Qualinesti corruption seeks to undermine this
new beginning. A new generation of elves and humans must band
together if the noble experiment of Kith-Kanan is to be preserved.

www.wizards.com

ENTER THE EXCITING, NEW DUNGEONS AND DRAGONS® SETTING... THE WORLD OF

THE WAR~TORN TRILOGY

THE CRIMSON TALISMAN
Book One
Adrian Cole

Erethindel, the fabled Crimson Talisman. Long sought by the forces of darkness. Long guarded in secret by one family. But now the secret has been revealed, and only one young man can keep it safe. As the talisman's powers awaken within him, Erethindel tears at his soul.

THE ORB OF XORIAT
Book Two
Edward Bolme

The Last War is over, and it took all that Teron ever had. A monk trained for war, he is the last of his Order. Now he is on a quest to find a powerful weapon that might set the world at war again.

AVAILABLE IN 2005!

TWO NEW SERIES EMERGE FROM THE RAVAGED WASTES OF... THE WORLD OF

THE
LOST MARK
TRILOGY

MARKED FOR DEATH
Book One

Matt Forbeck

Twelve dragonmarks. Sigils of immense magical power. Born by scions of mighty Houses, used through the centuries to wield authority and shape wonders throughout the Eberron world. But there are only twelve marks. Until now. Matt Forbeck begins the terrifying saga of the thirteenth dragonmark . . . The Mark of Death.

THE
BINDING STONE
TRILOGY

THE DRAGON BELOW
Book One

Don Bassingthwaite

A chance rescue brings old rivals together with a strange ally in a mission of vengeance against powers of ancient madness and corruption. But in the haunted forests of the Eldeen Reaches, even the most stalwart hero can soon find himself prey to the hidden horrors within the untamed wilderness.

AVAILABLE IN 2005!

ENTER THE NEW WORLD OF

EBERRON

THE
DREAMING DARK
TRILOGY

Written by Keith Baker
The winning voice of the DUNGEONS & DRAGONS® setting search

CITY OF TOWERS
Volume One

Hardened by the Last War, four soldiers have come to Sharn,
fabled City of Towers, capital of adventure. In a time of uneasy
peace, these hardened warriors must struggle to survive. And
then people start turning up dead. The heroes find themselves
in an adventure that will take them from the highest reaches of
power to the most sordid depths of the city of wonder, shadow,
and adventure.

THE SHATTERED LAND
Volume Two

The epic adventure continues as Daine and the remnants of
his company travel to the dark continent of Xen'drik on an
adventure that may kill them all.

AVAILABLE IN 2005!